"I want to buy you, Ms. Tinsdale."

"Of course," Rachel said, wishing her gun was in her hand instead of in her purse. "Did you have a payment schedule in mind, Mr. Slick?"

"You can name your price," he said. "And this is no joke. I need a woman with guts and looks. You've got both. But they won't do me any good unless you're willing to stand on an auction block." His gaze raked a path from her head to her breasts, and she was shocked to feel an electric reaction. Instinctively she crossed her free arm over her chest. "Good," he said. "The more innocent you appear, the better."

"What *are* you talking about?"

He leaned closer to her face. His breath was warm, and she inhaled the subtle fragrances of bay and night spice. "Three words," he said in a low, uninflected voice. *"White slave trade."*

Dear Reader,

Ready for something a little different? Something tantalizing and daring? A real page-turner that's more than a little shocking? Here it is—a lush, evocative, frankly erotic romance set in the world of white slavery. Hard to believe? Just turn the pages....

Love Slave by Mallory Rush is all that and more.

At Temptation, we're never afraid to push the boundaries to bring you the best books possible. And the widest variety. Lovers & Legends, our yearlong miniseries, captures the magic and fantasy of romance, while Candace Schuler's glamorous Hollywood Dynasty trilogy begins in July. Glenda Sanders again weaves a fascinating paranormal tale in *Lovers' Secrets* (August). Comedies, adventure stories, emotional dramas, chilling Gothics and suspense novels, paranormal titles—both light and dark—make a compelling mix each month. And, every once in a while, a book that is sensationally shocking....

Love Slave—read only with a loved one close by....

The Editors

LOVE SLAVE

MALLORY RUSH

Harlequin Books

TORONTO • NEW YORK • LONDON
AMSTERDAM • PARIS • SYDNEY • HAMBURG
STOCKHOLM • ATHENS • TOKYO • MILAN
MADRID • WARSAW • BUDAPEST • AUCKLAND

For Rachel McInnis Wallace—
Sister, writer, and friend who shares
The secrets that bind us

Published June 1993

ISBN 0-373-25548-9

LOVE SLAVE

Prologue

"TIME TO SAY GOODBYE to your sister, Joshua." Mr. Johns patted the twelve-year-old boy's dark head.

Joshua stared hard at the social worker until the man glanced away uneasily, his Adam's apple bobbing up and down, just like a turkey's when he gobbled. Josh shrugged the comforting hand away. Didn't want no pity. Didn't want nobody but Sarah to even touch him.

"I gotta do this right," Joshua said quietly, so his sister wouldn't hear. The man looked sad, even guilty. Josh played it for all it was worth. He stuck his thumb in the opposite direction, just like his daddy used to do when he sent him to his room. "Mr. Johns . . . please?"

Mr. Johns headed the other way, taking along with him the grown-ups who'd accepted Sarah into their home.

"C'mon, Sarah." Josh led the silent five-year-old into her new bedroom. She clutched her baby doll against her as Josh sat on the canopy bed and pulled her onto his lap. "Let's talk," he said, tugging on a long blond braid.

She didn't respond to his hair pulling. All she did was stare out the lace-curtained window and stroke her little hand through the doll's ratty curls.

"Remember the Christmas Santa brought you that?"

"There's no such thing as Santa Claus." She blinked her eyes, and out rolled two big tears. "He's dead, too."

"Now don't you start crying. If you do, you'll make me start, and big boys don't cry. That's what Daddy always said.

And we don't want to let him down. You and me, Sarah, we're gonna get through this and make him proud."

A huge sob shuddered through her small chest. Josh rocked her back and forth, the way he thought Daddy would have. And then he remembered his father telling him he was the man of the house and to watch after his sister while he went out for groceries that night he never came back.

"Oh, J-Josh," she stuttered out. "Josh, I'm s-scared. I think I killed Daddy."

"That's crazy talk, Sarah."

"No, it's not! 'Member when we got in trouble for laughing in church?"

"Yeah. My butt's still stinging from the licking I got when we came home."

"'Cause you couldn't quit laughin' at the old lady singing in front. But I quit. Know how?"

"How?" Josh picked up a coverlet from the foot of the bed and tucked it around them. He was going to miss his sister stealing the blanket when he went to sleep in his own strange bed.

"I pretended Daddy died. It was the horriblest, saddest thing I could think, and it made me stop laughin'." She stared at him with big, frightened eyes, guilt and remorse contorting her impish face. "I did it other times, too, and now he's dead. I made him dead from thinkin' it. I'm a bad girl. A bad, bad girl. And preacher says the bad ones go down there. You know, that place where the devil's at, with the brim and firestone? I don' wanna go there," she wailed. Sarah clutched the doll in her arms, twisting her fingers into the shaggy mop of hair.

"Shhh . . . shhh," he said, trying to soothe her. "Now quit thinkin' like that, Sarah. You didn't make it happen, and you're not gonna see any hellfire and brimstone. Don't go forgettin', you were always Daddy's angel, and you'll always be mine. Angels go to heaven, not hell."

"Josh, you know you're not s'posed to say the *H* word. That'll earn you a licking for sure."

"And who's gonna give it to me? You?" He tweaked her nose, and she giggled past her receding tears.

"You're sure I'm safe?" she said hopefully.

"Absolutely, positively sure." Josh swallowed past the lump in his throat. They'd be coming for him soon, to take him away from Sarah. Then who would look at him as if he'd hung the moon? Mr. Johns? The warden at the orphanage? A vision of iron bars and prison beds made him hug her tight.

"You're squishin' me, Josh."

He forced himself to loosen his hold and fake an encouraging smile.

"This is sure a pretty new room you've got, Sarah. Lots better than the one at home. They look real nice, your new folks do, and they were so excited when you got here, saying you were the little girl they'd always wanted."

"But they're not you. They're strangers, and I want my daddy back."

"Me too. But that won't change anything, angel. We've got to say goodbye for a little while, but when I'm old enough I'm gonna take you away from here. That's a promise."

"When, Josh?"

He could visit on holidays. Big deal. He wanted his sister back, and all he could think of now was years and years of goodbyes like this. It was tearing his guts out just thinking about it.

And so he didn't. He thought about how he was going to keep his promise to Sarah. He knew he'd need a place for them to live and enough money to take care of her.

How could he do it? Mowing lawns? But maybe the orphanage wouldn't even let him out to do that. Just like they'd lock him in tonight so he couldn't comfort Sarah while she cried herself to sleep.

Something hard knotted up inside him and settled protectively around his heart. His hands clenched the sheet, and he held her as close as he could without making her yelp.

"I'll come back when I've got lots of money. Then I'll buy you and me a brand-new house where we'll live together again. No grown-ups around, so we can eat all the candy and have all the pillow fights we want. Whenever you feel sad, just think about that."

"You promise?"

"Cross my heart, hope to—"

She threw her arms around his neck and nearly hugged the stuffings out of him. Josh stared at the window, which was lifted a crack. The warm Mississippi breeze cut through his emotions and cleared his head..

Suddenly he had the beginnings of a plan.

"Can you keep a secret, Sarah? A real important secret? 'Cause if you tell, I can't come back to get you." She nodded her head, her braid bouncing up and down. "I'm running away."

"No, Josh! You could get in bad trouble."

"Only if they catch me." Realizing he didn't have any time to waste, he forced himself to put her down. His expression was stern. "This is what we've got to do. You lay down and pretend to be resting. If they ask you where I am, you say I went to get a drink of water. That way they'll look around the house before they go after me."

"But that's lyin'!"

"It's a good lie, Sarah. If I don't get away, I'll never be able to get you back, and you want me to, don't you?"

"More'n anything." She looked real scared as Josh tucked her in and kissed her cheek. He was suddenly torn between crawling under the covers with her and making a run for it.

"I love you, angel. Be sure to say your prayers every night. And when you get homesick, just think about me and the day I'll take you back home."

"I love you, big brother."

He untangled her arms from around his neck and gave her the baby doll to cling to instead. Josh turned before she saw the tears brimming his eyes.

Big boys don't cry.... Big boys don't cry....

He crawled through the window, then shut it back to a crack as soon as his feet touched grass. Blowing his sister a final kiss, he made sure the coast was clear, then ran as fast as his feet could fly.

Sure wished he had some of those Keds so he could take off like Superman outrunning that train.

Train! He hadn't known where he was headed, but now he did. They'd passed some tracks a mile or so down the road. He'd hop the first train that whizzed by.

Josh was winded by the time he got there. He kept looking over his shoulder, expecting the orphanage's guard dogs to hunt him down.

He'd followed the tracks a good mile when he heard a chugging that sounded like his own labored breathing. Then the train was passing, passing too fast, and no way could he be Superman and outrun it. Just barely, he made out the on-coming blur of an open side door.

He started to run, trying to remember how he'd seen it done in the movies. Lordy, he wished he was taller, as tall as Sarah thought he was, tall enough to hang the moon and swing her on a star.

Do it! He sprang high at a dead run and caught the side edge of the railway car. Wind sucked at him, pulling him toward the slicing wheels and onto the iron tracks. He screamed, his fingers sliding and clawing to pull the rest of him to safety. He looked down, his eyes wild. He felt the mean steel all but eating up his feet and knew if he let go he'd be mangled like a mouse chewed up by a tomcat.

And then he felt something grab his locked arm. He raised his head, the wind whipping it so hard he thought his neck would snap. His eyes were glued to a grizzled face, a mouth that was gnashing out some urgent command.

Josh nearly pulled the man out with him before he was safely inside. He fell into a trembling heap on the coarse floor. He heard the door being shoved nearly closed while the locomotive's deadly wheels sang a rusty lullaby against his raw cheek.

And then he was being nudged gently, and a brown paper sack filled his stinging vision.

"Drink some, young'n. Not too much, or you'll puke. Just a swig to make your innards quit shakin'."

It felt like liquid fire going down. Josh coughed and sputtered, trying to regain his breath. By the time he had, his new comrade was guzzling freely.

"Running away?"

"No, sir, I'm just on vacation."

"Sir?" The man cackled, revealing dingy teeth.

Then the liquor hit, and Josh felt warm and numb. His insides quit shaking, and he leaned back, exhausted.

"Thank you, sir. You saved my life."

"That depends. Just might've saved you for somethin' worse than you were running from." He coughed and spit on the floor, then wiped his mouth against the arm of his ragged shirt. "What's your name, boy?"

"Joshua Smith."

"Wrong. First thing you got to learn on the run is, don't leave no trail. Names are like Hansel with his bread crumbs, and no bird around to eat the tracks."

Josh nodded, feeling weariness overtaking him.

"What's your name?" he asked, covering a yawn with the back of his hand.

"Ain't got no name. Left it behind when I took off on my own vacation." He patted Josh's bruised arm, and Josh could smell body odor and the sweat he'd worked up saving him. It was a comforting touch, all the same. "You listen up good, boy. This train's headed for Chicago. Don't make a peep, and you might make it. Big city makes it hard to find runaways. Want to tell me why you're running now?"

"My dad died. They put my sister in a home, and they were going to tote me off to an orphan—"

"Don't know why you're running, don't care to know."

"Then why'd you ask?"

"I'm tryin' to teach you somethin', give you some schoolin' that's not in the books."

Josh considered that. Sounded like good advice. "Are you going to Chicago?" he asked hopefully.

"Me, I'm getting off at the next refuel stop."

"Can I come with you? I won't be any bother, I promise."

"Best you learn right now, the only way to travel is alone. Now get you some rest and don't say no more. Me and the bottle want to get cozy."

Josh shut his eyes, meaning to pretend sleep. If he was careful, he could sneak out and follow his new friend long enough to pick up more lessons before striking out on his own.

But the liquor, the ordeal, the lull of the train's constant movement, seduced him into sleep.

When Josh awoke, the train was still moving, but he was alone. He looked around the emptiness—dark now, since it was night. Rubbing his eyes, he tried to remember. . . .

And then he wished he hadn't. He was glad his father wasn't there, glad no one could see the tears that big boys weren't supposed to cry.

Reaching into his pocket, he found a torn-up Kleenex. And a five-dollar bill. He knew it hadn't been there when he'd jumped the train. Remembering that protective hardness he'd summoned in Sarah's room, he drew on it again, replacing his tears with something gritty and determined.

When Josh Smith hit Chicago, he had five dollars, the clothes on his back, and a promise to keep. In less than a week, he had a room in a deserted building where he fought the rats for space, a box he'd painted black and stuffed with clean rags and a can of saddle soap, plus a rickety chair he'd salvaged from an alley.

Joe at the greasy spoon next door loaned him a spot on the corner and leftovers from the grill in exchange for running errands and free shines.

Spotting a potential client, Josh wiped off the cracked vinyl seat of his chair and blocked the man's path.

"Shine your shoes, mister? Fifty cents'll get you the full treatment. Spit polished and shiny as a new penny."

The man sat down, and Josh had his first customer. "You got a name, son?"

"Rand Slick," Josh said, quickening his buffing strokes.

As good a name as any for a man with no roots. A man in a boy's body. A man who'd learned two rules from a bum: Trust no one, but if you do, make damn sure they earned it. And when you take the dark, endless road back home, go alone.

1

"MISTER?"

"What?"

"I said, shine your shoes, mister?"

Rand Slick blinked several times, willing the present to come into focus.

"Sorry, son, can't spare the time." He pulled out a wad of big ones and peeled off a fifty. "Grab a square meal, but put the rest in your college fund. Believe me, it's a wise investment."

Rand hurried on, skirting a bum hugging a brown paper sack. He hated this sleazy quarter of Vegas. The atmosphere made him feel dirty, as though his fine clothes and supple leather wing tips were melting away, leaving him in rags and battered shoes. Nothing but his ongoing quest to find his sister could induce him to relive the bad old days of his youth.

He entered a run-down building, his hopes lowering with each step on the threadbare carpet. His sources had said this PI was good, but these seedy surroundings made him wonder.

He scanned the faded lettering on the yellowed milk-glass office doors until he stood in front of one that smelled of Windex. The black ink scored into the clear beveled glass was carefully etched and looked new.

It read Rachel Tinsdale, Private Investigator. His flagging spirits climbed a notch when he opened the door and a tinkling wind chime announced his entry. The scents of potpourri and lemon oil masked the mustiness of age. The office was neat, the furniture secondhand but warm, vintage. A vacant desk with several stacks of paper, a cup of coffee, and only a mild litter of files rounded out the scene.

"Have a seat and I'll be right with you."

The invitation came from under the desk. He frowned. Voices could be deceiving, but this one sounded, well, kittenish, too young. An ingenue from an old Elvis movie. Not a good sign. Reflexes and courage and quick thinking were important for the job he needed done. Maybe his sources were wrong. If so, better to find out now. He'd check Ms. Tinsdale's rep out for himself.

His steps were muffled by a big oriental rug. Once he was positioned by the side of the desk, he got a view of flowing red hair, a slender back covered in white cotton, and what appeared to be a cute little tush bobbing on the edge of a wicker chair. The backside package was nice, but it was a minor credential. What he needed were skills he could trust. Yes, a test on how she faced unexpected danger was imperative.

"Don't move," he ordered in a low, menacing tone. "Stop what you're doing and don't move a hair."

"Just let me polish this last toenail, okay?"

Just let me polish this last toenail? Her safety was supposedly at risk and she was worried about the color of her toes? It was a cool and ridiculous response, but it certainly wasn't one that suggested she could handle this case.

"Before you ransack the office, you might as well know I've got ten bucks to my name. Why don't you save yourself the bother of tearing the place up, and me the mess? Here's my purse." A large, ugly handbag was shoved across the floor in his direction. The action made her rear bob a little higher, and Rand's seasoned eyes narrowed appreciatively.

"Go ahead," she said. "Pick it up. The billfold's at the bottom, and the money's stashed in the change compartment. But you'd better hurry, because I've got an appointment in one minute, and you're liable to get caught."

Rand had to give her credit for ingenuity—as well as bad taste in purses. She had his interest, though, so he decided to play along. He stooped down to pick up the bag.

How she did it, he had no idea, but Ms. Tinsdale was no longer under the desk. She was crouched on the floor and pointing the muzzle of a gun straight at his face. He was too stunned to look past the chamber, but he got the impression of fire bending delicate glass.

"Okay, you scumball, drop the goods and lie on the floor. Arms locked behind your head, legs spread, and don't *you* move a hair while I make a body search."

He should start talking—and fast. Then again, having his body searched by Ms. Tinsdale had a certain appeal. To check out her skills—investigator-wise, of course.

"Did you hear me? I mean business, buster. Lie down and spread 'em."

He'd never been one to argue with a gun, especially when a lady was fingering the trigger. He followed her orders.

Her free hand efficiently frisked his arms. Then, when she glided it over his ribs and back, he had the keenest sensation of stimulation. What was he, some kind of pervert? He was actually enjoying this! Rand frowned in self-disapproval.

"I think you'd better stop," he said gruffly.

"Getting too close to something you don't want me to find?"

I'll say, he thought. Her hand was nearly patting his rear, which was awfully close to an area that didn't care that his only interest in Ms. Tinsdale was business.

"Aren't you just a tad overdressed for the occasion? Or maybe you ripped off the threads, huh? No, don't tell me. You're a hood who likes to make a statement."

Her fingers gripped his ankles, checking for a hidden weapon, then clamped onto his calves. When she made a quick glide over the back of his thigh, he groaned.

"Ms. Tinsdale," he said raggedly, "why don't you save us both some embarrassment and stop where you are?"

"How do you know my name?" She did stop, unfortunately, her palm resting near his crotch. "The door, of course. Ah-hah! Thought you could fool me, did you?"

She grazed the interior of his thighs, then went for the other leg.

"Ms. Tinsdale!" he said urgently. "*Enough.* I'm Rand Slick. I'm here for our appointment to discuss a missing person."

"Rand Slick?" she exclaimed. "Oh my gosh!"

Deciding he was in no condition to expose his front side, he kept his position but lifted his head. His gaze collided with the most luminous green eyes he'd ever seen in his life.

A spark of recognition seemed to leap between them, and for a moment they stared at each other. Had he seen her somewhere before? Or maybe there was just something familiar about her that struck a chord with him.

Who was the more surprised, he couldn't have said. Ms. Tinsdale appeared speechless, embarrassed, and something else, something that mirrored his internal confusion. The situation had the feel of a tightrope, each of them tugging at opposite ends while the tension quivered through the charged air.

"Think you could put the rod away? I have an aversion to being on the wrong side of a trigger."

As quickly as the connection had been made it was broken. She turned and carefully put the gun in her purse. Rand was momentarily snared by the swish of long, vivid red hair, the sleek, poetic movement of her back twisting around, the exposure of slim ankle and white fabric riding up her thighs as she got to her feet.

She offered him her hand.

It was dry, but he caught a faint tremor. Or maybe it came from him. He must be having a belated reaction to the gun because he sure wasn't some prepubescent kid—not that he'd ever been a prepubescent kid, exactly. But looking at her, full in the face—a face that seemed fresh but was arranged in sweet, provocative angles—he wondered just how old she was.

Apparently not too young to know how to handle a pistol.

With surprising strength, she helped him to his feet. Standing, she came just beneath his chin. Her own notched up. For something so delicate-looking, it sure had a stubborn set to it.

"Do you care to tell me what that little stick-up act was all about, Mr. Slick? I could've blown your head off."

"Sorry. I wanted to test out your reflexes. Not a good move on my part, I'm afraid."

She snorted her agreement, then nodded to a chair facing her desk. As they sat opposite each other, his respect for her climbed a notch. She looked composed in spite of the test that had gone awry.

Or had it? She was good. She was also one first-class frisker. He shifted in the chair, feeling an uncomfortable reminder of that.

"So tell me," she said, "do you make it a habit to hit people out of left field? Or was this just a lapse into . . ."

"Stupidity?" He chuckled. "I've been known to be unorthodox in my methods. But I get answers and results, one way or the other."

"Mr. Slick, I think we just connected."

No, Ms. Tinsdale, we connected on the floor. Had she read his mind? Was that why she was suddenly busy shuffling papers, why she'd quickly averted her gaze from his?

Rachel could feel his shuttered dark eyes boring into her. Something was happening here that she wasn't comfortable with. Growing up in the PI business had left her with fine instincts when it came to first impressions. Rand Slick had a polished quality that hid some dangerously rough edges.

He was handsome, for sure, but there was nothing soft to balance out the stern planes of his face. His eyes, the color of slate, came close to matching his hair. He wore it a little long for an executive, brushed straight back from a well-shaped forehead. The severe style exposed several lines permanently creased into his brow; smaller lines edged his eyes. Great mouth. Nice jaw. Nothing weak about either.

For some reason he reminded her of Rocky Balboa. The kind of man who maintained an aura of the streets no matter how far he moved up in the world. Or maybe it was just those muscles of his, muscles that felt more brawler-tough than workout-lean.

"Okay," she said brusquely, "you tested me out and you're still here, so I take it I passed?"

"With flying colors."

"Then it's my turn. Before I take a client on I like to know exactly what I'm dealing with. We'll start with some questions."

"Shoot."

"I almost did."

Rand chuckled. Hard to stay tough with this guy, Rachel realized, struggling to maintain her objectivity. Just because he needed her services and had a terrific smile, that didn't make him an okay person.

"So what do you want to know?" he said, easing into a position that suggested comfort but struck her as guarded.

"Let's start with you. Harry Kline put us in touch, but he wasn't too liberal with facts. He said you're legit, you've got some mutual business interests and a personal reason to find someone who's missing. For knowing you a couple of years, he didn't seem to know much. I'd like to know more."

His smile dissolved into a thin, expressionless line. "I didn't come here to discuss myself. Let's stick to business—and any information you need to find my sister." His voice was the flat tone of unquestioned authority.

Rachel felt as though she'd just slammed into a concrete rail after cruising along at a smooth speed. She'd picked up on his rough edges, but she hadn't been prepared for them to emerge so abruptly. Whoever Rand Slick was, he definitely was not a man people messed with. He had a way of turning the tables.

She didn't like it. It took a lot to unnerve her, but he did, with his tense posture and his sharp but strangely distant stare.

"Never let nobody know you're shook," she remembered her dad saying. "Look 'em in the eyeball, and even if your innards turn to mush, don't back down."

Rachel made herself sit straighter. Fortunately, the desk hid the foot she was busy shaking.

"In that case, tell me everything you can, no matter how unimportant it seems. Her habits, her hobbies, and especially the kind of people she hangs out with."

For a split second she caught a glimpse of something vulnerable in his expression. He quickly replaced it with the implacable mask. The unexpected reaction caught her like a velvet uppercut to the right before she'd recovered from the brass-knuckled sting from the left. Against her professional judgment, she found herself growing more curious about this quicksilver enigma than about the sister who had brought him here.

"She's seven years younger than me. That puts her at twenty-six. I know next to nothing about her habits, what she does for kicks, or how she makes a living."

"Do you have a picture?"

Again, that flash of unguarded emotion. Again, the disguise. He reached inside his coat pocket and handed her a faded black-and-white snapshot. He looked away while she studied it.

Rachel's heart softened on a lurch. There was a story in this picture. A very sad story. It wasn't so much the faded image of Rand Slick as a young boy, hugging a little girl who stared up at him adoringly. It was the creased texture of the glossy paper, the edges rubbed smooth from years of constant touching.

She struggled to appear unaffected. This wasn't a person who liked to expose himself, and any sympathy from her would be deflected with the same stony look he was now wearing. Besides, there was the cardinal rule: A PI never let himself get emotionally involved in a case. It wasn't professional.

"Nothing more recent?"

"No. We were separated shortly after this picture was taken."

"How?"

"It doesn't matter. What does is that I've been tracking her for years. I've pulled strings, gone through litigation, and run into one dead end after another. The family she was living with died when their house caught fire. Any pictures there went up in smoke."

"She got out?"

"They lived in the country, and I understand from the closest neighbors, she ran off a year earlier with a drifter who was passing through. She was a senior in high school."

"There's an angle—high school. Did you check the yearbook? We could get a more recent picture there."

"I checked that out. Country school, and not enough students to go to the bother. Believe me, Ms. Tinsdale, I left no stone unturned."

"Do you think you'd recognize her if you saw her?"

"I do. I . . . I had occasion to see her twice. Once when she was ten, and then at fourteen. At least I thought it was her from a distance. A brother can spot his sister, no matter how many years pass."

"You didn't talk to her? Find out any facts we can use?"

"No. There were too many people around, and besides, I . . ." He passed a hand over his eyes, concealing what she suspected was some emotion he didn't want her to see. "It was an unusual situation. Don't ask me to explain. Please?"

That last word had seemed hard for him to get out, as though he were requesting a personal favor and asking favors didn't come easy. He'd kept his voice even, but there was no mistaking the undercurrent of something raw. If necessary, she'd probe later; for now she respected his need for privacy.

Rachel extended the photo to him. Their hands touched. They came to an understanding with that touch. She cared. He needed her to care enough to share his search.

They shared more. A distinct but disturbing current was passing between them. It was achingly personal, and something she couldn't acknowledge with a client. Especially not with a man as mercurial as this one.

"There's more." He pocketed the snapshot. "You might as well know, five different detectives have worked on this case. I've got a thick file that you're welcome to look over if we can come to terms."

"Go ahead and give me the rundown." She put pen to paper, ready to take notes.

"Sarah—my sister—moved around a lot after she ran away." He paused, and she sensed that some thought was troubling him.

"Do you know why she ran away? Could it have anything to do with why she stayed on the move?"

"I don't think so. The family she was with seemed pretty solid. Who knows? Maybe it was just a crazy whim, or an idea she picked up from . . . a bad influence." He cleared his throat and shifted as though the chair were a bun warmer and he wanted to get away from the toasty heat. "Anyway, I got pretty close several times, but either she had wanderlust or she was on the run."

"Any guess why?"

"My sources indicate the man she ran off with had some shady connections."

"Were your sources reliable?"

"They were shady enough themselves to make the connection."

Her pen stopped in mid-scratch. "Back up a minute. Are you telling me you're in with some undesirable characters?"

As he raked a hand through his back-brushed hair, light filtered through flecks of silver. How many of those flecks had been put there by his quest? she wondered. Didn't matter. Even if she sympathized with him, no way was she getting mixed up with the wrong crowd. Her reputation was more important than getting kicked out of this office because she couldn't pay the rent.

"Look," he said, sighing. "I'm clean. I've got no faith in the system, and I do know some people outside it who've gotten me information that money can't buy. I don't set myself up to owe favors, only to collect them. Relax. Whatever my connections, they're not who I am."

Rachel tapped her pen against the paper unconsciously and studied him intently.

"And just who are you, Mr. Slick?"

His jaw tightened; a muscle ticked in his cheek. Rand got up and leaned over the desk. Any vulnerability she had sensed in him before had been snuffed out. This towering man with the face of granite was intimidating the living daylights out of her.

She'd be damned before she let him know it.

"Since you seem as concerned with my background as you are with this case, I'll give you a little bio, and then we'll drop it. What do you want to know? The ID I can't give for my sister?"

Don't back down. If you do, he's out of here. You keep hitting a nerve, and now he's turning the tables. Again.

Rachel swallowed hard. "I like to know how my clients tick. If I'm risking my hide, you can't blame me for that."

His expression said that he could and did.

"Okay, we'll start with the fact that I find it grating when people tap their pens." He whipped the pen from her hand and tossed it to the desk. "As for habits, I brush my teeth two times a day and shower every morning. I drink moderately, avoid emotional entanglements and practice safe sex. My favorite hobby is making money, but I like to play racquetball and poker. I can't stand to lose, and it's rare that I do. As for palling around, I prefer to fly solo." He smiled without warning, and she was reminded of a barracuda contemplating lunch.

His turnaround bothered her as much as the thought that being devoured by Rand Slick had a certain frightful appeal.

"Now," he continued smoothly, "since you know as much about me as the next guy, you can drop the mister and call me Rand. Turnabout being fair play, it's your turn, Rachel."

Belatedly she realized she was staring at him, mouth agape. So much for being her father's daughter, master bluffer and A-1 private eye.

"What—what do you want to know?"

"Everything, actually. But for now I'll stick with some important specifics. Do you like to visit faraway places? Could you possibly endure being stripped in public? And, by some miracle, is your virginity somewhat intact? If the answer is no to any or all, can you fake the first two if I make it worth your while?"

"*What?*"

"You heard me." He gripped her wrist, his fingers biting urgently into her skin. His touch was compelling, even as it set off a shrilling alarm. "I need a woman with guts and looks. You've got both. But they won't do me any good unless you're willing to stand on an auction block and go up for sale."

"You've got to be kidding."

"This is no joke, Ms.—Rachel. I need your skills, and I need your body." His gaze raked an incisive path from her head to her breasts. She was shocked to feel an electric reaction. Instinctively she crossed her free arm over her chest. "Good," he said. "The more innocent you appear, the better. If you've got the courage, I've got the in."

"What *are* you talking about?"

"The reason for this meeting." He fixed her with a level stare. "I want to buy you."

Funny, he didn't look nuts. Of course, Jack the Ripper probably hadn't, either. Her wisest move would be to humor him until she could buzz security.

"Of course," she said, forcing a smile and wishing her gun was in her hand instead of her purse. "Did you have a payment schedule in mind?"

"You can name your price. And quit fumbling for a way to flag the guards. Hear me out and I'll leave if you don't want to cut the deal."

"I think you'd better get to it."

"All right. I tracked my sister down, but I can't get to her without a special ticket." He leaned closer to her face. His breath was warm, and she inhaled the subtle fragrances of bay and night spice. "Three words," he said in a low, uninflected voice. *"White slave trade."*

2

"Did you just say 'White slave trade'?"

Damn, he thought. He'd let his desperation overcome his good sense. Hadn't he been turned down enough times without scaring this one off before she gave him half a chance?

Rand released her wrist, absently noting that he could easily break it. He was nearly twice her size. He also noted, and not so absently, that her skin was as soft as feather down and disturbingly pleasant to the touch.

"I think I came on a little too strong." He smiled apologetically, having decided charm might be his best tactic. "It's a long story, Rachel. If I can buy the rest of your day, I'll be glad to pay generously. No strings, just a chance to have you hear me out."

She was silent, probably weighing whether to take him seriously or question his mental stability. He caught her glancing at her purse before turning to an appointment book. She shut it quickly, but not before he saw that it was blank except for a space with his name. Rand looked away, not wanting her to know he'd seen.

"My fee is fifty dollars an hour."

"Why don't we make it an even five hundred for the day?" Rand shelled out the cash and laid it on her appointment book. "This shouldn't take ten hours, but I'd like to compensate for interfering with your schedule."

She looked from the neat stack of bills to him, a startled expression animating her face before she quickly disguised it. Rand decided then and there that he had himself a good actress—a little unseasoned maybe, but lots of potential. He tucked the fact away for future reference.

"Well . . ." she said slowly, appearing to debate with herself. "I suppose I could break free, since this seems to be urgent. Have a seat, and we'll pick up where you left off."

"If you don't mind, I'd rather discuss this over lunch." Not that he was hungry, but putting her at ease in a relaxed atmosphere seemed a better way to lure her in. He didn't like to get overly personal with people, but from what he'd seen of Rachel, she might respond best to exactly that. "Tell me what you're hungry for and we'll head out." Rand went to the door, not wanting to give her time to balk.

When she hesitated, he twisted the knob. She made her decision, quickly stashing the money in her wallet and rummaging around for her keys. Five hundred dollars! Enough to pay the back rent and buy groceries for the month. If Rand Slick wanted to eat lunch on her time, she was in no position to quibble.

She just wished he'd quit throwing her equilibrium off, not to mention getting her sidetracked by the way he was waiting, his hands shoved into his pockets so that his shirt strained and his pants did the same. Lord, she hoped she looked calmer than she was.

"How about a sandwich at the corner coffee shop?" she suggested, relieved her voice was deceptively steady.

"How about a nice place on the other side of town? No offense to the neighborhood, but I prefer other surroundings. We can flag a taxi if you're uncomfortable driving in a car alone with me."

She was uncomfortable, but it came from the proximity of their bodies as they stood—too close—at the door. She could feel strange waves of energy generating an even stranger heat between them. It was as if radio waves were riding the air and tuning in on the fine hairs prickling on the back of her neck.

Rachel did her best to ignore it. He'd paid in advance, and the least she could do was show some good faith by allowing him to drive. Besides, in a taxi they'd be forced to share a cramped seat.

"Starting now, we're on your time, Rand. My office is officially closed for the day. Since my car's in the shop, we don't have to flip to see whose wheels we take."

He smiled, seemingly pleased, but the quirk of his lips only managed to make her awkward. At the moment, Cool Hand Luke she was not, and she cursed softly when her keys slipped from her grasp and clattered to the floor.

"I'll get them," he offered.

They almost knocked heads. Their hands connected at the keys. For breathless seconds, she couldn't move. Meaning to laugh the accident off and pretend there wasn't something so physically startling in the contact that it snuffed out her remaining composure, she slowly raised her face.

His breath was on her. There was a dark room behind his eyes, one that was as unchaste and ominous as it was lush with invitation. Leather and lace. Black velvet sheets and white silk curtains trailing the floor. Haunting. Erotic. And so dark that she was momentarily blinded by his slate-eyed eclipse.

Rachel blinked, trying to get her balance. What was she doing? Decorating his bedroom and checking out his lighting scheme? Rand was way out of her range of experience, and this was a professional meeting, even if the roiling in her tummy insisted it was more.

She took an unsteady breath and managed a faint smile.

"Not a smooth move, huh?"

"I like the way you move."

Rachel quickly rose and shoved the key in. *Damn, why couldn't she get it to lock?* She was jiggling it frenziedly when he caught her hand. Her breathing was not normal. Nothing had seemed normal since he'd walked through this stupid door that she couldn't get locked.

"Let me." His hand glided over hers, working the key. It clicked. For several seconds they remained still, but then he broke the contact, and Rachel exhaled the breath she'd been holding so long her lungs shuddered with relief.

"Thanks," she said as Rand led the way, guiding her by the arm. His grip was polite but firm, and disconcertingly provocative in the subtle pressure of palm to elbow. "That's a testy door," she added, to fill up the taut silence. "It takes a special touch to get it to cooperate."

"Reminds me of some people I've known." He grinned devilishly, and Rachel felt as if she'd just tripped over something. She glanced down, almost expecting to see her heart doing a tap dance. "Take me, for example." He chuckled. "Believe it or not, I can get testy."

"Why, surely you jest." Rachel laughed, glad to break the tension. "And here I thought you were always laid-back."

"Laying back is something I could be tempted to indulge in—given the right person and circumstances."

Rachel looked at him sharply. If Rand had picked up her not-so-subtle reaction to him, he was certainly being forward about letting her know it. Or maybe she was just so shaken by it herself that she was getting her signals crossed.

"Why don't we talk about the circumstances and people in question? That is, faraway places and your sister."

"Here we are." He opened the passenger door of a Mercedes convertible. She got in without getting an answer. Rand lifted an edge of her skirt that was trailing the ground, then draped it over her lap. "Buckle up. I've got a vested interest in keeping you safe."

The door shut, and Rachel shook her head, hoping to clear it. For some reason, she'd never felt less safe in her life, or so aware of a man, as the one in question climbed behind the wheel. Rand put on a CD, surprising her with his selection. Strange music: dipping flute notes, the rippling, cascading sound of some exotic stringed instrument. Winding. Mellow. A musically sensual ache wisping round her mind with tantalizing images.

"Do you like it?" He glanced at her keenly as he negotiated the early-afternoon traffic.

"It's very...intriguing."

"Tell me what it reminds you of, what picture it draws in your imagination."

The low, mesmerizing appeal of his voice blended into the hypnotic lull of the clear, undulating notes. She closed her eyes, and for a moment she was transported to a faraway world.

"I see...camels, people in long white robes, sand, palms." She laughed softly. "A hookah on a carved teakwood table next to a brass lamp that might have belonged to Aladdin. Persian rugs, dark rich silk. It's a scene from the *Arabian Nights*."

"And do you smell anything?"

"Sandalwood, incense, and..." *Bay and night spice.* Rachel's eyes snapped open. Good heavens, she'd almost described his cologne! Feeling her cheeks grow warm, she rushed on, "My dad always did say I had a vivid imagination. I get carried away with it sometimes."

Rand stopped the car, and she realized they were parked in front of an exclusive establishment, the kind of place where she was afraid she might not know which fork to use. She'd just watch Rand and follow suit; she was good at bluffing when she had to be.

And now was one time she had to. The exotic setting she'd conjured was still with her, and she was caught up in the tendrils of the music. Rand was studying her closely, not making his expected move to get out. So why was she sitting here, mooning over some steamy, sensual and purely imaginary scene with a man who was, after all, nothing more than a potential client? Reminding herself that this wasn't a date, Rachel reached for the handle.

"Wait." He caught her hand. There was something very intimate in the innocent gesture. "Your imagination's more than vivid, Rachel. It's very close to reality. Have you ever heard of a small Middle Eastern country by the name of Zebedique?"

"No," she said quietly, acutely aware that he hadn't released her hand. Could he feel her small shake, the one that hummed to a sweet vibration through her nervous system? This was not appropriate to the situation, not in the least. Hadn't her father trained her better, taught her never to get involved with a client?

She willed herself to be immune, but failed. So she tried to withdraw her hand from his, because it felt too good holding hers. But Rand didn't seem inclined to let go unless she pried it loose.

"I'd like to tell you a little about Zebedique," he said, running his thumb over hers so lightly that she wondered if she might have imagined the brush. "It's very similar to the place you described. Rich, a little excessive, and hedonistic. I own a house there. Quite a bit different from my place in New York."

"A vacation getaway?" And what was he doing in Vegas, if New York was home? His sister, she supposed. The sister she'd almost forgotten about. Rachel winced, upset with herself. This was no way to start out her new practice.

"I guess it could be. But that's not why I bought it."

"You think your sister's there?"

He nodded. "I do. And I need a woman to get us connected. A very special woman who's savvy and brave and can pose as my—well, someone who has access to areas where only women are allowed. It's very segregated, and men can't approach other men's, ah . . . territory."

He watched closely for a reaction, and Rachel managed not to show her apprehension. He was choosing his words very carefully, obviously not wanting to scare her off. No need, she thought, she was scaring herself enough. Suddenly she realized that she was now stroking his thumb in a way that was not at all imaginary. With a mental slap of ruler to wrist, she stopped the nonsense.

"Go on, Rand. You're paying me to listen. I'm all ears." *And sweaty palms.* She felt his fingertips brushing over them, making her nerve ends leapfrog, then collide with each other. She needed to get her hand back.

She left it in his care. Rachel told herself that he was holding her captive with his grip. The fact that she was a willing prisoner was something better ignored.

"Okay, I'll be blunt. I have a plan that can get you in, as, shall we say, a desirable acquisition. No one would buy you but me, and once I did, no one else would dare touch you. You'd be considered my personal property."

"Your...personal...property?" Rachel stared at him hard. Surely her imagination was going berserk. All this illicit hand touching must be affecting her brain, shading his words with intimate overtones he hadn't intended. "You're not telling me that women are being sold there for sexual purposes to the men who buy them?"

"Not just any men. Wealthy men from around the world. I understand virgins go for a premium, due to supply problems, and American women are especially in demand because the slavers are afraid to risk many abductions. The ones they acquire seem to be without family to trace them. A local casino is where Sarah disappeared."

For a moment she was beyond speech. Then came a surge of sympathy for Sarah, and her heart went out to Rand.

"How horrible for you. You must be worried sick."

"Worrying doesn't solve anything—action does. I need you, Rachel. Once we're there and the transaction's made, I can protect you, since you'll belong to me." Something troubled and haunting was in his gaze, and she puzzled over it, and then she puzzled over her desire to soothe it away. "Experience has taught me to take care of what's mine, whatever the opposition."

"Sarah?" she said softly.

His nod was curt. She left it alone.

"You mentioned a house in Zebedique?"

"Where we'd live—the two of us. We'd have to give the appearance of our expected roles." He smiled that disarming smile of his that scrambled her mental faculties and made her wonder what hid beneath the smiling surface. "You can act, can't you, Rachel? It wouldn't be unpleasant. The house has quite a layout. I've got an office already set up, there's a pool, a sauna, servants around to do the cooking and cleaning. You'd have your very own handmaiden. I understand she used to be a masseuse. Just think, in your off time you could get back rubs."

He patted her hand. If it was meant to be comforting it was anything but. Back rubs and strong masculine hands provoked other images.

"But our roles—what would they entail?"

Rand reached for his door; when she followed suit, he caught her wrist.

"For one thing, it would mean I act like the sultan of the house while you pretend to stroke my ego. If you're half as good at that as you are in the hand-holding department, I'll be strutting for a month."

Rachel flushed and jerked her wrist from his grip.

"Now," he continued, drumming her clenched fist with his fingertips, "just in case we can strike a deal, what say we give it a little practice? You stay put, and I'll come around to get you. Then, once we're in the restaurant, I'll order for us both, and you look like you're hanging on my every word while I bore you silly talking about my arbitrage business."

"Do I have to laugh if you tell a bad joke?"

"I understood all good concubines do."

"Concu—"

His door slammed shut, and Rachel stared at it, mouth agape. Concubine? Hadn't that word gone out with the Ol-

Testament? The CD had shut off, but Rachel was left with the uneasy impression that the music and the word went together strangely well.

As well as his hand and hers, and the lingering ripple that seemed to mesh warmth with a dark, forbidden thrill.

3

RAND TOPPED OFF their champagne flutes while Rachel excused herself and went to the ladies' room. He watched the alluring combination of slender ankles, shapely legs and hourglass curves that swayed in time with her gliding stride. He liked her walk. It had an attitude.

Fact was, there was a lot he liked about her. Maybe a bit too much. He'd have to be careful, or she might slip under his skin, which was more than any of the string of women who had passed through what he supposed was a personal life had ever done.

Rand sipped his champagne, mentally toasting his good fortune. If he was going to buy a woman, Rachel was definitely the one he wanted to own. He hadn't gotten her to agree yet, but he would.

If exposing enough of himself to evoke her compassion—and playing on the surprising physical tug between them—didn't work, money should do the trick. Then again, Rachel didn't seem to be all that interested in money. For some reason, that bothered him. Maybe because it made him feel devalued, reminded him of things he'd lost along the way—emotions he couldn't afford, and qualities that didn't have price tags.

"Now, where were we?" Rachel smiled, and he felt an unfamiliar throb penetrate his senses. Before she could reseat herself, he got up and pushed in her chair. "Imagine, a bona fide gentleman—and chivalry's supposedly dead."

She laughed softly, and it was as if effervescent bubbles were seeping into his pores. Natural. Wholesome. Lush. *Whew.*

"Imagine, a woman who accepts it as chivalry and doesn't growl 'You chauvinist.'" He saluted her with his glass, and she hit him with a hearty burst of laughter before he'd recuperated from the aftereffects of her full-lipped grin. "What's so funny? I haven't even told you a bad joke yet."

"When you said 'growl,' it reminded me of a silly toast my dad used to say." She giggled and sipped at her champagne. When she looked over the rim, her eyes were sparkling. Rand was startled to feel something jolt him dead-center like a bull's-eye zap into a runaway target that had never been hit.

"Now I'm curious." *And a little shook, and I'm juggling an arousal that's got nothing and everything to do with getting you to agree to share sleeping space with me.* "You were going to tell me about your dad and how you grew up anyway, so why don't we start with his toast?"

"I couldn't possibly say it in here."

"Why not?"

"Because this place is so classy."

She glanced around, and he noticed that she seemed ill at ease. He'd also noticed the way she had emulated his choice of fork or knife during the meal. Discreetly, with a PI's ability to play a charade, but he'd deliberately used an incorrect one, and she'd followed suit.

He knew. Rachel had a sharp eye, but a lack of savvy when it came to protocol and etiquette. He could relate to that. Years ago he'd spent many a hard-earned dollar to order salad and soup in ritzy places like this. Watching. Assimilating. Mimicking the manners of the elite, then returning to his hole-in-the-wall to wolf down a substandard pizza or hot dogs with pork and beans.

No, she didn't fit here any better than he did, and it gave him a sense of something shared. Sure was a strange feeling, but he did find it a pleasant one. Comforting, even.

"Look, Rachel, you're classier than that highbrow bitching at her husband at the next table—and I'm a paying customer. I'd say that gives us the right to say anything we damn well please." Rand lifted his glass. "C'mon, indulge me. Then you can indulge me some more and tell me about your dad."

She shrugged. "We still have a lot to discuss. You're sure this is how you want to spend your time?"

"We will. I am. And let's hear it. Sultan's decree."

"In that case, touch your glass to your nose." Rand did as instructed, though his attention was on the cute way Rachel's nose turned up and crinkled as the tiny bubbles tickled it. There was a light sprinkling of freckles across the delicate bridge that made her appear younger than the twenty-two years he'd learned she was.

"Next you have to growl." She demonstrated, and he growled along with her. It was a low animal sound that provoked thoughts of similar noises in the heat of passion. His lids dipped to half-mast, and hers opened wide.

"Uh, that's . . . that's very good, Rand. A little ferocious, but definitely in the spirit. Kind of."

"Maybe you should show me again," he suggested, pulling his chair next to hers. Leaning in close, he inhaled her unique scent, a scent that was unencumbered by perfume. Money smelled good, but Rachel made money smell like dirt. "Growl for me. Soft, but deep in your throat."

Something that sounded like a faint squeak emerged.

"You can do better than that, Rachel. Once more, but with feeling. C'mon, I'll even do it with you."

He made a noise like an animal's mating call as it began to rut. She hesitated, then joined him, and this time he heard a sweet undulation shift into a kittenish purr.

"Purr-fect," he whispered. "What's that old saying, something about the cat's meow?"

She quickly reached for her champagne. Rand intercepted her and put the glass to her lips, raising it slightly so that a trickle escaped the side of her mouth. And what a mouth, he thought with a sensual pang. Made for kissing and kissing back until those lips were even fuller than they already were.

He felt his body shift, felt his tongue dancing against his teeth. Dying to lap up that stray drop, he bit down before he could act on the impulse. Quickly salvaging the napkin she was twisting in her lap, he dabbed the liquid away.

"Rand," she said in a strangled voice. "Rand, those people are watching us."

"Oh? Then let's do the toast, since we've hooked an audience. Maybe it'll give them something to talk about besides what they were arguing over."

"But it's for a noisy bar, or a party with friends."

"Then let's be friends and have our own private party." Friends. He'd like that with her, he realized. And then he found himself exposing his truer colors. Even as his mouth formed the words, he could scarcely believe he was lowering the guard that was his constant companion.

"Pretentiousness doesn't score many points with me," he heard himself say. "And, believe it or not, I'm more at home in a corner bar than hobnobbing with the likes of our fellow diners. I like you, Rachel. Just the way you are."

"Rocky," she said, almost to herself. He quirked a brow in question, and she claimed her glass. "Okay, here goes. Look out, mouth." His gaze settled on her lips. She wet them, and he managed not to try for a taste of her little pink tongue. "Look out, gums. Open up, throat—here it comes!"

Rand nearly choked on a growl, while a belly-deep laugh tickled his grinding lust. Oh, it did feel good to laugh. If Rachel only knew . . . It was like a gift tied with a bow of joy.

"Lady, you are dynamite."

"I am?" Rachel couldn't believe what she was hearing. "Open up, throat—here it comes!" wasn't exactly crème de la crème.

Whatever standards he judged people by, they sure weren't the norm. Then again, Rand was anything but the norm himself. They were a pair in some way she couldn't finger. Him, with his brutish but suave exterior; her, with her bungling attempts at sophistication, which only magnified how out of sync she was in this uptight, budget-straining joint.

As far as she was concerned, her Caesar salad was wilted lettuce, this pâté de foie gras stuff was nothing but fancy chopped liver, and the beef whatever-you-called-it—bourguignon?—reminded her of Dinty Moore, with some Carlo Rossi stirred in for good measure.

"I think maybe you mean Rice Crispies, Rand. I'm closer to snap-crackle-pop than dynamite."

"Says who? You? Or some significant other I'd like to know about if there's one hanging around."

Rachel hesitated as his eyes narrowed on her. Rand Slick wasn't someone to toy or flirt with. If she was smart, she'd nip this in the bud, tell him she was heavily involved with someone who didn't exist. That was what she'd do—lie. Lie, and get this meeting back on track. Forget his dark charm, ignore the delicious push-pull between them, and settle for safety.

"No significant other." Rachel closed her eyes, angry with herself. She'd lied right nice, just to the wrong person. If the road to hell was paved with good intentions, she ought to be frying any minute.

"In that case, you are definitely dynamite. A lit stick that's giving me a charge I haven't had in . . . well, maybe never." A waiter appeared and took his plastic. "Now tell me how you turned out this way. I get the impression that dad of yours taught you more than a toast and how to frisk a hood making a statement."

Rachel laughed self-consciously, reminded of their hands-on intro. Those muscles of his were . . . better left unremembered.

"He raised me. My mother died before I was old enough to remember much about her."

"And did your mother have beautiful red hair?"

"She had red hair." Rachel smiled, greatly pleased by his compliment. She touched her hair, then stroked her fingers through it before she realized what she was doing. Preening! She was preening for him, and wishing he was doing the touching instead of her. She jerked her hand away. Rand looked as if he longed to pick up where she'd left off.

"Anyway, Daddy did the best he knew how bringing me up. He signed me up for a softball team when I was six, and taught me to throw a punch when the boys said I pitched like a girl."

"Did he teach you to throw the ball, too?"

"You bet. Especially when I almost got kicked off the team for bloodying the biggest bully's nose."

He laughed, and she enjoyed the deep sound; it was a far different kind of pleasure from the illicit one she'd felt upon hearing his sexy growl. She liked to make him laugh. Maybe because she was pretty sure the faint lines fanning his eyes weren't caused by laughter.

"Was he protective when you started dating?"

"I'll say. He told me boys had one thing on their minds, and he should know, since he was one of them. He had this test for judging them. Handshakes. Said you could tell a lot about a man by the way he shook hands. A limp handshake? Wimp. A firm handshake meant guts."

As he chuckled, Rand stretched. Her gaze slid to his chest. When he didn't have his suit coat on, she could discern the width and proportions of his musculature. Again she was reminded of a street tough with a smooth veneer. Rocky. Slamming his punches into a side of beef instead of a punching bag. The underdog coming out on top, compensating for life's shortcomings with grit and character. She hadn't tested his handshake, but she was certain he had guts, and then some.

"I can understand his wanting to be protective. It's something I've felt in the past. The distant past." His expression let her know that he hadn't missed where she'd been looking and he rather liked catching her at it. "So. Besides playing ball, throwing punches, and screening your dates' handshakes, what else did you pick up from your dad?"

"Target shooting. Hanging around his office, learning the business. Sitting in on poker games with him and the boys while they drank beer and swapped jokes. If you were expecting fancy dresses and cheerleading practice, I don't qualify. Disappointed?"

Rand tapped a finger to his lips. She wished he'd quit doing that. It kept drawing too much attention to his mouth. In fact, everything he'd said and done had drawn too much attention to him as a man and to her as a woman, and too little to the real reason they were here. It should bother her; it bothered her that it didn't.

"Disappointed? Hardly. Intrigued? Very. But I can imagine it must have been hard growing up like that. Setting you apart from other kids your age." He hesitated, but then she felt his hand cover hers. "I know what that's like."

A small silence fell between them, one that was easy and yet not easy at all. She felt a sense that they were sharing a common bond, but she could feel him pulling back, as though he'd confessed more than he'd wanted to and was struggling to understand why.

The waiter broke into their tentative liaison before she could explore the lure of the unknown. How much of this man's exterior masked a self-protective nature, a nature born of a past that marked him as different from others? The question tugged at her, even as the marvelous sensation lingered that Rand found her intriguing.

As they walked to the car, he kept his hand at the small of her back. The light touch sparked a tingle at the base of her spine that shot out in all different directions. It felt like the lightest of kisses, traced by the tip of his tongue, and oh, Lord, why was she thinking such a thing?

Some PI she was. Her conduct in the restaurant had been anything but professional, and her thoughts had been even less. She felt miserable about it. Miserable and fantastic, what with this glow that packed the punch of ten hot toddies in a single gulp. It simmered, then expanded, as his hand shifted to settle at her waist. Then she felt a slight squeeze that was pure *mmm.... Magic. Madness.*

Distance. She had to get some distance, and quick. If she hit that nerve of his, maybe he'd keep his distance, since she couldn't seem to.

"You didn't tell me about how you grew up. Or how you came to lose your sister."

For a fleeting moment, something poignant, tortured, softened his features. But then he erased it, and his expression was as blank as a washed-down chalkboard. Rocky was transformed into a renovated high rise, all the cracks and damage disguised by plaster patches, fresh coats of paint and tightly sealed windows. One-way windows. The kind designed to let somebody look out but deflect the view of anyone trying to look in.

Funny thing about windows, she thought. They had a way of getting broken or left open. Glass was fragile, and accidents did happen.

"I lost Sarah to fate, Rachel. As for growing up, my home was on the streets. Alone."

"And?"

"And arbitrage is a risky business, with big returns if you've got a knack for juggling two things at the same time. I buy and sell securities simultaneously when I detect a discrepancy in the going price. The way I operate is by getting rid of what I buy almost before I acquire it. In rare cases, I hang on to something for myself. If you're good, and I am, big profits are reaped. If you screw up, and that's easy to do, it's immediate death."

She frowned, disappointed with him for being so reticent, and for giving her the distance she needed. But most of all she was upset with herself for telling him so much and so freely, and for wanting more than she could possibly have.

"You think I told you nothing, don't you?"

"You explained your line of business but left out much of personal importance."

"Wrong. Read between the lines, Rachel. After all, you're a PI. You should be good at this." He waved her into the car, and she got in. Rand leaned in close, bay and night spice evoking images of exotic music. "While I drive, you can think me over. Who knows? Maybe you'll figure me out, which is more than anyone else has ever pulled off."

"I don't guess you're feeling generous enough to spare a hint or two?"

His lips thinned, and then slowly shifted to a sly smile. "Think of me as a Rubik's Cube. But even if you solve it, the colors won't quite line up, because a few slots are missing. Oh, and the hinges are stubborn, too. Comes from some jagged edges on the inside that've been there too long to budge from their old groove."

As he drove, Rachel stole glances at his profile while she puzzled her way through the maze. Missing: Sarah. But what else? And what caused the jagged edges that he seemed to find more comfortable than exposing even a small bit of himself?

The music hovered between them again, slipping into the crevices of her mind and playing tricks with reality. She could see him dressed in a sheikh's flowing white robe, autonomous and mysterious, until he shed it and revealed all his missing pieces, rough edges, and multicolored hues to a special woman. She saw the woman in a long, flowing dress of white gauze, her arms open wide and trembling as he slipped away her veil.

Rachel couldn't see her face. Yet she couldn't deny that, more than anything, she wanted the woman to be her.

4

RAND STRETCHED, then leaned back into the cushions of Rachel's old couch, feeling an odd delight in simply being close to her after the way their first meeting had been cut short. He'd had to rush back to New York after their lunch to straighten out a potential mess in a high-stakes acquisition.

Two things had struck him in their three-day separation: For once he resented the intrusion of his work, finding the manic pace annoying rather than exhilarating. Moreover, he'd caught himself calling her on several occasions with tidbits of information that could easily have waited.

Truth was, he liked the sound of her voice, the kittenish freshness of it. But, most of all, that breathless little catch that made him think they were sharing this peculiar sensation of light-headedness—as if the earth had changed the rules of gravity, causing his jaded senses to be buoyed up on the air while his feet moonwalked New York concrete that had about as much substance as a marshmallow.

Staring at her bent head while she studied Sarah's file, Rand marveled at this internal out-of-syncness. He'd all but run to her front door, anxious and yet certain he was imagining the whole crazy thing. And then he hadn't been certain of anything, not even his name, because she'd knocked the supports out from under him with a single dazzling smile.

Whump! He'd felt the ground tilt as a soft, tingling blow clobbered him right between the eyes. He didn't know what the hell it was. Not lust; it went beyond that. And surely not love. He'd never been in it, never expected to be, and he most certainly didn't believe in love at first sight.

Rachel's brow was furrowed when she suddenly looked up. "You're staring at me."

"Caught me. Want me to stop?"

"No—I mean, yes. You make it hard to concentrate."

"Do I? Sorry," he lied. Then he managed a half truth. "I'm trying to judge your reaction to what you're reading." He leaned over and tapped a well-thumbed page. "I see you've gotten to the meat of the matter."

"The investigator you hired did a good job. Several slavers operating under a single umbrella and shipping to one port. Zebedique." She tossed several photographs from the file onto the coffee table. "I thought you said you didn't have any other pictures of Sarah. I do assume this is her—or at least what I can see of her, covered from head to foot in the local costume."

"That's her. The men I hired to keep Sarah under surveillance managed to snap those before her guards joined her. As to why I didn't show you these before—two reasons. First, there's not much to see. Just a pair of eyes peeking out, and the rest of her face under a scarf. Second—"

"You thought it might scare me off if I got a gander at these too soon."

"Bingo. You do have to admit our first meeting was enough of a shocker as it was." Fearful of the effect the Polaroid images could still have on her decision, he tried to get a fix on their impact. "I felt the nature of these photos was more graphic than if she'd been wearing nothing. Maybe you can understand why I held out on you."

"I do, and it was probably a smart move on your part. Even knowing what I know now, I can hardly believe what I'm looking at. It's another world, and not one I'd ever care to be in. Imagine, living without the freedom to walk alone or even choose how you want to dress." Rachel studied the pictures a moment longer before replacing them in the file. She shook her head and said bluntly, "This is a very nasty business. It needs to be exposed, Rand."

"As soon as I've got Sarah. Any tip-off before then would implicate a casino manager who's rolling in dirty payoff dough. If I finger him now, and he squeals on his crooked buddies, any chance Sarah's got is snuffed."

"But this has been going on too long. Sarah disappeared months ago, and Lord only knows how many women were abducted before her. Surely there's another way besides the one we've discussed."

"Don't you think I've considered every other angle? I've kept round-the-clock surveillance in Zebedique since I traced her there. They've located the house—"

"Conveniently close to the one you bought when you went to check the country out yourself?"

"Of course. Unfortunately she's too heavily guarded to make a successful snatch. Unless you can come up with a better idea, I see no other way but to make the connection at the bathhouse she's taken to every Friday."

"Women only, right?"

"That's right. Massages, whirlpools, saunas. I understand from one of the servants I hired—the masseuse who would be your guard—that the concubines are left unattended in the sauna."

"They're not afraid their prisoners might escape?"

"Hardly. Not when they're naked and have to be covered from head to toe just to walk down the street."

Rachel tapped the pen she'd been using to take notes, and he stared at her hand, struck again by the delicate structure of tapered fingers he would love to feel sifting through his hair, flexing against his neck, reaching for his—

She abruptly stopped the tapping. And then he remembered his unbecoming little speech that first day. Abrasive. Typical of the man he'd become, who didn't quite seem to be the same man, the man within the skin that felt this inexplicable need for her touch.

"This handmaid, or guard . . ." she said.

"Jayna."

"How do you know she was telling you the truth? That she wasn't suspicious and might be setting you up?"

"Because she's under the impression I'm going to take up residence with a concubine of my own and I want to be sure said concubine would have no chance of escape. She's retired from the bathhouse, and I'm paying her well. Jayna has no need to be suspicious, and every reason to want to keep a generous paycheck."

"You've been thorough."

"So have you." He smiled when she arched an expressive brow in surprise. "You checked up on me while I was gone. Were you satisfied with what you discovered?"

"I was impressed," she admitted. "You're very high profile. Respected. Successful to the point of embarrassment. But even the business magazines say you're as much a mystery man as a boy wonder. No one knows where you came from. There doesn't seem to be a trace of your whereabouts until you hit the arbitrage business eight years ago. You've been elbowing and plowing your way to the top ever since."

"Surely you don't believe everything you read."

"No. But apparently you found out I made a few calls. I was left with the impression that you're not necessarily liked by your competition, but you are feared. Even by other cutthroats in the business. Mr. Slick, you have a reputation for playing dirty pool."

He usually regarded such a comment as a compliment of sorts. But when it came from her he felt a sudden need to defend himself.

"I play to win, Rachel. It's the only way I know to survive. And before you swallow someone else's sour grapes, keep in mind we're all products of our circumstances."

"Meaning?"

"It's true I'm less merciful than most, but maybe it's because I have reason to be hungrier than they ever thought about being." He could see her weighing that, turning it this way and that and coming up with something that might have been sympathy.

Sympathy for Sarah's case—that he wanted. Any other kind he wanted no part of.

"Sliding that around the Rubik's Cube? Careful of the jagged edges, Rachel," he warned. "My competition is, and they're ten times tougher than you."

He instinctively kept his expression challenging. And guarded. But the hardness he usually felt knotted in the pit of his makeup was struggling against an alien force. Something vulnerable. Something that was nudging his defenses with a persistent whisper that escalated into a cry for understanding. Acceptance. A distant but gripping need for a gentle and all-encompassing embrace.

Their eyes were locked in a revealing gaze. His were doubtless saying more than he could ever bring himself to admit, and the exposure, even unspoken, was tearing at years of protective masking he was urgently trying to slap back in place. Her returning gaze, asking for access to those hidden areas he hadn't even allowed himself to breach for so many years, was so soft that it began to hurt to look at her.

Rand glanced away.

She touched his hand. He commanded himself not to grasp it and bring her into his arms. Arms that felt so open and empty that he clamped them against his ribs to keep from filling the void.

"I hope you're not upset that I ran a check on you."

"Of course not," he said, more curtly than he'd intended. Steeling himself, he chanced another meeting of eyes, and found the gentlest shade of green. They could have been pastures of soft, dew-kissed grass, beckoning him to rest after years of ceaseless running.

"I wasn't trying to pry," she explained.

"I know. In fact, I would have been disappointed if you hadn't taken the precaution. You just proved you're careful and professional. Exactly the kind of person I need."

The person I need...I need...I need... Rand drew a deep and none-too-steady breath as his words came back to him with unsettling overtones that left him stranded between the need to yank her out of the chair and onto his lap and the urge to run for the front door and get the hell out while the getting was still good.

"I need to finish reading this file before we discuss whether or not I'm a willing candidate." She began to read, then muttered, "I can finish this sooner if you quit staring."

Rand managed to focus on her apartment, which wasn't easy since she held his attention as captive as he needed to hold her in Zebedique to free his sister.

And perhaps someone else. A boy buried so deep he'd been all but forgotten, but who seemed bent on putting in a belated appearance.

Was it the feel of easy comfort here that whispered to Joshua? His eyes settled on a nearby bookcase. How many women kept a can of Mace next to an old doll?

Shaking off the threat of memories, Rand glanced at his watch. It was getting late, and Rachel was turning the last page of the file. He anxiously scanned her face.

"So what do you think?"

"I think the findings seem accurate, and the plan you outlined for hooking the slaver—with me as the bait—would probably work."

"Then you'll do it?" He gripped the arms of the chair where she sat—next to the couch that he wanted to pull her onto so that he could roll her beneath him. Chemistry wasn't new to him, but when had he wanted to hold a woman just to have her hold him back, give him some companionship so that he didn't have to keep going through this treacherous search alone?

"What you're asking me to do is infiltrate a highly dangerous society of pleasure seekers."

"I am." He took the file and tossed it on the coffee table. Grasping her hands, he forgot about his pride long enough to expose his desperation.

"I need you, Rachel. Five women investigators have already turned me down. With each 'no' I get, more time passes. Precious time, Rachel. I'm working against the clock. The slavers could move their operation any day, and then where would I be? Square one, scrambling to find their whereabouts, which could be fifty miles away—or fifty thousand."

"And meanwhile your sister remains prisoner."

"That's right. I've already invested more time than I can afford, working out of motels, burning up the phone lines, catching red-eye flights to New York to keep my business together. I can't do this indefinitely."

"But once you make it to Zebedique, how will you cope?"

"Hopefully we can move quickly. If it takes a while, I'm prepared. An office is already set up in the house. No need to fly out until the job's done." His jaw tensed. "I won't leave there without her."

"How much time have you spent looking for someone who'll agree?"

"Too long. That's why I need a quick decision from you." He leaned in toward her, signaling his urgency. "There aren't many women who can fit the bill for this job, and no one could be as perfect for it as you. I need you. Desperately. After everything you've read and heard about me, surely you realize those are words I don't use lightly."

Rachel was experiencing a meltdown that turned her objectivity inside out. She felt for Rand, and for the sister she had caught glimpses of in the file. Black type had heartlessly translated Sarah into a statistic. But to Rand she was flesh and blood.

She felt Rand's warm human flesh pressing against hers, and the blood that flowed through his veins seemed to course into her own. Could she do it? Did she dare try to crack the slavery ring when simply holding his gaze made it impossible to think?

Just the facts, ma'am, she ordered herself. She was working hard to establish her reputation, one that wouldn't depend on her dad's and would transcend the liability of her age. Rand was in a position to help her get a leg up.

He was also capable of compromising her ethics. *No emotional involvement allowed.* As in a picture of a heart with a diagonal slash through it. Only her heart seemed heedless of the slash.

It pounded rebelliously as she looked at him now, the strong, enigmatic male, the caring, desperate brother. She tried to force away any outward softness while it was there, shifting, catching her up inside. If their first meeting had left her breathless, the dizzying momentum that continued to gather was enough to send her scrambling for escape from this emotional vacuum that was sucking her in. She couldn't see any exit except his arms. The very arms she needed to escape.

If only she could forget the case and search that dark place behind his eyes, a place that must have its roots in a faded black-and-white photo. If only...

Drawing on reserves of professional strength that denied the woman inside her who was reaching out for him, she confronted the stark, brutal facts that she could not ignore.

"You want me to work the casino, look lonely and lost. Hook up with the slaver, let him buy me a drink at the bar, lead him to think I've got no family and I'm sexually innocent. And I'd have to do this without even a gun for protection."

"The gun would raise suspicion, since they'd go through your things after getting you alone. But I'll watch from a distance. And we'll bring in another PI to tail you. If you've got a colleague you prefer to work with, we'll go with your recommendation, no question."

"Jack. Jack O'Malley. He was my father's best friend, and he sponsored me for the five years of training I had to put in before I could take the state exam. Jack's better than good, he's great. But no matter how savvy a PI is, there's no guarantee things will go according to plan. Even Jack might not be able to get close enough to switch drinks with me." Rachel exhaled a shuddering sigh. "I don't relish the thought of downing a designer drug, if it comes to that."

"And it could. Much as I hate to spell it out, you deserve the unvarnished truth. What it comes down to is that there's a good chance you *will* be drugged. If you are, they'll do whatever it is they do in transit, and getting through that just might be easier if you're flying high. If you manage to stay sober, you'll have to give the act of your life."

"For how long?"

"The auctions take place every Saturday, so it depends on when the nab is made. Chances are you'll have at least several days of sheer hell when you'll have nothing to depend on but your wits. All I can promise is that once I get you off the auction block, we'll be in this together. Even when we're staging a performance for Jayna, or anyone else who might be listening at the bedchamber door."

Rachel paused to consider the implications of that. Rand, enacting his role as her owner, master of her body. The body that, at the moment, was eager to get the show on the road.

Stop it, she ordered herself. Any hormonal urges or forbidden thrills she felt had no place at this moment, had nothing to do with his dire straits or her ability to make a rational decision.

"You're sure you're not being set up yourself? What if it's a fake invitation and you get hauled away to a foreign prison? What if I'm stranded and go to the highest bidder? I could end up just like Sarah, with no one there to get either of us out, since you refuse to go to the police."

"It won't happen. My connections are paying back a debt that comes to a staggering sum. My seat's reserved, and I'll be watching you closely. Don't worry, I've made sure the invitation's legit."

"I do worry. These go-betweens don't sound too ethical. What if they double-cross you?"

"Do you actually think I'd drag you into this without having some assurance myself? We're talking heavy leverage."

"How heavy?"

"Let's just say that an unnamed third party has a sealed envelope with names, places and lots of incriminating evidence on its way to *The New York Times* if there's so much as a single screwup. My associates have plenty of incentive to make sure this goes off without a hitch."

This was definitely not a man to cross, Rachel decided. As tempted as she was to explore some things she was probably better off not knowing, a sense of self-preservation demanded she put up a final defense.

"It's dangerous."

"I'll protect you. That's one promise I won't break."

"You said I'd be stripped. Put on an auction block." *Stripped. Auctioned off.* Could she actually endure such a violation of her modesty, being bartered like a slab of human meat, while Rand sat in the audience with a clear view of her body? She shivered, imagining the ordeal.

"It's the only way. I'd never ask such a thing of anyone, and especially not a woman as special as you, but I have no choice." His grip tightened. "You can name your price. I'm willing to pay whatever you ask."

For some reason that hurt. He was reducing this to money. Then she hurt a little more, remembering the cash he'd laid on her desk to induce her to hear him out. Money talked; she'd listened to the seductive jingle of his coin.

"And what happens, Rand, if I say no deal?"

"Then I pay you some hush money and you promise not to leak a word about what you've learned here. I'll walk out, and we won't see each other again—at least not under these circumstances."

Money again. As much as she needed it, the thought of it had never been so distasteful. Just as the thought of never seeing Rand again left an empty ache in the region of her chest. Somehow, the idea of saying goodbye disturbed her more deeply than the idea of being stripped.

"But what would you do, where would you take this?"

He shrugged, a determined look spanning his face and radiating into the tenseness of his posture.

"I'd keep hunting until I found someone who would agree. I'm sure they wouldn't be half as intriguing or entertaining, or come close to being as tempting to look at as you. But I have a sister to find, and those are optional qualities that didn't enter the picture until now."

His laugh was short, humorless. "You know, Rachel, the too little time we've spent together, the conversations we've had when I called on any trumped-up excuse just to hear your voice...they've done something for me that money can't buy. I've actually found myself feeling something so good that work and Sarah weren't the only things on my mind. Even if you don't take the case, I'd like to thank you for that."

What those words did to her. Words that assured her that these topsy-turvy feelings that she couldn't acknowledge were alive and well in Rand's dark and vibrant persona, too. A persona that would have no choice but to go to another woman if she refused. One who would share his house. One who would take his case—and likely for the money she herself disdained.

None of these were reasons to agree, and yet she couldn't deny they were playing a crucial role in her decision.

"The ink's still wet on my license, Rand."

"Doesn't matter. You're good, Rachel. In fact, you're better than good. You'll be successful no matter what, but this case just might get you there a lot quicker. I have a certain amount of clout that I won't hesitate to throw in your direction if you say yes."

Rachel weighed the future ordeal, trying not to listen to the voice chanting in her head, *Say yes.* If she did, she could reunite a sister and brother and right a terrible wrong while she took a giant leap forward in her chosen profession.

Though, at the moment, her profession didn't seem nearly as important as the man waiting on edge for her answer.

Once she shook on it, there was no turning back.

She extended her hand.

"Put 'er there, partner."

5

"YES!" RAND SHOUTED a victory whoop. His hand closed over hers. "Quite a handshake you've got, lady. Shows guts."

"I like yours, too." She returned his beaming smile, feeling buoyant inside.

"Wonder what your daddy would think?"

She glimpsed another window. No daddy for Rand Slick. But he was human, and he wanted approval as much as the next man.

"He'd think you were no mark. He'd like you, but he wouldn't trust you. At least not with me."

"I can understand that. Sometimes I don't trust myself."

"Why not?"

Rand shrugged. "Guess it goes back to certain promises I didn't make good on. Mistakes I've made along the way."

"We all make those."

"True, but some are more irreversible than others."

She wanted to probe, but his eyes told her this was private territory not to be investigated just yet. Best to stick with a more immediate concern. One her feminine instincts hearkened to while her business ethics demanded she avoid this part of the deal.

"About our roles, Rand. Think you could enlighten me a little more on just what they might involve?"

"Better than that, what say we give it some practice? Pretend I've just taken you into the master's chambers." He pulled her from the chair and onto his lap. Before she could stop herself, a small gasp caught in her throat, followed by a tiny purr. "This is the scenario—the servants are listening at the door, wondering how I'm going to stake my rightful claim. Do I seduce you with tender words that they don't expect to hear any more than I'm used to saying them?"

Wondering if this was truly a game, and too aware that she didn't want it to be, Rachel forced herself to back away from exactly what she wanted to explore.

"I'm not sure if this is such a good idea, Rand. Maybe we should forget this and ad-lib when the time comes."

"No. Rehearsal is part and parcel, Rachel." Her behind was anchored against his groin. He was . . . Sweet heaven, he was thick against her, large. *Aroused.* She felt an immediate, answering response that tensed her belly and tingled the tip of her womb, then reached up and increased the weight of her breasts. "God, you feel good in my arms. Where have you been all this time? And how can we have just met and fit together like this?"

"We can't do this." She said the words even as she felt herself settle deeper against him and realized she'd draped her arms around his neck. Her head rested against his shoulder, and she inhaled the marvelous scent of him. The light growth of whiskers at his jaw grazed her cheek. He was nuzzling against her, or maybe she was doing the nuzzling. "Please, Rand," she said unevenly. "We have to stop this. Now."

"That would be an appropriate response. To which I would reply, 'We haven't even started.'" He locked his hands at her hips. "Then I'd add, 'How can you say we have to stop when I can feel you pressing deeper, deeper, and wanting the same thing as me?'"

A cry of need all but strangled her as she struggled to silence the instinctive sound.

"You want me to help you get your sister back, don't you?" She forced her mouth from his neck, his warm, strong neck, where she could feel the steady, reassuring beat of his pulse. "You have to understand, a private investigator can't get emotionally involved with a client. It can muddy their judgment, even leave them open to make mistakes."

"Is that a certainty? Be honest with me."

"It's a possibility."

"Anything's possible. Give me a concrete reason."

"Professional protocol."

"Protocol isn't something I bow to, and mistakes are possible no matter what the climate. Give me something, anything, to make me believe my holding you is going to jeopardize my sister. Facts. Examples. C'mon, Rachel. Remember, we're in Zebedique, and you'd better have some solid reasons to keep me on the other side of the bedroom door."

Was he testing her mental reflexes, just as he'd tested her at their first meeting? She didn't know, she didn't know anything, except that she wanted to forget possibilities and protocol and the missing sister so that she could embrace the brother, who had more facets than a crystal, more forbidden allure than she could possibly deflect.

"You're a client," she told him in a strangled voice. "A client. You're nothing more than a case to be solved and filed away once we're through."

"That's it? If that's the best you can do, then I must insist that you don't let the servants hear you say I'm nothing more than your client and you can't get involved for a mere technicality. Your flimsy protest would jeopardize our plan a lot quicker than any amount of involvement you might have to fake." He searched her eyes. "Or not fake?"

With one incisive look, with the sweet bite of his fingertips tightening at her hip, she felt more naked than she possibly could on the auction block. In self-protection, she denied the truth by emphatically shaking her head.

"You would still refuse me, the master to whom you belong? Then I would have no choice but to persuade you with logic." He traced her lips with a fingertip, then veered off to her throat. His smile was intimate as he monitored the rapidity of her pulse.

"This isn't logical, Rand," she said urgently. "This is not a businesslike position for us to be in."

"But it is business, and exactly the sort of position we will be in. And given that it's business, humor me so we won't have to completely wing it."

"Okay." She drew in a deep breath, needing some oxygen to clear her head. The oxygen didn't help. Reality and fantasy blurred together while she struggled to hang on to a fact she knew to be real. "I just told you, I won't have you, no matter what you say or do. It's impossible under these circumstances, and no amount of logic can sway me."

"That's good. Challenge me." He traced a pattern on her knee. She thought it was the shape of a heart, but he rubbed it away with the pressure of his palm before she could be sure. "What do you suggest I should say in a crucial moment like this?"

She shut her eyes while the world tilted to a skewed angle. "I think you should tell me that you like your women seasoned and sure, and that you're way out of my league."

"Am I now? You mean you can wave a pistol and likely hit your mark, bluff your way through a game of penny-ante poker and win with a pair of deuces. But you're off your turf when I'm hard and you're all but melting against me while we're both thinking of a dozen different ways we'd like to be kissing . . . and more. Oh, yeah, a whole lot more . . ."

He touched his forehead to hers. She could hear the mingling of their breath; they were sharing the air, and sharing the illusion he was weaving with consummate skill.

"Now it's your turn," he murmured. "Do you fight me? Do you succumb? Or do you simply fight yourself, because you want to believe this is only business, and business can keep you safe from the man who owns you and shares your desires—even perhaps, your bed?"

She'd been kissed. She'd been fondled. But she'd never encountered anything like this. Whether his words were sincere or not, he was right. She was off her turf.

She was also scared crazy, because she wanted to believe they could kiss a dozen different ways, and more. Lord, so much more. But to do that would dictate that she remain as emotionally removed as she'd have to in a relationship with a man who could hurt her with his distance if she let him get too close.

Then she remembered their earlier conversations: She always told him too much, while he returned little more than hints, dark looks that reached for her, only to retreat behind a shuttered window. *That* was the root of her resistance. His sister, yes—and that should be what had her drawing the line.

But it wasn't. When she finally gave her heart to a man, Rachel knew, she wouldn't be able to hold anything back. She needed a man who could return his heart just as freely.

Rand didn't seem to be that kind of man.

"Rachel? What do you say?"

"I would say that I'm not easy. And that succumbing to you, for any reason, is not going to happen. At least not until this case is over and Rand Slick's a mystery to everyone but me." A Rubik's Cube. How apt his self-description.

"But unraveling mysteries is your job. And while you're doing that, I'd have to give every appearance of trying to sway your judgment." He tugged at her hair and wrapped a strand around his finger, only to tease it to her lips, using the silky texture to arouse her. He did it amazingly well. Her breasts, pressing intimately into his chest, throbbed almost painfully, while her lips ached with wanting. "If tender words or logic didn't work, I would have no choice but to pretend force."

He tangled a hand in her hair and tugged until her neck was arched. It was a maneuver she'd never encountered, though his adeptness was that of a man very much in his element. His mouth grazed over her throat, and he whispered words that were rough, demanding.

"Fight me, Rachel. Just remember that whatever you've uncovered on me doesn't even scratch the surface. So if you really want to escape, you'd better fight me tooth and nail."

She pushed at his chest, while an unstaged cry of desire caused her to grip his shirt and begin to pull him closer, rather than thrust him away.

"Let me go. Get your hand out of my hair, quit rubbing against me, and leave me alone."

"Not convincing enough. You don't say it like you mean it, and therefore I'm not buying." He jerked his hips forward and tightened his hold. "You're no match for my strength anyway, so fight me by telling me the real reason you can't be doing this. Don't use Sarah as an excuse, because you've told me involvement is a potential risk, not an absolute. Get me where it counts. Up front and personal."

"It's you, Rand." Honesty, she decided, was her only means of escape. And if she didn't escape soon, she wouldn't have a chance. This time she pushed him away, with more strength than she thought she possessed.

"What about me? Specifics."

"All *right*." She groaned, while her woman's needs screamed for more, more, more. "I can't afford to tangle with a man who lives on the edge and gets his kicks from outwitting the devil. A man who's probably had a lot of triple-X-rated nights but slips out before the sun comes up. Long on technique. Short on stayability. I'm sorry, Rand. As much as I wish otherwise, that's not the kind of résumé I'm in the market for. You're one puzzle I'd be better off not trying to solve. Jagged edges have a way of drawing blood."

He released her hair and turned so that she couldn't see his face. The silence was taut, distorting the seconds that passed into an immeasurable length of time.

"Let me tell you something, Rachel. You did a damn good job of reading between the lines, but maybe, just maybe, there comes a point in a man's life when he wonders if it's time to revise his résumé." He paused, seemingly caught by what he'd just said—and not quite able to believe he'd said it. "Guess that's an item I'll have to put on hold. After all, we're just playing. Aren't we?"

"I don't know," she admitted, then realized how ingenuous she must sound to him. "Yes, of course we are."

"Of course. But this game's left me with a very real problem. I've only got so much discipline, and at the moment it's too thin for my own comfort. Comfort, actually, is the last thing I'm feeling in our current position." He shifted, and a pained expression twisted his lips.

"You're right. This is uncomfortable. I'd better move."

"No, wait." He tightened his hold, but it was the softening of his tone that kept her in his arms. "You did give me some comfort tonight. A kind I didn't expect. It's something I'm not quite sure how to deal with." He seemed not to have finished. The clock tick-tick-ticked in the background, stretching out the elastic silence. When he spoke again, he rushed his words, as if to get them out before he could take them back. "I don't know how to deal with it, but I'd like to try."

"Deal with what—comfort?"

"Accepting it, that's what."

"I don't understand."

"Don't you? Tell me why you agreed, and don't play any games. Your answer's important."

Tell him, when she couldn't accept the reasons herself, couldn't even completely understand them? Reasons that reduced her to a refrain from *The Wizard of Oz: I'm melting, melting, melting... Ahhh...* It was the same tortured sound, the same sense of being thrust into a fantasy world that dazzled her even as she chanted, *There's no place like home...*

How could she tell him this, when her control was too precarious? If Rand had been dangerous before, he was lethal now. Holding her close, stroking her hair, letting her see inside just enough to touch the softness beneath the razor edges that could indeed draw blood.

Go ahead, Rachel, tell him, came the inner taunt. *You know it's about as safe as handing an arsonist a Bic. You're about to go up in flames as it is, with his mouth flirting with your neck. Don't you want to feel his teeth take a bite or two, before you find out how good his tongue feels slipping around yours? He's bound to be good at it. Maybe he'd even stick around long enough to teach you a few tricks to remember him by. Go to bed with him and get some more practice for the case. You can handle it. Right?*

Oh, God, so wrong. Her every instinct rebelled, but desperation demanded that she pull some of her own shutters closed before she could commit a very foolish and irrevocable act.

"Why did I agree? You promised to pay me well." How brittle her voice sounded in her ears. And as abrupt as his mouth jerked away from her neck. "My career's just getting started, and this is the chance of a lifetime to make my mark."

6

"No." Rand's fingers tightened, and his eyes narrowed to mere slits. He looked as if he wanted to shake her, and kiss her senseless, too. "You care. You're a good actress, Rachel, but not good enough to fool a master of the game. Whether you'll admit it or not, you do care."

He got up so fast she nearly tumbled to the floor. Then he grabbed his coat and slung it over his shoulder.

"I'll be leaving now. We can discuss details tomorrow. Call me at the motel if you need a ride."

Rachel smoothed her skirt with shaking hands, feeling too ashamed of what she'd done, and too unnerved by his sudden brusque demeanor, to look at him.

"That's okay. My car should be ready in the morning. What say we meet at 10:00 a.m., in my office?"

"Fine." He was leaning against the door, his chest filling her vision, when the smooth tip of his finger insistently lifted her chin.

Rachel stared into a face that was both filled with and devoid of emotion, a perplexing face that had upended her safe world in a matter of days. If this was what he could do in so little time, where would he leave her in a month, or maybe three? She shuddered to think.

"If it's a matter of money, Rachel, be warned—I always get the most out of my investments." He leaned in, his mouth hovering perilously close to hers. "Judging from your convincing performance, I'm certain that, whatever the price, you're going to be worth double."

She was still staring at his mouth, thinking of the threat it posed, when threat became reality—and from an unseen source. She felt the hard length of his leg slide smoothly between hers, felt the shock of her immediate moistening. She tried to protest, but no words would come, only a moan escaping her lips.

Into the wedge he lifted, shifting to a sure, steady rhythm. Slow and deep. Quick and teasing. She tried to move, but she seemed paralyzed, unable to tear herself away from his intimate stroking. Leg strokes that were so incredibly wonderful that her body turned traitor, her own legs parting, then clenching, now returning thrust for thrust.

She thought she must be half-crazed. Her breathing, so strange and choppy, quick rushes of it like gasps, and then no air at all. His palms were cupping her hips and urging her higher, faster. He was saying things that were disjointed and arousing, and she was trying desperately to hang on to his murmurings.

Beautiful… Yes, angel, that's it, so good… Feel the heat… But you're empty… Poor angel… Care…care…you do…

What was happening to her? She didn't know.… All she knew was this thing she was grasping blindly for, this thing that escaped her reach, while she was so empty she hurt.

She whimpered his name, knowing he held the means to her release. He made a low, pleased sound, then quit moving his leg. Her own were trembling, and he gentled her frantic hips, which she couldn't stop from jerking against him. He soothed her with a touch that was generous and tender until she found a measure of control. And then his palms pressed tight on either side of her hips, stilling the last of her movements.

"You're okay," he said in a quiet, reassuring voice.

He kissed her forehead. Then he slowly moved away.

Rachel couldn't catch her breath. He thought she was okay? She could hardly stand. She was close to hyperventilating. She hurt between her legs, and she felt a frustration so terrible that a scream was trying to claw its way out of her throat. Did it show on her face? Was that why his held a mixture of kindness and male satisfaction that came close to smugness?

His gaze lowered and she suddenly realized what held his attention. Her skirt was hiked up to her panties. She glared at him and jerked it down with shaking hands. Actually, she was shaking from head to toe. In passion and passionate anger.

He turned to leave. She caught his hand at the doorknob, not knowing what she would say, because she was speechless. She only knew her pride demanded retribution for his blatant coup de grace. It staggered her, humiliated her, and worst of all, good Lord, it aroused her. *What kind of man was he?*

And what kind of woman was she to respond to him?

"What you just did— It wasn't fair, or appropriate, or—" She was sputtering, unable to string her feelings into a simple sentence. Rachel had never been so upset in her life; she silently counted to ten and took a shuddering breath. "Manipulative, that's what you were. You manipulated me, and I don't like it."

"Oh?" His gaze angled to the apex of her thighs. "Could've fooled me."

Her cheeks burned while her stomach bottomed out. Rand played dirty. Well, he was going to find out she could, too.

"Don't you dare try something like that with me again, or you'll be looking for another PI."

"Don't worry, I won't. You gave me the answer I was looking for. Too mad to ask? Since you're probably curious, I'll tell you anyway. I needed to find out if money was the only thing that's really motivating you. Now I can leave with the feel of you riding my thigh and know that at least that much was genuine."

She was compelled to disguise her weakness, to cover the shame of the lie that had caused this with another one.

"An impromptu performance. Nothing more."

"Are you up for an encore to convince me you're telling the truth?" He took a menacing step forward, and she quickly moved from his reach. He chuckled, apparently satisfied with her reaction. "Just kidding. You pulled out the big guns. I'll behave."

"You'd better. And don't even suggest another rehearsal. We have our roles down as pat as they'll ever get."

"Bravo. With an exit line like that, you deserve an Oscar." He winked. "Curtain's closed, angel." The door shut.

Rachel rested her forehead against the hard grain of wood. At least it was solid, while she was coming apart at the seams. She rolled her head back and forth. Something wet slid down her cheek.

The tears of a clown, she thought. Some were for Rand, alone in his ivory tower, where he knew how to cope, and probably too well, even if he might want more. But mostly they were for her, because she didn't know how to cope when she needed more from a man than he might have the capacity to give.

For all she knew, it had been nothing but a power play, a well-executed performance on his part, or a test of her stamina, to see how she held up under undue duress. But not for her. She *felt*. Her emotions, her words, the physical responses he commanded, were very, very real.

Rachel wiped her wet cheeks with a determined swipe of her arm. "Get a grip on yourself," she growled aloud. "You're being ridiculous. He turns you on. So what? He won't pull this crap again so you're safe. Now quit crying. He's a client, nothing more. Take his money, do your job, and you'll be okay."

You're okay, came the wisp of a voice, his voice. She heard the soft reassurance again, felt his gentleness when he could just as easily have taken her on the floor without a protest from her. She still burned for him to do just that. How in heaven's name was she going to cope in Zebedique?

Exotic music. Palm trees and sand. Minaret swirling into an indigo sky. Sandalwood and incense and . . .

Bay and night spice.

The image she'd conjured up in Rand's car that first day was suddenly too vivid. She was there again, could see the woman turning her head as Rand released the catch of her sheer veil.

Her fair skin was flushed with anticipation. She wore passion's maturity well, standing proud while he shed the fragile garment, and then naked as he leaned her into the bed with a mating growl.

Rachel swayed against the door, her legs refusing her their support as she stared into the vision. She saw the woman's face—and something more.

Fate winked, then vanished through a dark, steamy window.

RAND'S FOOT PRESSED DOWN on the accelerator, as though the faster he drove, the farther he could distance himself from what he'd spent nearly a lifetime outrunning.

Unfortunately, he just got himself to the motel that much sooner. Rand gripped the wheel, hearing his own harsh breathing fill up the silence. Claustrophobia pressed in on him. But he didn't move, didn't want to go to his empty room, any more than he wanted to sit at a bar alone or waste his time picking up a willing woman. He'd done it before, knew the emptiness of waking up next to someone he cared nothing about.

Care. He still couldn't believe he had the capacity to hurt as much as he had when Rachel had said she didn't. But he knew better; she did care, and nothing could have prepared him for the shock of realizing that he desperately wanted her to care. He'd actually called her "angel." He had always been miserly with endearments, and *angel* was the most treasured of all.

The sound of a couple laughing as they strolled through the parking lot arrested his attention. His eyes narrowed as they kissed and exchanged a verbal intimacy. A tight sensation stitched through his chest. He wanted what they were sharing—intimacy. A commodity that was rare in his life. Until now, the lack had been of his own choosing.

What was happening to him? How had Rachel filtered into the ice-water blood of a man most people considered little more than a moneymaking machine? He felt as though she had triggered twenty-odd years of gathered momentum that smashed his hardened heart with the grace of a two-ton velvet hammer.

It hurt. It felt damn good. A lot like doing emotional gymnastics after decades of no workouts. But was it worth riding out the pain to get to the gain? And how much hurt would Rachel have to endure while he bungled his way through?

He had to give this some careful consideration. Sarah was a commodity he couldn't risk—though there was a good chance she might resent him more than welcome him. What he had to know was whether Rachel had been honest about the potential consequences of getting involved. She could simply have been groping for an excuse to avoid exploring the boundaries of a relationship with a man as risky as him. He suspected it was some of both. That left the burden on him of figuring out the priorities.

He frowned as a final, crucial question emerged: Could he play his role convincingly and manage their proximity until Sarah was found? Even better, could he navigate a dual mission, save Sarah, and explore this compelling relationship with Rachel, too?

Rand flipped on the CD player, and music filtered through the whirlpool of his thoughts. Zebedique. An exchange of money and paper. Rachel, his possession, in a country that gave men absolute control over their women.

A slight smile tugged at his lips. Quite an amusing concept, really. That hair of hers was nothing compared to the fire within her. A fire that had challenged him to throw down the gauntlet before he'd had the good sense to leave. What he'd taken was a minor victory, the memory of her whimper, the sweet grip of her riding his leg.

He knew exactly where she'd been, could still feel the pulsing warmth radiating beneath his pants. He'd remember that tomorrow.

And remember was all he'd do. No more dress rehearsals. Zebedique would give them plenty of opportunity to walk the tightrope in a high-stakes game.

Rand came to a decision and shut off the music. Passing the lovebirds on the way to his room, he smiled. Funny thing about life, he thought. Just when a man believed he'd be happy if he could find his sister and make everything up to her, he discovered someone else that he'd nearly forgotten.

Joshua. Just as deserving as Sarah. Joshua, a poor kid who'd had his heart stripped out by his own childish misjudgment. He hoped Rachel wouldn't regret what she'd unwittingly done, peeling away his layers to expose some kernel of tenderness and need that belonged to a long-lost boy.

Rand, or Joshua, or whoever the hell he was, had to discover the truth: Was Rachel the key to giving Joshua a fair shot at the life he might have had if he hadn't run? And could Rand Slick stop running, after a lifetime of dodging the odds?

He made love to her in his sleep. When he awoke, Rand knew that for once the sweat drenching his sheets was owed to a kinder source than the old demons who liked to pay their visits in a dream. One he jeeringly called See Rand Run.

7

SHAVE AND A HAIRCUT, two bits. Rachel glanced at her watch. Eight o'clock on the nose. Not only had Rand proved to be a man of his word, he was so punctual she could set her clock by him.

She couldn't get to the door fast enough, even though she was dreading the inevitable war of want versus will. Though she could look all she liked, Rachel didn't trust herself to touch him. The problem was, the more she looked, the more desperate she was to touch, to give up this farce of friendly allies pretending that that night a month ago hadn't happened.

But it had happened, and the memory was there, always there. Between them, and escalating, like the building tension felt by two estranged lovers riding in an elevator. Together but alone, separated by pride and more as they slowly inched up to the same floor while they stared anywhere but at each other.

Yet it didn't stop her furtive glances of longing. Or prevent her heart from deeply caring for him—at least as deeply as their slipping guards and their uneasy hands-off truce allowed. He was still a mystery to her. The better she got to know him, the more it seemed she didn't know.

Rachel took a deep breath and mentally snapped out an order to her nervous system to stop this crazy nonsense. And realized it was an exercise in futility the instant their gazes locked.

Rand let go a low, admiring whistle. "You could stop traffic in that getup."

"Let's hope it stops some trafficking. By the way, thanks for the lift. As soon as this job is over, I'm shopping for some new wheels."

"You could have caught a ride with Jack." He raised a brow in a silent challenge. When she refused to rise to the bait, he smiled warmly. "I'm glad you called me instead."

"Let me get my purse so we can get out of here," she said hastily, before he could press her for reasons she couldn't accept herself. "Jack's probably already at the casino. I hate to keep him waiting."

"Do you? You certainly haven't had any qualms about keeping *me* waiting. Do you realize this is the first time we've had a minute together since that night—"

"Don't be ridiculous, Rand." She wanted to cut him off before he could speak her own thoughts aloud. *Why had she set them up like this?* As if she didn't know. "Except for your quick trips to New York, we're constantly together. Planning, trial runs at the other casinos. And don't forget the two weeks running that we've laid the bait."

"Without a nibble. So what do we do? The *three* of us drink coffee till we're floating and swap jokes at some damn greasy spoon. I suppose you think that qualifies as time together, too."

"Of course it does."

"The hell it does. We're never alone. Jack's a great guy, but—"

"No 'buts' about it, he's the best backup your money can buy."

"Money." Rand snorted. "That again. Is it possible that for once, just this once, we could forget money and Jack and have an honest conversation about something that's been on my mind since before the first stakeout? We need to discuss it, and I want to do it *now*."

She wavered, on the cusp of giving in to the never-ending temptation to turn her back on her profession and confront head-on what always went unsaid.

"Later, Rand. Jack's waiting."

"Let him wait. This can't."

"Too bad, because it'll have to," she said sharply. Rachel was angry at herself for the weakness of needing some last, stolen bit of him to take with her as a talisman against the whims of fate. She turned, intent on a quick exit.

He caught her arm. She stared at the connection of his dark skin and her own pale flesh. Where his fingertips touched, she felt a glow. It spread until the room seemed to shrink in size and fill up with charged emotions and an energy that hummed of intimate whispers and hot sex.

"It's not too late, angel," Rand said quietly. "You can still back out. Do it."

Knowing how much his sister meant to him, she could only meet his probing stare with her own look of wonder and confusion. His brutally handsome face was softened by the same edge of concern she heard in the current of his voice.

"Do you actually think, even for a minute, that I would?"

"No. But I had to offer. I've got a gut feeling that tonight we'll hit pay dirt."

"I know. I feel it, too."

"Do you? Is that why I can feel you shivering like it's ten below zero instead of eighty degrees in here?" When she averted her gaze, he caught her chin and searched her face. "Is it?" he demanded.

"Of course," she said firmly, praying her eyes didn't give her away. "It's only natural to be nervous with stakes this high. But if anyone can pull some sleight of hand in the drink-switching department, it's Jack. And you'll be there, too."

"But not when you need me the most. Then you'll be on your own, without even a gun or a tracing device on you. I don't like it. Not one damn bit."

"We knew from the start that it's the only way, Rand. A hundred bucks and a false ID is my best insurance. They'll go through my things. They'll search me."

"I know." His grip tightened until she nearly winced. "When I think of what those bastards might—"

"Don't think about it. This is my job. It's what you hired me to do. I'm prepared."

"Yeah, right. The truth is, no matter how prepared you believe you are, it's going to be a nightmare, being helpless in the hands of strangers. A nightmare for you. A nightmare for me. When I first came into your office, you were a means to an end. Things have changed."

"This isn't a good time to talk about—"

"There's never a good time for us to talk, is there? You've seen to that. What are you afraid of? *Me?* When I haven't so much as tried to kiss you again? You're my friend, or at least the closest thing to a friend I've let myself have for more years than I can count, and you won't even look at me. *Look at me.*" He gave her small shake. "That's better. Okay, *friend,* I'm giving you one final chance to back out. My instincts are almost always right, and they're telling me after tonight there won't be any turning back."

As she stood there and filled herself up with his forbidden touch, Rachel knew to a certainty that there had been no turning back from the moment they met. Even if she could lie to Rand, she couldn't lie to herself.

She'd never been in love before, so she wasn't yet sure, but she was terribly afraid she was falling in love. In love with a man she knew, and yet knew not at all. She'd dated her share, had her share and more of kisses and heavy petting. But never had she met anyone like Rand Slick. And *never* had another man made her want, desperately want, what she couldn't have at this moment, and made her want it with nothing more than a look, a palm that swept to the small of her back, or a soft kiss pressed to her temple.

"Tell me you're off the case," he whispered sharply. His embrace was urgent as he kissed her again, only not so soft, because it was fierce and had trailed to her neck, where his teeth lightly scraped. "I don't want you to go through with this. I'll find someone else, and—"

"Stop it, Rand. Stop it!" Summoning up the core that was strength, belief in the rightness of what she was compelled to do, Rachel thrust him away. They stared at each other, both breathing in harsh, syncopated rasps. "I told you we couldn't get emotionally involved. If this doesn't prove my point, nothing does. You have a sister who needs you, who needs me because I can get to her where you can't. And not only her— what about the other women who are at risk while you shop for someone to take my place?"

"I don't know those other women. I don't care about them. You I care about."

"Don't," she snapped, flinching at her own sharp warning.

"Too late, Rachel. I do. Not that you seem to care that I . . . care."

Steeling herself against the flow of something that felt like liquid nirvana coursing through her veins and making her head spin like a top, Rachel glared at him.

"Care later, Rand. Care when you can afford to."

"When I can afford to?" His harsh bark of laughter was derisive. "Here's another little tidbit to slide into the cube. Caring's the one thing I *can't* afford. Not yesterday, not today, not tomorrow. Sister or no sister. I won't be forgetting you threw back in my face what I'll never be able to afford. Just remember, I don't offer anything without the intent to reap my benefits tenfold. And I will, Rachel. *I will.*"

His gaze burned so hot it was freezing, rooting her to the floor and making the imprint of his hold on her arms chafe. But her heart he still held, held it so tight she could feel it squeeze out each erratic pump.

"If you're trying to scare me into backing off from this case, it's not working. I'm in, Rand. I'm in and I'm not bowing out until Sarah's safe and you're a file I've filed away. As, I suspect, you'll do with me once this is over. Case closed."

Hardly was his silent response. Rand studied the stubborn tilt of her chin, which quivered ever so slightly, revealing her hard line as nothing but a sham from a woman of substance who didn't believe it herself. Who did Rachel think she'd taken on? Some horny kid who didn't know the difference between lust and whatever it was that she'd done to his insides?

Those insides balled into a hard knot, deflecting the blow of her rejection. One he couldn't accept, *would not* accept. He all but chortled because it was so obvious she *felt*, she *cared*, just as much as he did. It made her rejection a hell of a lot easier to handle than the fear for her safety that overshadowed his reason.

"Know what? I can almost pity that slaver once he gets his hands on you. Your tongue is sharper than any knife he might be tempted to cut it out with." His short laugh was accompanied by a sneer. It was directed at himself, fool that he was, for feeling too much. Not love, surely not, but something she called up inside him that kept growing and growing until he thought it might eat him alive. "Forget I ever said that I cared, okay? Like everything else between us, we'll pretend it doesn't exist, and maybe it'll go away. God, I hope so."

She hesitated, then touched his hand. Softly, a soothing brush of ruby-painted nails over clenched fist.

"I'm sorry I hurt your feelings, Rand. This isn't how—"

He knocked her hand away, and she covered her throat, as if he'd jammed a finger into her windpipe. Rand smiled coldly. Rachel was going to learn he didn't go down easy, and when he did he latched on to whoever dared tried to top him.

"Get your purse. And please, not the ugly one. The one with black sequins should match that dress you can hardly even breathe in. Maybe you'd like to change into something closer to decent? You do seem to be having trouble sucking in air and—why, Rachel, your cheeks are turning such a lovely shade. They even match your lipstick and nails."

"What's the big idea, slamming the way I'm dressed?" she retorted hotly. Rand was perversely pleased, quite certain that it was his refusal of her touch, not his comment on her taste in purses or her choice of dress that had her steaming. "*You* picked this out! Or don't you remember?"

He remembered and only too well. He remembered his command: "*Turn around. Slow.*" His finger circling the air, while her feet pivoted on a platform at a by-appointment-only designer boutique. His gaze roving hungrily over her person, touching her with an intimacy that his hands didn't share.

True to his promise, he'd kept his hands to himself. All that day she'd modeled and he'd sipped champagne while drinking her in from his slouch in a Queen Anne chair. He'd bought ten knock-'em-dead outfits, though she'd insisted two should do.

What a joke. Everything she'd put on was transformed from cloth to class. The only urge greater than to buy out the store was to strip her down to nothing and drive into her so long and deep there was nothing left of either of them.

"I remember, angel," he said smoothly. "But that was for my eyes only. I might be a lot of things, but I stop short of scum. That's who you're peddling your wares for tonight. He'll bite. Sink his teeth right into that sweet, delectable top-dollar flesh of yours. I can't help but wonder how much he'll sample before I buy up the leftovers in Zebedique."

"They're not in the business to deliver damaged goods. Not if they want top dollar. And your dollars, no matter how ill gotten, are just as good as the next bidder's, Mr. Slick."

He had to admire her grit. It caused him to quirk a brow and smile inwardly, silently acknowledging defeat. He couldn't let the smile reach his mouth, because it was impatient to crush hers with a lip-eating, tongue-thrusting, can't-get-my-fill hunger.

"But of course it is, Rachel. Money *is* the universal language, and it's the one I speak most fluently. Far better than

English, so perhaps you can understand my lack of elo-
quence when I say—" his gaze feasted on the swell of her
breasts "—pull up that damn bodice before you fall out. Your
job is to lay the bait, not to feed the shark."

She gave him her back and marched into her bedroom. But
not before he saw the fleeting expression of hurt on her face.
Then, sequined bag in hand and bodice a good two inches
higher, she brushed past him with a haughty disdain he didn't
buy for a minute.

With a brisk twist of the wrist, she locked up and stalked
to his car. Rand beat her to the passenger door.

Instead of thanking him, she sliced him cleanly with a
stony, madder-than-hell squint.

Rand guided the mean machine with a sweating palm over
the leather-bound steering wheel. His guts turned to water
just thinking about what might lie ahead for her once she was
stripped of his protection.

The problem was protecting her from himself, once foreign law gave him owner's rights and Rachel was handed into
his own greedy keeping.

RAND SCANNED the crowd in the casino until his gaze connected with Jack's, who gave a small nod before moving to a
gaming table a discreet distance from where Rachel stood.

It was tremendously difficult for him not to stare. In profile, she appeared to be enmeshed in a game of roulette. The
black cocktail dress did indeed hug her too well in all the right
places. It set off her red hair and green eyes so vividly that he
was reminded of Christmas at night. Holidays were something he detested, since he had no family to share them with,
but Rachel sparked images of youthful hope and a stunning
feminine fire that crackled in a hearth called home.

She bent closer to the wheel, and his attention narrowed
on her too-generous display of cleavage. Rand took a bracing swig from his glass, commanding himself not to go jerk

the bodice higher, even as his fingers itched to plunge it down until her breasts tumbled free.

Rachel slid him a sidelong glance and smiled sweetly before turning the smile that was his on the man who sidled up beside her. The guy was wearing enough gold chains to put Fort Knox out of business, and he had a motor mouth that wouldn't quit. No way was this bozo their target.

The bozo rested a palm on a smooth ivory shoulder. Rand's grip tightened on the glass and he felt a distinct urge to hack the SOB's hand off at the wrist.

To his relief, Rachel cut the touchy-feely short and headed for a blackjack table. Jack cut his losses and moved in closer. Rand cut through the crowd, tailing her at a judicious distance.

His attention eventually focused on an elegant man in evening attire who approached her with a questioning smile and appeared to be confused as he asked her something. Then he shrugged expressively and shook his head, his smile so charming and sincere it immediately made Rand suspicious.

As the man continued to engage Rachel in what seemed to be an entertaining conversation, Rand bent down and pretended to tie his shoe, never releasing them from his peripheral vision.

Was it the too-smooth moves from the too-oily operator that caused his skin to crawl? Was it Jack's curt nod to Rand—he had a seasoned eye for a con—that made him shudder? Or was it the way Rachel was playing her role with a flawless finesse, appearing friendly and interested but not overeager, that had him swallowing against a dust-dry throat?

And then the man was gesturing toward the bar, and Rachel was appropriately hesitant before slowly smiling in agreement.

She dropped her sequined purse—the sign they'd hit the jackpot. The guy was good, so good Rand would've staked the cool ten mil he'd made on yesterday's coup that this was *it*.

He didn't give respect easily, but Rachel had won it, and it climbed several notches as he slyly observed from his post. She was reeling their mark in like a pro. If she was scared, she wasn't showing it, although his own heart was banging against his ribs and adrenaline was rushing through his system.

But as he followed them into the bar, an image of plump pillows, a feather-down bed, and Rachel his, all his, muted the apprehension clawing at his gut. Dear Lord, how he wanted to protect her, even knowing that if any woman in the world could protect herself it was Rachel.

Jack beat someone to the bar stool next to the one Rachel took beside the slaver. *It had to be the slaver.*

As Rand watched her doing her job, so incredibly well, even better than he'd dared hope, he did a double take.

For an instant he could have sworn she wasn't dressed to kill in black, but was naked beneath a loose, flowing gown of white gauze.

8

RACHEL'S STOMACH rolled over for the hundredth time in ten minutes. The cucumber cool she'd felt in rehearsal was nowhere to be found as she confronted the real thing. *Help, Rand! You were right! This is too scary, and I want out!* She battled the instinct to hightail it into his arms, which were less than twenty feet away.

Managing to stop her foot in midshake, she tilted her head so that the soft lighting would show her hair to its best red advantage.

"Beautiful hair on a beautiful lady," Maurice said. At least that's how he'd introduced himself. His voice dripped with enough culture for Barrymore and Olivier combined. He was so convincing that she might have bought it, if her trained eye hadn't spotted some subtleties that marked him as a counterfeit. His nails were clean, but needed clipping. When she'd dropped her purse, she'd noted that his shoes could use a shine. His cologne was way too strong. Little things, telling things. A man of true wealth and breeding would have seen to the finishing touches. And he sure as heck wouldn't be squirting his mouth with breath spray as she watched and forced a smile and gushed an ingenuous reply.

"I'm glad you like my hair. But really, Maurice, such an outrageous compliment, it's enough to make a woman blush."

"Don't tell me you don't get at least a dozen a day."

"Are you kidding?" She looked shyly away, her gaze brushing Rand's across the room, where he was making small talk with a woman who looked like a hooker. The momentary connection steeled her resolve and escalated her running pulse to a gallop. Her cheeks burned as she noted Maurice's quick, calculating assessment of her bosom. Rachel pressed an unsteady hand to her cleavage, hoping the material would absorb the trickling beads of sweat.

"Kidding?" he repeated, laughing softly. "My dear, I have never been more serious. You are, in fact, *exquisite.* I'm a worldly man, in experience, not to mention travel. But my acquaintance with women of your ilk—intelligent, divinely gorgeous, and most pleasant to converse with—is, shall we say, unfortunately limited. Surely you've had many men, besides myself, appreciate those attributes."

"Oh, no! You see, I was an only child, and my parents were very protective, and—and I'm not exactly what you'd call, um, overly experienced when it comes to worldly men."

At least if she didn't count Rand, whose compliments were often left-handed and unembroidered. Still, she'd take them any day over this stuff, which was so thick she wanted to gag. As for the protective parent, that much was true. Dear Daddy had run off many a boyfriend with his inquisitions and his bone-crushing handshakes. If he could see her now, he'd roll over in his grave and pound at his coffin lid to get out.

"You, inexperienced, when everything about you is the epitome of sophistication? You must be younger than you look. How old did you tell me you were?"

"I didn't." Her nervous laugh was genuine. "But I turned twenty-two last month. I hope you don't think I'm a baby."

"Rubbish. Why don't I buy us a drink, and we'll toast to your birthday?"

"That would be really nice. After all, I did spend it alone, and I would so like to share it with someone special." She paused for effect. "Someone like you."

"But what about those protective parents of yours? Surely they sent their love and presents, even if they were too far away to join you."

"Farther than that, Maurice. Mother and Daddy died in a car accident two years ago."

"How tragic. Surely you must have other relatives that miss you. Aunts or uncles or grandparents?"

"Unfortunately, no. My parents were only children, and my grandparents passed on when I was quite small."

"Oh, my dear, this *is* tragic." The glint in his eyes reminded her of matching fruit rolling up on a slot machine and spitting out a stream of silver to be fingered greedily. "Please accept my condolences, *and* my belated wishes for a happy birthday." He raised a single finger to the bartender, who had thus far stayed too busy to acknowledge them. "It seems the bartender is finally coming our way. What shall I order for you?"

Your slimy guts skewered on a toothpick umbrella and drowning in a Mai Tai for me to throw in your face, scumbag.

"A glass of white zinfandel would be wonderful."

"But not half as wonderful as you," he deftly insisted.

Rachel tugged down the hem that had ridden up her thighs an uncomfortable few inches. Maurice's appreciative note of the small act suggested that he more than liked her sense of modesty. He was lapping it up. The creep.

Refusing to consider the inevitable investigation of her body, Rachel managed to quell the queasy swishing of her stomach, and leaned back so that Jack was a few inches closer for the little while longer she would have him to count on.

Maurice placed their order, then kept the conversation running with an anecdote that she laughed at in all the right places. Stolen glances alerted her to the bartender's deceit. While he'd fixed her companion's Stolichnaya straight up in clear sight, he poured the wine, and took a half minute too long to do it, beneath the counter's ledge.

Drugged. The wineglass he set before her with a flourish and a smile was drugged. Rachel deflected her immediate impulse to recoil from Maurice and dump the drink in his lap.

She could feel Rand's gaze on her back, and with it came the familiar prickling of the fine hairs on her nape. He was anxious, worried, and sending her a silent message that it wasn't too late to get out.

She reached for the wine, meaning to slide it a few crucial inches closer to Jack's identical goblet.

Maurice caught her trembling fingertips with his own. They were smooth, dry and insistent. He lifted her glass and inhaled the bouquet before gallantly handing it over.

"A sip and a toast. To you, my sweet, and especially to our most fortuitous meeting."

A quick glance to the left, and she saw their bartender disappear in a swish of ruby velvet doors. Her educated guess was that he had a fast call to make so that a driver would be meeting them at the entrance.

Rachel pretended to take a small sip, then set it next to Jack's, just as they'd planned. What they hadn't planned on was Maurice's quick retrieval of the glass, or his admonishing shake of the head as he urged the rim to her lips.

"Come now, you don't *really* consider that to do justice to your birthday, or to our delightful acquaintance, do you? Let's try this again. To you. To me. To a night we'll never forget."

Had Jack switched the glasses? Not unless he was faster than David Copperfield and Houdini rolled into one.

"Here, here!" Rachel faked another sip. Before she could and the glass on the bar and stall for a few precious seconds, Maurice caught her wrist and tilted, tilted . . .

Deciding that if she didn't drink up she'd risk blowing her cover, Rachel took several quick swallows. It had a slight bitter flavor, but otherwise there was no telltale taste.

From what she knew about the drug of choice, she could expect it to hit within ten minutes. *Let it hit*, she decided. Maybe she was better off drugged than enduring more of this hell that she knew was nothing compared to the hell awaiting her. At least this way she wouldn't have to fake the effects.

The effects kicked in before she could polish off half the glass. Something tickled the back of her throat and emerged as a silly giggle. Maurice was stroking her calf with the unshiny tip of his shoe, which had begun to gleam like Tinkerbell's wand in the shimmering darkness. And how agreeable she felt when he whispered that they should leave here and do the town in style.

Sounded good to her. But it shouldn't. Rachel frowned, then laughed as she scrambled for a wisp of comprehension. The room had grown hazy, and so had her brain. She reached for her purse and knocked it to the floor.

"I'll get it, my dear," Maurice offered graciously, swiping it up and leading her out on his arm.

If she had to be drugged, Rachel decided, this one—whatever it was—wasn't half-bad. She laughed gaily, feeling wildly uninhibited and loose. Everything struck her as funny. The way Jack was getting up and taking her glass along with him. And Maurice patting her purse, which he wouldn't find a gun in. Of course, in her current state of hilarious insanity, she'd have found it real funny to blow his miserable head off. She would have liked to say as much, but her tongue felt plumper than an overstuffed quilt.

As they made their exit from the bar, she was aware of an electric sensation stitching up her spine. Someone had touched her at the small of her back.

Even flying high, she didn't need to look to see who it was. Only one person had ever affected her like that. Rachel tilted her spinning head and caught a parting glance from Rand before he was swallowed by the crowd zooming in and out, then whirling round and round in kaleidoscopic Technicolor.

Unlike her, Rand hadn't been smiling. So what? she thought as another lilting giggle erupted. Those stern lips of his were made for kissing like crazy, and crazy as she was for him, she'd gladly return his dumb dough in exchange for a taste of that gorgeous, sexy mouth.

She hoped he hurried up and met her in—well, wherever the heck it was that he was going to buy her. Too bad it was going to cost him, when she'd gladly be his for free.

9

THE LONG WHITE ROBES fluttered against Rand's sandal-clad feet. He quickened his pace, sidestepping a peddler hawking gaudy jewelry from a brightly colored cart. A drunk, thrown through a tavern's swinging doors, landed in his path.

Rand stepped over him without a cursory glance, his mind locked on Rachel. A queasy feeling twisted his insides with each thought of what they might have done to her.

His utter inability to help her when she'd needed him the most was a bitter reminder of past failure. Shutting it out, he concentrated on the surroundings.

Zebedique. Just as he remembered it. Beggars and whores and stinking-rich sultans milled together in narrow cobblestone streets lined with casinos and massage parlors, opium dens and exquisite jewelry stores.

It was a twenty-four-hour party, as rich as it was sleazy. The thick smell of spice permeated everything. He caught himself sniffing his pores as he rounded a familiar corner.

He headed straight for a voluptuous building composed of stained-glass windows and swirling gold turrets that looked like butterscotch-dipped Dairy Queen cones. Rand adjusted the long, scarf-type hood covering his head.

"You are invited?" the guard said in broken English.

Luckily, English was the common language used by the international travelers who gathered here in Zebedique. Rand had had no reason to hire an interpreter, as many here did, or to pretend he was anything but what he was: a visiting American with enough money and contacts to grant him entry to this high-stakes den of iniquity. Even so, he'd studied up on the local dialect, and he could get by. Better yet, he could eavesdrop.

"I am invited. Do you wish to see my papers?" At the curt nod from the guard, Rand produced a letter of introduction and proof of an unlimited line of credit at a Swiss bank.

The guard waved him inside. As he took his indicated seat, Rand declined a drink and the sexual favors a servant girl offered. He scanned the crowd, aware that anticipation seemed to pulse through the air. Low murmurs filtered through the musical strains of a flute. Fat men, handsome men, old goats, fast livers, all lounged and drank and greedily fondled the girls who were in ample supply.

A loud clap sounded. The flute was joined by a stringed instrument, and a line of exotic, heavily made-up women took their places, then began to dance, to strip and undulate sinuously on the stage.

So this was how the slavers worked their customers up, he thought, almost dazedly. He wished he could say he was immune. But as he looked at the bronzed bodies glistening with oil, he could only envision Rachel, her fair skin, her flowing red hair, her lips, lush with invitation, beckoning to him to take her home.

Rand groaned, feeling the rush of his blood, the rise of his sex. His groan was echoed by many, and he wished to heaven they'd just get on with it.

He got his wish. The women finished their dance and left. A dark, sinewy gnome of a man took center stage. The room, charged with lust, now went silent.

"Bring the girl out." He clapped his hands twice, and two men struggled with a dark, slender woman who was twisting and screaming and trying to break free of their hold, in spite of the rope binding her wrists.

Rand was appalled. The rest of the crowd seemed excited, judging from the murmur of approval sweeping through the room.

"She's spirited," noted the auctioneer. "A fine Egyptian woman to warm a man's bed." He signaled, and a large hook attached to a rope dropped from the top of the stage. With practiced ease, the two assistants looped the bonds on her wrists over the hook and left. At another signal, the rope was raised until she was balanced on her toes.

The woman was crying, and Rand toyed with the notion of buying her just so that he could set her free.

He couldn't. There were going to be a lot more women exactly like her, and buying all of them was out of the question.

"You like her breasts?" said the gnome. "Then see how you like the rest!" With a jerk of his hand, he whipped the sheet from her body, exposing her in full frontal nudity.

The woman shrieked, and the audience applauded.

"Unfortunately she is not a virgin." The gnome caught her around the waist, the rope turning as he pivoted. "But she's very tight, and why should virginity matter, with such beautiful buttocks, and thighs you can train to wrap around your waist?"

The bidding lasted several minutes, the auctioneer forcing up the bids, constantly extolling her merits.

She sold for the equivalent of fifty thousand dollars. The new owner claimed her. Amid polite applause, he carried her off the stage.

Rand wished he'd taken the drink he'd been offered. He needed something to get a hold on himself before Rachel was similarly disgraced. Something to dampen this sick anticipation. He couldn't bear the thought of seeing her so horribly handled, of these other men looking upon her while they fondled themselves and placed their bids.

While he would outbid each one and doubtless be filling himself up with the sight of her nakedness.

The thought left him with a load of self-disgust—and the familiar arousal that thoughts of her always evoked. By the fifth girl, those two warring qualities had twisted together with his gnawing anxiety: overt references to sex, nudity, and concern about Rachel bombarded his senses.

"And now, gentlemen, the most intoxicating beauty we have ever offered. American. Educated. And, best of all—" he clapped his hands, and Rand watched, numb and yet, as he had feared he would be, hideously enthralled, as Rachel was led onto the stage "—she is a *virgin!*"

Flanked by the guards, she held her head high and walked silently, dressed in nothing but a sheet and her attitude, to the center of the platform. Rand could see her scanning the crowd, eyes guarded but alert.

Lord, she was beautiful, standing proud and aloof from it all. He sensed the other patrons' anticipation as excitement swept them into a taut, hushed frenzy of lust.

Rand lusted, too. Her eyes caught his, and he knew she was pleading with him to end this quickly and take her away from this horrible place. He couldn't claim her soon enough, to whisk her away to the haven they'd share.

Something shifted in the middle of his chest, heaping sympathy and tenderness on the caldron of emotions he was struggling to control.

But then the auctioneer was teasing them, sliding the sheet from her breasts. One plump alabaster breast spilled out, her nipple haloed by a large, dark areola.

Feeling himself grow so stiff that he hurt, Rand told himself he was no better than any other barbarian here. How could he, a civilized man, be nursing this aching arousal, when it was Sarah's identical plight that had brought him here, to right a terrible wrong? He didn't know. But his need for Rachel was immense, and he'd never imagined being faced with such raw carnality before assuming his position on the tightrope.

Rand drew in a shuddering, hot breath, tasting spice and the anticipation of woman on his tongue. He commanded himself to raise his gaze again to her face and support her with that until she was his, only his, by virtue of his filthy lucre.

Nonetheless, this atmosphere was bad for a man's morals.
And it seduced his to sink lower with each second that passed.

RACHEL LOCKED HER EYES on Rand. He was the only solid
thing in the madness that had surrounded her since the minute she'd left the casino with the slaver. She held fast to his
presence, to the reassurance she read in his gaze.

But there was more. Something dark and earthy that permeated the room and was focused on her. She shivered and
vowed not to cry or scream.

Or dissolve into hysterical laughter. The whole thing was
so absurd, so bizarre, that she felt as if she were trapped in
some B-grade movie, playing the starring role while another
part of her observed, in disbelief, from a distance.

Distance. Maurice and company had kept their distance
from her throughout the flight. Had, in fact, seemed eager to
hand her over to this end of the business—which had, mer-
cifully, proved to be *all* business. After a medical examination had established that she was indeed a virgin, she had
been treated as if she were an investment to be handled with
the greatest of care. She'd been bathed, massaged, mani-
cured and pedicured, her hair washed and brushed so that it
gleamed like the pennies she'd scrubbed with an eraser as a
child until they'd glowed copper red and new.

An exclusive club for slaves in the making. No clothes allowed. She'd counted twenty naked bodies besides hers, and
the treatment of each one had been so luxuriantly cavalier
that she'd begun to feel oddly liberated by her own nudity.
Her ingrained modesty, at home in the Western world,
seemed a quaint, outdated custom in this anachronistic,
backward society.

Rachel was strangely grateful for the five days that had
passed since she'd been a free woman in Vegas. The time had
allowed her to adapt to these foreign surroundings. She could
deal with this, she told herself—no problem.

A sense of calm enveloped her. The guards departed, leaving her hands bound but unhooked. Why, she wasn't sure. Maybe it was her condescending glare, or the lack of struggle that accompanied it. Whatever, it apparently increased her value, judging from the mercenary smile the auctioneer turned on her. The terrible little man pried the wrapped sheet from one breast and then the other. The audience oohed and ahed their beastly approval. The auctioneer winked, and she managed not to spit in his face.

Instead Rachel thrust her breasts out, taking pride in her sculptured femininity. And it was more than pride. She taunted them with it, while Rand maintained his outward cool....

Which disintegrated before her stunned eyes.

Attuned as she was to his body language and to the silent support of his gaze, she was struck dumb by the metamorphosis in him. First, the steady rhythm of his breathing became agitated to the point of panting. Then the clear focus of his eyes on hers lowered to her upper nakedness and became transfixed so long that he appeared to be in a trance. His tongue snuck out, but rather than retreating, it repeatedly traced a hungry path, around and around, as if it were her inner thighs he was lapping at rather than his own dry lips.

Her savior was suddenly no savior, but the devil himself, considering the spoils of his ill-gotten gain. She was horrified to realize that Rand had relinquished his ally's support to stare at her breasts with a hunger unrivaled by that of his lust-in-the-dust colleagues.

A rope dropped down, and she felt the auctioneer lifting her arms to a hook.

"I can do it myself, you cheap little runt," she snapped, taking her anger out on the nearest scapegoat.

"So you can talk after all," he said in halting English. "Cooperate and I won't hurt your dignity."

"You can go to hell. Dignity's something you don't have to give." Warm air swirled around her breasts, and she ignored the agony of feeling more exposed than she had during the examination. Rachel raised her hands with a grace befitting a ballerina and defiantly notched her chin upward.

She shut out the rippling noise of the buyers, the drone of the auctioneer's wheedling voice. If only she could do the same with her hurt, her deep disappointment in Rand, looking at her as if he were even more crazed than the rest of them. After the time they'd spent together, the bonds they'd forged, bonds she'd believed to be of friendship, how could he turn into this—this animal? The fine edge of longing and unspoken emotions had never left, but never in her wildest dreams had she expected this kind of betrayal. It made her want to weep.

The hell she'd cry. Rand could destroy her illusions of him, and the disgusting men sitting with him could drool all over themselves while she was helpless to cover her near nakedness, but no one could strip away her pride.

Her body was another matter. Without warning, she felt the thin sheet whipped off. An outraged cry ripped from her throat before she could stop it.

"You sleazy little bastard, get your grimy hands off me!"

"A spirited virgin, gentlemen. And see the lovely hair between her thighs, matching that of her scarlet head."

"You stupid jerk, you despicable creep, you low-down, no good—"

"But let us not stop there." He yanked her around and stroked her buttocks.

Gone was her earlier calm. In its place came a flash-point rage. Rachel was on tiptoe, but she had her balance. With a quick self-defense move, she pulled up and kicked sideways, landing a blow to his groin.

He bent over, groaning and cursing and calling for a whip.

"One hundred thousand American dollars!" came a shout.

"One hundred and fifty!" echoed another.

Voices slashed her ears, dozens of men scrambling to outbid their competition with ruples, yen, pounds and marks.

By why wasn't she hearing Rand through the mayhem, while she dangled helpless, naked, and up for grabs?

The auctioneer was quickly gaining his footing, turning her around, gesturing to her breasts, her thighs, then stepping a safe distance away.

"Five hundred thousand American dollars from Prince Dominic," he said triumphantly. "Do I hear a higher bid?"

Rachel stared in shock and fury at Rand. His eyes were almost glazed, and even from here she could see his labored breathing. What she saw was the look of a man in the throes of passion, but his passion was overlaid by the raw anger she saw in the clench of his jaw, simmering in his gaze.

Unlike the rest of the men, who had remained seated throughout the fanfare, he stood.

"One million American dollars."

Every head present turned at the commanding sound of his projected voice.

Then silence was followed by murmurs of speculation and respect for the amount of money.

The auctioneer called for silence.

"One million American dollars from the new member. Do I hear more? One million and a half?"

The question was directed to the prince. Rachel held her breath, or at least what she had left of it.

The prince shook his head.

"The beautiful woman goes for one million." The greedy slaver nodded to Rand. "Come and claim your prize."

She watched as he strode forward, his eyes fluctuating between her face and her naked body. When he gained the stage, he stooped and swept up the sheet. He positioned himself between her and the sea of watching eyes, shielding her from every view but his.

"You will enjoy taming her?" said the auctioneer with a sly smile.

"I will. But don't ever let me catch you touching her like that again, or you'll be using this sheet for a shroud. Beat it, and don't come back until we're gone."

Rand spanned the sheet wide between his arms, but he didn't immediately cover her with it. The spread of white muslin blended into his robe, the hood of it contrasting starkly against his dark skin. Her mind was spinning, casting him as Valentino in *The Sheik*. But he was no actor, he was a man she'd spent the past month with, craving the touch he withheld and wondering if she might be falling in love.

This was not the same man. This was a dark stranger more dangerous than the one who'd asserted his hold with a sexy ploy at her door. He whispered to her now, as he had then, saying, "You're okay, angel. I'm here, and I'll protect you."

He was protecting her, all right. Protecting her from prying eyes, only to devour her with his own. She bared her teeth, not trusting herself to speak.

His gaze hungrily trailed her body, and she was torn between fury and a quivering spark of—desire. No! How could she even think it? She wanted to tear his head off for daring to look at her like this, for subjecting her to such degradation, even if no one else could see.

"Remember the Oscar," he said in a low, gritty voice. Slowly he put the sheet to her back, his hands grazing over her fevered skin, relaying a proprietary feeling that spoke of the protection he'd promised. As he wrapped the covering beneath her raised arms, she could feel him shaking.

His fingertips hovered over the top of a breast, then slowly closed the distance, as though drawn by a force beyond his control. He touched the tip of a single nipple. His touch became a stroke. Once. Twice. A rolling, gentle squeeze that brought forth a tortured groan from him.

Rachel was appalled to feel both nipples harden and thrust out as if seeking more. Her legs shook, and her belly tightened. A tiny, mewling sound escaped between her parted lips in answer to his inarticulate murmurings.

Why wasn't she fighting him for all she was worth? She didn't want this, not this way. She abhorred him for what he was doing, for making her acknowledge a shameless facet of herself in this obscene place, making his conquest in the privacy of her home seem trivial and pale.

She wanted to cling to him. She wanted to bolt and return to a time that was safe and familiar, when she was late with the rent and had never laid eyes on Rand Slick.

"Mine." The word was a thick whisper, and if she hadn't seen his lips move, she might have thought she'd imagined it.

Quickly, then, as though he didn't trust what he might do next, Rand wrapped the sheet around her twice and secured it between her breasts. She was still dangling from the hook when he pulled her insistently against him.

Even beneath the folds of his robe she could feel him hard, pulsing. He unhooked her arms, and she fell limp against him. The bindings stayed her from thrusting against his chest. Her bound hands caught between them. She squirmed to break free, but he subdued her by quickly shifting. Her fists pressed intimately into the harbor of their nearly joined groins. She was too close to hurt him, and too shocked by the stunning arousal the feel of him evoked even to try.

Vaguely she realized that the audience was craning for a better view as he fanned a palm over her buttocks and tangled a hand in her hair.

"What are you doing?" she demanded, fighting tears of horror and need.

"I'm sorry for what you went through. Dear God, I am. But I'd be lying if I apologized for this."

His mouth came down on hers. Greedily. Possessively. His kiss was compelling and tender and fierce. His lips slanted against hers, rubbed them, learned them, and ate from them. Then the tip of his tongue dipped into the groove of her lower lip before taking it into the warm haven of his mouth. Such was his wooing that her teeth unlocked, and with a pleased murmur he pressed between them, in a smooth glide that was so hungry it intensified her own mounting greed.

An absorbing, ravenous kiss. A shared kiss of mutual need held too long in check. He was making her crazy. Yes, yes, she must be losing her mind. Because if only her hands were unbound she would grip him to her, stroke her hands through his hair, wind her legs about his waist and—

And why had they waited so long for this rapture, this physical bond that felt like whispered words of a deeper bonding, an aching, unspoken vow? She couldn't remember—something about pride and manipulation and threats, a twisted part of the puzzle with the jagged edges.

Then she lost even that memory. He was kissing her madly, and she was opening her mouth, begging for more while she searched for the thread. *Pride, jagged edges, so twisted up...*

Through her moans, the faraway rush of rippling applause spread in her ears. It cut through, and she remembered where she was, and good Lord, if she didn't stop this insanity she wouldn't even care if he took her right here.

Rachel tore her lips from his and reared back. Eyes that lapped at her with dark, ominous fire stayed her from demanding the release she didn't want.

"Let's get out of here and go home," he said hoarsely.

She tried valiantly to keep something of her independence, pushed harsh words past her kiss-swollen lips. "First you call that pig back to give you a knife and cut me loose."

"So you can slap me? The answer is *no.*" Rand hoisted her over his shoulder, one hand locked over the backs of her legs, the other cupping her behind with a possessive caress.

"Stop it," she demanded as the sound of music blended into the scent of spice and uncurbed desire. "You have no right to do this."

"The papers that are waiting say that I do."

"You don't own me. I don't belong to you."

"I guess that's something we'll both have to find out. I just spent a million bucks to have the chance, and from what I saw on that stage, the answer's going to be worth every dime."

"This isn't a joke, and I'm in no mood for theatrics. Put me down. Do you hear me? Put me down!"

He ignored her screams of demand, but as they exited to a standing ovation she heard him chuckle and say, "Once we're home, angel, we'll take our bows."

10

"DAMMIT, RAND, STOP! Let me walk!" Rachel hung over his shoulder, smacking his rear with her bound hands, since he had the rest of her in a clinch. They'd passed through the massive entryway of a house and been bowed to by servants who promptly disappeared; and now he was carrying her up a marbled staircase and through some kind of maze. She felt him shift, kick, heard a door slam.

"Did you hear me? I demand that you put me down right this instant."

"If you say so."

Suddenly she felt herself hauled upright, and then he was cradling her in his arms. Then he stooped low and let go. She fell a short distance before the softest sensation imaginable greeted her back.

Rachel sank into what might have been a pillow of clouds. A white canopy that was so huge it could have passed for a tent was fanned out overhead. A quick glance to either side informed her that she was lying on a bed, the likes of which she'd never seen before. Round, voluptuous, a gigantic silk pincushion.

Rand's face, still partially concealed by his hood, stared down at her. His dark brows were knitted together, making his eyes seem like twin obsidian stones glittering darkly beneath two horizontal slashes.

Rachel couldn't catch her breath and she knew it wasn't from the gentle fall. It was the way he was staring down at her, seeming larger than life from her vantage point, dominating the room with his powerful frame enfolded in the robe.

A grand sultan in his domain. The torched expression he wore as he stroked her visually told her more than she wanted to know.

He wanted her. Now. And they were all alone.

Suddenly she wished for even the company of that disgusting crowd.

Rachel followed his gaze and realized the sheet had come loose. Her breasts were covered, barely, and so were her hips, even more barely. Her legs were exposed to her upper thighs and sprawled out in a most undignified way. She squirmed, trying to pinch them together. Her eyes dilated with alarm when she realized she'd succeeded only to loosen the sheet more. Her breasts were all but spilling out, and she could feel the rush of warm air tickling her feminine parts.

"Welcome home," he said in a thick voice. "I hope you find our bed comfortable."

"*Our* bed?" Her apprehension soared, as did her indignation that he was taking advantage of this. Staring at her with even more heated rawness than he had at the auction, and making no effort to disguise what it did for his masculine urges. "The audience is gone, Rand. You can drop the act."

"Hardly. The act's just begun." He thrust his hood back and sat on the edge of the bed. It gave under his weight and rolled her against him.

"You're a civilized man . . . aren't you?" she said desperately, fearful she might soon find out just how barbaric he could get. "Quit looking at me like that!"

"Like I want to strip what's left of that sheet off in no civilized manner?" he said in a booming, authoritarian tone.

"Stop it," she hissed. "I don't like this."

"Good. Very good," he whispered, then returned to a forceful volume. "Whether you like it or not makes no difference. We play by my rules, woman, not yours."

"*Your* rules!" She struggled to move away, but he caught her upper arms and hoisted her upright until they were almost nose to nose, mouth to mouth. Her rapid, choppy breathing mingled with his, which was maddeningly deep and even. "Get your hands off me and take your rules right out the door with you."

"I have no intention of leaving!" he bellowed. "We're going to do this my way. Give me your hands and be quick about it!"

"Why? So you can loop them around a hook and dangle me from the bed while you rape me?" She heard something that sounded close to hysteria rise in the pitch of her voice.

"Don't be ridiculous. When I choose to take you to bed, you'll be more than ready." His words were arrogant, but his gaze reflected an intensity of emotion she was too unstrung to decipher.

Again he spoke low. "Listen to me, Rachel. You weren't the only one in agony while you were being paraded on that stage. It practically tore my guts out to watch what they did to you. Every time I think about that creep touching you, I—" His grip tightened, and his eyes took on a distant sheen. Was it anger? Frustration? "I've been in control for so long that—God, I forgot how it feels to be without it, to be helpless to protect someone that I—"

She whimpered as his fingers bit deep into her shoulders. His vision seemed to refocus to the present, and he abruptly let go. "I didn't mean to hurt you." He swept a soothing stroke over the red imprint he'd left and murmured, "I'll do what I can to make up for what you went through, and I'd say that excludes rape. So relax. We're home. You're safe." Then he said brusquely, "The wrists?"

When she hesitated, he took it upon himself to place them in his lap. Working the fine knots, his fingers were deft and agile, belying their size and strength. Would she ever understand him? This paragon of mystery, whose touch veered from the harsh to the sensitive, while his expressions and words rushed in so many different directions she couldn't keep up.

For the moment, she was still too jangled from the ordeal to even try. All she knew was that he'd wanted to protect her, and as vulnerable as she was now, half-nude and responding to his gruff concern, she wanted to protect herself from her protector.

Distance. She had to get some distance from this dark edge of intimacy that she'd succumbed to on the stage with an abandon that she was too ashamed of to remember, even as she could feel it threatening to overtake her again as they sat, too close, on the bed.

"You might have hated it, Rand, but I was the one being terrified, disgraced and—"

"And you never showed it," he said quietly. "I was proud of you, Rachel. You should be proud of yourself for handling it as well as you did. Oh, and, by the way, great shot. Made me want to whistle and clap when you decked that munchkin."

"Are you as proud of yourself? The way you stared at me, keep staring at me, makes you look as depraved as the rest of those slobbering heathens."

"That's because I was." He flung the rope to the gleaming marble floor. "And still am, though I imagine you gathered that with your hands in my lap. But as for your question, the answer is no. I wasn't proud of myself. I was ashamed. And more aroused than I've ever been in my life. Be honest, Rachel. Didn't you feel the same things, too?"

She didn't want to be honest with either of them, and so she looked away. He already knew, anyway. No need to give him the satisfaction of confirming their base bond.

Pulling her wrists to his lips, he kissed the abrasions marking her skin. "I'll tend this after you have the bath I ordered drawn."

He hadn't offered her an apology for his behavior, and so what if wanting one was hypocritical. She wanted him to say he was sorry, not make a statement that sounded suspiciously like a master's dictate. A solicitous one, but a dictate nonetheless. He'd said it so smoothly, with an ease of command that didn't expect to be challenged.

"You'll tend this? After I take a bath you ordered?" She met him with a level stare, determined to assert some independence before he started taking his role to heart. "I can tend myself and draw my own baths, thank you, Mr. Slick."

"So the auctioneer didn't lie," he shouted. "You are a spirited wench! Now get this, my virgin possession. I said *I'll* do the tending. And you will let me do it, like it or not. You will obey your master or suffer the consequences of your impertinence."

He grinned. Rachel couldn't believe his audacity. Why, he was actually enjoying this! Throwing himself into his part with relish, while the weakness of her position left her wide open to his whims.

"I'll most certainly do no such thing," she informed him sternly. "Leave, just leave before I scream loud enough to bring the servants running."

His low chuckle antagonized her. Her eyes blazed a path of outrage that he deflected with a spark of supreme delight.

"Why, you arrogant, pigheaded—" she sputtered. Pointing a shaking finger at the door, she gave an order of her own. "Get out! Did you hear me? Go away and don't come back until you can wipe that stupid smirk off your face. Do it before I scream these walls down on your head, you ... you ... *dictator*."

"Scream all you like, my hot-blooded beauty," he boomed. "The servants won't save you from the master of the house." He hooked a thumb in the door's direction, indicating there might be prying ears. "And don't forget I am your master, too. I own you, woman. Lock, stock and barrel."

"Why, you ... you ... Ooh!" She lunged at him, ready to punch him good for everything he'd done and everything she'd let him do. She aimed for his nose, which seemed apt, since he was rubbing hers in the situation that he had the nerve to gloat over.

She was fast and on target, but Rand reacted with the reflexes of a street fighter. He caught her raised fist and jerked her against his chest. The sheet fell away and Rachel's heart turned over. Her naked breasts were pressed into his robe.

"Scream again," he instructed in a low, rough voice. She tried to, but her voice was caught in her throat. "Then maybe you need some help."

He hesitated, then quickly loosened the folds of material to expose a large expanse of firm muscle and dark sworls of hair. His skin was warm, the color of coffee cream. Their nipples touched. Her breasts parted and rode against his. The way he held her to him rubbed their flesh together in a sinuous rotation, tight but shy of a crush.

"My way," he said in an intimate whisper. "Be careful, Rachel, or you might end up enjoying my way more than yours. Open your mouth and scream."

She did. She screamed in frustration, because he'd assumed his role so effortlessly, when she wanted something real and lasting. And then she screamed again, because perhaps if he thought she was pretending she could convince herself, too, and he wouldn't stop what he was doing, making her breasts grow heavy, weighted. A healthy dose of self-disgust spurred her on, the ease with which he could play her tasting like a bitter truth shoved down her throat.

Even as her cries faded, the tingle spawned by the brush of his hair spread in widening ripples.

"Perfect," he whispered. "Almost as perfect as your breasts gliding over my skin, so soft I could swear they're melting into my chest and you're feeling something more for me than you do for every other client. You do. Admit it."

"No," she said brokenly. "*No.* It's—it's what you're paying me for. You're a job, my ticket up. After today, I don't even know if we can still be friends."

"In that case, we should be safe, shouldn't we? You have no emotional attachment to me, and so even if I feel something very special and dangerous for you, we're both protected, and Sarah's future isn't threatened. Though more than ever I wonder if she's really the one at risk, or if she's simply a convenient excuse."

Footsteps sounded in the hallway, and he shifted, hastily pressing her down into the giving cushion. His weight was on her, and their upper bodies were joined. And then he moved until he lay fully on top, his thighs hugging hers, his erection straining against the material of his robe to seek her out.

"Please, Rand . . ." Pleading with him, pleading with herself because her instincts were screaming at her to part her legs and discover the dark secrets yet to unfold, to take them and the resulting risks without confronting the truth he had suggested. "Get off of me. Get out. We'll pretend this never happened."

"Pretending's something that we've been doing too long. Since the first day I walked through your door, we've skirted the edge, and it's been about the hardest thing I've ever had to do, keeping my hands to myself while all I could think about was touching you, and touching you a lot more intimately than this." He spread her hair out against the sheet. The tug of his fingers against her scalp shot downward, radiating to her belly, and to the place where she began to clench, to ache.

"You're forgetting about Sarah." It was her only defense. She didn't hesitate to use it, to cling to it like a cross that could ward off a vampire.

"No, angel, I never forget about her. Though chances are she's forgotten about me. Hold me. Help me to forget, too."

He said it so gently, and with so much appeal in his voice, that she could feel her muscles go lax with the soothing flow of his words. And then she remembered that he was most dangerous when vulnerable. She tried to resist, but his lips were soft, feeling, asking for the comfort she wanted to give. She almost reached for him; the urge to grasp his head, to kiss him in reassurance and soothe him with loving strokes, was so strong she hurt with the wanting.

But she didn't. Instead, she gave him a comfort that was safer for her.

"Don't worry. I'll find Sarah. You'll get it worked out. Then maybe you'll be the one doing the forgetting—about me."

"You're so wrong. We'll find Sarah, but together. You and I, we're partners, Rachel, not adversaries. And no matter what happens after we get out, I could never forget you."

No, she didn't think he would. But chances were he'd leave her. Patients did cling to their physicians in their time of need, only to regain their health and send a bouquet with a thank-you note once the crisis was over. How easily it could happen with them. If it did, she doubted she'd ever recover. It was that threatening possibility that caused her to shove at his chest rather than embrace him.

11

HE BORE DOWN, all tenderness forsaken, demand spiking his tone.

"Don't push me away, dammit. You know as well as I do that what's happening now has been a long time coming."

"Nothing's going to happen except what we came here for. Get off me, Rand. You've been here long enough to satisfy the servants."

"The servants, maybe. But not me. I'm not leaving this bed until we've got a few things straight."

She renewed her struggles, frantic to avoid this confrontation. His hands were on her, grappling with her flailing arms until he had her wrists manacled above her head in a single hand, his grip firm but unhurting. She squirmed, but his body pressed insistently, pinning her down.

"Quit fighting me," he whispered sternly. His mouth was too close, so close that the heat of his breath fanned her face and she felt more drugged than if she'd inhaled ether. Then she quit fighting, praying he'd say what he had to and leave.

"That's better." Better? She could only hope it wouldn't get worse. "We've been hiding behind this case, because that's the way you wanted it. No more, Rachel. We're on new turf, and my patience with the sham has run out."

"I don't want to talk." She buried her head in the downy texture of a pillow. He took the access to her neck the position offered, running his lightly bearded chin against it, then soothing the slight abrasion with his tongue. "You're being unfair," she charged, trying to shift away, only to have him follow.

"I never said I was fair."

"I can't think when you're doing this to me."

"Good. Can I take that to mean that I am something more to you than a bank draft, a rung on the ladder you're climbing?" He released her hands.

"No." Her automatic denial was contradicted by her palms' refusal to obey her mental "Don't touch" message. They sought his bare skin, the flex of her fingers gripping his back tightly.

"Liar," he softly accused. "Admit it. You're more distracted by what you're afraid to confront between us than any amount of distraction that would be there if you risked confronting it."

His words rang of truth. She was desperate to escape them—and desperate not to. Once she owned up to them, there was no turning back, and that terrified her, because she knew her own fate could prove worse than Sarah's. Rand had the power to take more than her innocence. He could break her heart.

Rachel forced her hands away from the warmth of his skin, skin that she could easily grow addicted to touching, and played the trump card that was wearing thin from overuse.

"As much as you want to find your sister, that's a risk you shouldn't gamble on."

"Maybe I'm gambling on the fact that you're a woman of depth, who would stop at nothing if she was committed to a personal cause. One who would do her best if she's got an emotional stake involved."

Rachel shut her eyes, feeling the bed beneath her, his weight so solid and so good covering hers. But his words, the ones just spoken, sparked a horrible suspicion. Oh, how it hurt to think it, that he might play her as heartlessly as he had his mean competition.

"If you're trying to barter my body and my emotions for a vested interest in your sister, you're not going to succeed. You can't manipulate me like I'm one of those commodities that you scarf up then liquidate to make your profit."

"Is that what you think?" he demanded. "Dammit, quit hiding your face in the pillow and look at me."

She shut her eyes tight. There was a sharp burning behind them, the threat of accumulated tears that she would not cry.

The insistent pressure of his grip at her jaw forced her face from the pillow. His breath was warm; she inhaled spice and the hint of bay. How could she compete with this? He was older than she in more than years, and she was floundering. No, worse than that. She felt as if she were staggering, banging into walls and sliding headlong into a revolving glass door that was going too fast for her to escape out the other side.

She reached for something, anything, to stop this crazy spinning that was more disorienting than any drugged wine.

"I'll tell you what I think," she said in a cracked voice. "Once this is over, your old life will be waiting. A life that's as alien to me as mine is to you. You're a man who plays to win and bails out before he can sink. Anyone else on board had better be a good swimmer, because they'll be cutting through the waves you leave in your wake."

He was silent for a while, and then he whispered, "You cut me, Rachel. You just cut me deeper than any insult that's ever been hurled in my face or any knife planted in my back. Including the one you drove in our last day in Vegas. You're still twisting the knife, and I'm still going against everything that defines my life to tell you I *do* care. *You* care. Don't deny it. Just tell me what it is that makes you want to."

His genuine hurt touched her in a place that quivered in empathy. Her emotions weren't the only ones on the line, and his honesty deserved the same from her.

"All right. It's because caring does go against what defines your life. Maybe I am more than a means to heal your missing-person affliction or to gratify a mutual lust. But for me, it's not enough." She could feel his laser-sharp gaze against her still-closed eyes. She had to leave them that way to say what she had to. "You're driven by instincts when it comes to survival. Mine tell me that my ultimate lesson could come from you. I can't be a ship passing through the night for any man. And because I more than care, especially not for you."

His curse was soft and curt. "You're right," he said roughly. "It could happen. But unless you can find the courage to take the chance, neither of us will ever know if you can teach me something I need to learn."

"And what is that?" she asked hesitantly, hopefully.

"It goes back to what you said about ships. After a long haul, they can run out of steam. Even the ocean liners, angel. Not an easy thing to accept when they like to think of themselves as autonomous. That is, until a sister ship comes out of nowhere and throws out a line."

He pressed into her. Deep and insistent was the grinding of his need. With a small cry, she arched upward, not meaning to, but somewhere, somehow, she had lost her own command.

Her eyes opened to search his, to discover if they were open and honest or simply those of a man in heat.

Steamy windows. Open windows, open as they had never been before. There was a depth there that she'd sensed, but sensed only. Staggering, yes, and frightful, because she saw him in all his darkness, beckoning her into his haunted, eerily vacant room.

"You know, Rachel, it's awfully disappointing when the line disappears before the captain can decide whether or not to take it. But I guess that's a moot point when the decision's already been made for him."

There was heavy disappointment in his statement, mingled with undisguised need. It touched her deeply, stoked a tender desire to share a mutual lifeline.

She touched his lips with her fingertips. His mouth drew taut with the stern clamp of his jaw.

"Who are you?" she whispered. "For once, Rand, tell me who and what you are."

"I'm afraid it's not that simple. In fact, since I met you, I'm not so sure myself. But I do know that at the moment I'm a man who's waging a real battle. You're innocent. I haven't been for a very long time." A struggle was taking place inside him, one she could feel in the sudden jerk of his hips, the simultaneous narrowing of his eyes. "Right now I'm wanting to take you somewhere that I don't think you should go."

Rachel's need to explore this unfamiliar path was great; so, too, was her fear. She swallowed convulsively, her throat dry.

"You're probably right. But before you make that decision for me, at least let me see the place you go."

"It's a walk. A walk on the dark side." He smiled without warning. A chilling smile that she sensed was meant to frighten her away from the danger he posed. She didn't recoil, as she knew she should, but stared at him as though she were a doe paralyzed by a headlight in the night.

"You really want to know who and what I am? Then welcome, angel, to one very intimate facet of me. If you're wise, you'll steal a glimpse and leave it at that. Take my warning as a sign that you're not a passing ship."

Her palms bracketed his shoulders. She was stranded between the urge to grip him to her—to rush headlong, without looking back—and the realization that she should heed his warning and shove him away while she had the chance.

"Why do I get the feeling that you're trying to protect me from yourself? That part of you is so good it's the real danger. But that's another man who's moving against me, tempting me to stay and take the risk."

"You see too much and you see too deep." His lips bore down on hers, plundering in no polite way. She responded before giving herself the option of escape, letting him take her down, down, to a place where there was no light, just this blind spot where she groped for the feel and taste and smell of him. But then he was pulling back, done with his ravaging, and slowly shaking his head.

"Run, Rachel. Run while you can. Against everything I want, I'm giving you a head start. Take it. I'll catch up, but by then you'll be much safer, if not out of my sight. You deserve that much, even if it's more than I want to give."

"I see through you, Rand." She threaded her fingers through his hair; it was clean and thick and arousingly rich. "Heaven help us both, because I'm still here."

"So you are." The tempering she had sensed, had read behind the inky blackness, retreated, leaving a gleam of danger that both beckoned and menaced. "You're either very brave or very foolish, Rachel. Because I'm ready to give you a closer look at just who you're dealing with. A man who knows when a woman's aroused, and knows that you are in no small way. It would be so easy for me to touch you, just so . . ."

He insinuated his hand between their bodies and stroked her cleft. The teasing whisper escalated into a merciless vibration. She cried out. She arched, and her body shook as though in the grip of a palsied madness. His expression hardened with some purpose she was too far gone to care about.

"Help me," she moaned. "Protect me." And then she gripped his shoulders, the broad slope that loomed above her. "Ahhh . . ."

"That's right. I could have you right now, and well don't I know it." Swift and sure was the glide of his finger into her entry. The sensation was too great, and painfully unsatisfying.

"It's not enough. What you're giving me, it's not enough."

"No, angel. It's more than I've ever given any woman before." He began to thrust slightly. Gently. With guarded strength. "You said I was no different today than those other barbarians. But I'm going to prove to us both that you were wrong. That I can feel this soft heat inside you and leave it at that. Because there's so much more that I need, something you've got that I've lost. If I can manage this, then maybe, just maybe I can get it back. Believe it or not, I am protecting you now."

"Rand," she sobbed. "Please, Rand, I can't stand it. You're making me hurt inside. Where you're touching me. But even more, here. In my heart. Don't do this to me, not unless you can be what I need."

"Unless I know what that is, I can't give it. Tell me what you need, and don't hold out."

"You," she cried brokenly. "*You.* But I want it all, and I don't know if you're able to give it."

"Neither do I . . . yet." His strokes gathered momentum, now fuller, deeper, a tactile invasion that made her reach with each retreat and weep for his possession of her. "More than anyone could possibly know, I do care about Sarah," he said, in a voice ragged with frayed restraint. "But I also care about us. In fact, I care enough not to strip off my clothes and take what my body's demanding. I'm stopping this right now, Rachel, while I still can. Protection. From me."

He made to withdraw, and she grabbed blindly for his wrist.

"How can you leave me like this?"

"With great difficulty, that's how. But knowing that you do care, apparently more than you want to, gives me enough reason to leave you like this."

"You make me need you and then you leave? It's cruel, Rand. How can you say that you care and be so cruel?"

"Do you think what I'm doing is easy for me? Sweet heaven, Rachel, if you can't sense how close I am to the edge, surely you can feel me against you, so hard that I hurt. The way I see it, I'm not being cruel. I'm being kind."

"Damn you, Rand." This was kindness? This horrible, empty ache he had created yet again and was leaving unappeased was kind? It seemed the cruelest punishment a man could devise. "Damn you for inviting me inside just to slam the door in my face."

"Damned if I do. But more damned if I don't. You see, angel, there's more I need to know before we take this all the way. What I'm leaving you with is some time to think. As much about your motives as mine. We both deserve it." He shut his eyes, and she thought he sighed. A sad sound, a distant whisper.

"Joshua deserves it."

12

"JOSHUA?" How could he spin riddles at a time like this? His reasoning was madness, and his timing was even worse. She opened her thighs and wrapped them about his. Arching, all but begging, she clung to his waist, demanding that he not desert her.

Rand's head fell forward, and he stared down at her with more complexities in his expression than she could possibly interpret through her distress. She knew one thing, and one thing only: the instinct to mate with him, to bond.

"Joshua's very close to Sarah. Probably much closer to her than he is to me, though lately he's been paying me some surprise visits. But enough about him." His teeth clenched as he growled a final warning. "Unwrap your legs, Rachel, before I decide to finish what we've hardly started. My more honorable nature just clocked out, since it's already put in some overtime."

She shook her head in a stilted negation, more torn and confused than denying. His face discarded the wisp of tenuous discipline and bore down on her with carnal force.

She glimpsed something, something she couldn't quite define. It tugged at her, this nagging sensation of having brushed the gentlest core of him, only to have him jerk it away before she could touch it. Her physical need peaked and interlocked with the need to reach out, to go where he had withdrawn to. Her frustration was more than sexual; it came from being denied access to what made him the man he was.

"You're hiding something from me, aren't you? You managed to get what you wanted out of me, and now that I want something in return you're shutting me out. You're running."

"Be glad I'm offering to run. We're in a country that gives me absolute rights to your body, and those are some rights I'm way past being ready to claim. This is our bed. This our bedroom. It's only the possibility that we could have something we both need that's keeping me in check. But just barely." He thrust down. Up. Then down again. A hard, rolling grind. "Unlock your legs," he commanded. Then he snapped out, *"Now."*

She forced herself to release him. A sensation like glass shattering sliced through her extremities.

"It wasn't supposed to be this way." It sounded like an accusation, and at the moment she did blame him for all the terrible things she felt. "This wasn't part of the deal."

"Apparently the deal has changed. Seems to me we've both been guilty of lying to each other as well as ourselves."

He got up and adjusted his robe. She clutched at the sheet with shaking fingers. Rand caught her wrist and covered her himself. She glared at him, in outrage he'd dangled the bait, hooked her, and was leaving her floundering alone on a deserted shore. Her begging cries were still in her ears, and she winced at the memory of his rejection. He'd refused her body, her need to know him. One refusal was humiliating, the other hurt. She lashed out for both.

"Sounds like you've got it all worked out, Mr. Slick."

"Not yet, but I'm getting there."

"With your rules, right?"

"That's right. After I tend your wrists, we'll share a nice dinner." He paused, then gentled his voice. "I'd like us to enjoy a pleasant evening our first night together."

"Since you want it to be pleasant, I suppose I can count on you disappearing into another bedroom?" God, she hoped so. He'd found her out, and no amount of acting ability could disguise that.

"Another bedroom?" he shouted toward the door. "You will warm my bed, and that's final. Sultan's decree." He kissed the top of her head and murmured, "You and me, Rachel, in some ways we're one of a kind. Should be interesting to see what kind of bed partners we make."

"Something tells me you steal the sheets."

"And something tells me you're a natural cuddler. Can't wait to feel you snuggled into my backside."

"Don't count on it." Drawing on the remnants of her bruised pride, she sought to get back at him where it hurt. "This whole setup smacks of stacking the deck in your favor. Devious. Underhanded. Just the way you work your business. You've turned out to be just as much a shark in the relationship department as you are behind a desk."

"Maybe. But I wouldn't exactly call you merciful at the moment. I'd think you might be grateful. After all, you're in bed alone, aren't you? If I didn't have some morals, we'd both be screaming by now."

Rachel didn't want to be merciful, and she sure as hell wasn't shelling out any gratitude. Her fingers closed around the first loose pillow she could grab. She hurled it at him, and he caught it as neatly as a pro player handling a pass.

"Don't bother coming in here tonight. Just get out! Get out and leave me alone."

"I would have gone sooner, but those thighs of yours have quite a grip."

Her cheeks burned at the reminder. "That's right! Run for the control panel!" she screamed at him. "Hit the right knobs! Touch her breasts, blur the lines between what's acting and what's not. You, the master, so smug and full of his own power. But I know better, Rand. See how you run."

"Actually, I'd prefer to stay for a change, even with the nasty turn your temper's taken. And as for running, you're doing a good job yourself. Admit it, Rachel, your feminine ego's been pricked, and you'd rather throw me out than have me walk."

"Don't flatter yourself." Damn the man, standing there looking so insufferably sure of himself, while she felt more stung and discarded than ever in her life. "I wouldn't sleep with you if you were the last man on earth."

"As far as you're concerned, I am. You do belong to me, and we can't let anyone think otherwise," he said in a subdued, stern tone. "Therefore, you do sleep with me, Rachel. Sex or no sex. But judging from this little encounter, it won't be long until we're both too far gone to forget about pride, and who's right or wrong. I just hope by then I've got a few things resolved myself."

"What things?" The question was out before her pride could intervene.

"Stick around and we'll both find out."

"Do I have a choice?" she retorted, miffed at his easy deflection.

"You have choices, and so do I. It seems we've both made some important ones already. By the way, there's a wardrobe in your closet. You will wear the white silk tonight?"

"Not if that's what you want." She'd wear black or green or purple. Anything but white silk or a muslin sheet.

"Suit yourself. They all end up on the floor for the servants to see anyway. Enjoy your bath, Rachel."

"Go to hell, Rand."

He stopped, his hand at the polished brass doorknob.

"Too late, angel," he said softly. "I've already been there and back."

A click sounded just before another pillow could hit its mark. Rachel dropped her head in her hands, vowing not to scream or cry, in case he was listening at the door. Taking deep, unsteady breaths, she realized the smell of spice was on her palms, mingled with the scent of bay. She sniffed her arms and realized she was covered with his scent. It was doubtless on her neck, her breasts, even in the haven of her thighs.

She hurt there, almost as much as she hurt in the twisted-up, inside-out span of her chest. What had Rand done to her?

What had she done to herself? She didn't know. Hell, she didn't know anything except that she craved him, resented him. This lesson in emotional survival with Rand Slick had left her jarred, stunned and terrified of any brutal lessons he was capable of administering in their uncertain future.

If she'd had any doubts before, she had none now.

He did have the power to break her heart.

The sound of water splashing in an adjoining room was a soothing contrast to her chaos and turmoil. The bath he'd ordered drawn beckoned her to cleanse herself of the cloying musk that had tainted her at the auction. She would try to rid herself of the musk Rand had called from her own body, and wash away the hold he exerted, even now that he was gone.

"Your bath is ready." A weary, olive-skinned face peeked through the door that Rand had exited. "You may go through the side door in your bedroom. The master has given his permission."

"The master can die and rot before I need his permission to soak." Rachel felt bad when the woman ducked her head in a subservient manner—but not before a flicker of admiration and surprise flashed in her eyes. Accompanied by the trace of an approving smile. "Have you got a name?"

"Jayna."

"Jayna." So this was her guard. Rachel wrapped the sheet around her body as she rose to her feet, sizing Jayna up as she did. Trusting her gut instinct, Rachel decided she liked her. Maybe it was just that she was upset with Rand and Jayna seemed to sympathize. Whatever, if she had to have a guard, Jayna seemed like an A-okay one to have.

"Thanks, Jayna. I could use a bath. Maybe get my head on straight while I read a good book. Have you got anything around here I could read? Something the, uh—" make that *ugh* "—*master* would approve of?"

"The master left instructions to give you this." She smiled and extended a thick volume. "It is in English so that you might read and gain knowledge."

"Thanks. It's probably a travelogue, judging from his twisted sense of humor." Rachel accepted the book and headed for the side door. "Take the day off, Jayna."

"But the master—I cannot—"

"Sure you can. If Mr. Master has a problem, you tell him to come see me. I've got the only goods he's interested in getting under control." Rachel winced, remembering just how under control he'd had her goods. "Now go on. I can see to myself. Go watch a soap opera or eat some lunch. Or better yet, go round up some cards and chips. I'll teach you how to play poker tomorrow."

"You think to play cards tomorrow?" She laughed behind her hand. "It is not likely."

"How come?"

"The master. He is young and strong. And his eyes, they glow darkly when he speaks of you. No, I do not think he has plans that you should play cards with me tomorrow."

"You mean I need his permission for something as simple as playing cards?"

"Of course. He is the master. You are his bed slave. You would be wise to obey him." Jayna smiled sympathetically. "Even wiser to please him and gain his favor. He is your master but he is also a man, no? Even a bed slave might have power over a man."

If the auction and Rand's bedchamber performance hadn't driven home the absolute control he could wield over her in this perverse country, Jayna's observation did.

Shaken, Rachel grasped the gravity of the situation she was in the thick of, a danger far different from any she'd considered before.

"Thanks for the advice, Jayna. If you don't mind, I'd like to be alone and think on it awhile. Check you later."

"As you wish."

Jayna bowed out of the room, and for a long time Rachel stared sightlessly at the closed door. The rich mahogany took on the substance of iron, the engraved design resembling vertical bars. Shaking herself out of her trance, she looked around, absorbing the elaborately carved teak furniture, the walls draped in raw silk, the central location of the bed proclaiming its importance.

A gilded cage. And here she was in it, a woman in a country where a woman had to be covered from head to foot just to walk the streets. No freedom there, either, because she had to trail ten paces behind the man she was bound to—or, if a concubine, as Sarah was, and as she was, too, she was guarded by a servant of the master. Rand possessed a master's rights. She had none, other than those he chose to grant her.

The harsh reality of it hit her harder than the unreal memory of the kidnapping. Her hands clenched the binding of the book. By golly, he'd better be generous, or else . . . Or else what? What leverage did she have besides the tangled web of emotions they shared? Sarah? No bargaining chip there. This had become a personal mission, and she an avenging angel.

What it came down to, she realized, was her trust in Rand and his respect for her. *Talk about testing a relationship.*

Rachel padded into the bathing chamber and dropped the sheet. How could anything so decadent be for the purpose of washing up? Water spouted from a dolphin's gold mouth. She turned the handles—they were crafted in the shape of golden starfish—then got in. With a weary sigh, she leaned back.

The deep, sunken tub could easily accommodate four of her, which was good, since she felt trapped in one of those tri-fold mirrors, which multiplied her into a dozen different images. She shut her eyes, willing the perfumed warmth to ease away everything that had happened to her in these mind-boggling few days. She couldn't begin to piece it all together. She was too exhausted even to try.

In spite of her resolve to block it all out, images played in cinematic fashion behind her lids.

Rand in her office. Rand in her home. Desperate and sensitive, hard and mean. Rubik's Cube spinning on jagged edges until it blurred with too many colors, none of them matching. She felt as if she were screaming inside with frustration, and then in horror as the auction revisited itself. The velocity of it propelling her into the bedroom, where he made her feel too good, too weak, and then he was leaving her, leaving her still screaming, wanting, hurting....

Rachel grabbed for a nearby towel that had been draped next to something she thought was called a bidet. Pressing the thick cloth against her mouth, she gave in to the need to scream, purging her system with a long, agonized wail. The towel absorbed her volatile grief again and again. When her throat was too raw for her to do more than whimper, she thrust the towel aside and took in deep gulps of air.

"Buck up," she ordered herself. "Quit wallowing in what's past, hold out till you know if this is the real thing, and get your act together. Read a book. Maybe he left you P. D. James."

Determined to escape her troubled thoughts, she fingered the bound volume on the marble floor beside the tub. She hoisted it up and flipped to a page halfway through the volume.

Her eyes bulged, or at least they felt that way. The green of her irises nearly tumbled onto a well-thumbed illustration. With a burst of frazzled nerves, she flung the book out the door like a spitball over home plate. Her aim was a little too appropriate, under the circumstances.

The *Kama Sutra* landed neatly in the middle of the silk-cushioned bed Rand had dictated they were to share. Sex or no sex, according to him.

Well, Rachel thought with a little huff, no sex, as far as she was concerned. She had a job to do, and Rand's earlier manipulation—and rejection—was too slick to be trusted.

But she wanted to trust him. She steeled her wayward heart against the flowering softness he commanded with shameful ease, and concentrated on how to go about getting the information she needed. The first questions were there already: Who was Joshua? And just what did he have to do with Rand, Sarah, and this relationship that was spinning beyond her control?

Rand could determine her physical responses, and he'd probed the tender emotions she was losing the battle to. But she'd felt the proof of his body's need, had glimpsed his deeper regions and felt his protective sensitivity. It put them on an equal footing of sorts. Their hunger cut both ways, and that meant she'd get her answers. Her dad had taught her a lot, but table-turning was something she'd learned from Rand.

And what of the lesson she'd learned from Jayna? *He is also a man, no? Even a bed slave might have power over a man.*

She was no slave, but Rand was all man. She had let him call too many of the shots, and it was high time she exerted some influence of her own. Feminine influence. Potent stuff.

That decided, she lined up her strategy.

Tonight. The bedroom. Answers.

A showdown. His turf.

But her way.

13

RAND PAUSED outside the bedroom door, hesitating as he remembered the volatile exchange that had marked his earlier exit. He'd won a minor but significant battle for Joshua—and, he thought, for Sarah—at the expense of Rachel's self-exposure. And, unfortunately, her wrath.

Listening, he heard nothing of her movements. Of course, she just might be standing inches away, ready to clobber him with something more substantial than a pillow. Like more slurs about his character. He was still licking his wounds. Rachel possessed the uncanny ability to hurt him, and the equally disturbing ability to summon Joshua's ghost from his past. Did she realize she held that power? Whether she did or not, he most definitely felt the internal struggle as Rand and Joshua slugged it out.

How vulnerable he felt standing here, dreading to enter, and so eager that adrenaline made him feel like a car shifted into park with the accelerator pressed to the floor.

He had to mask it. Taking several deep breaths, he gained his composure. He didn't want a power struggle, and if Rachel sensed the depth of his vulnerability to her he would feel even more at risk than he already did. And yet, when he'd allowed her a glimpse, she had responded with physical abandon and a tenderness he needed so much it made him ache.

It had stuck with him like a sweet lump of sugar wedged in the back of his throat. Likely the reason he'd given in and bought the two dolls he'd picked up, put down, then paced the marketplace for an hour before returning to buy. They were just bisque and cloth. Just sentimental memories.

Just his longing for the woman who held the key to reuniting him with his sister. One who was also unlocking some parts of himself he'd been stunned to discover still existed.

Keys. Locks. Doors.

"Do it," he commanded himself aloud.

His hand was poised to knock. But then he remembered his role, and that allowed him to solidify his hold under the pretense of acting his part.

His jaw clenching, he went directly for the knob.

His breath left him. She was facing the window, looking out at the indigo sky, her hand clenched in the voluminous drapes. The white gauze spilled through her ruby-painted nails and trailed the ground, blending into the white silk she wore. One shoulder was bare, the other half-covered by flowing, sheer fabric. Her back was partially exposed, revealing skin as rich and soft as cream icing on a cake. It contrasted with the cascade of her hair—a study in scarlet temptation.

He thought she must be driving him a little crazy.

Rand leaned against the door. She gave a small start before whirling around to face him.

Holy heaven above, what is she trying to do? Get ahead instead of even? He'd raised the stakes, but Rachel seemed to have decided to make it all or nothing.

"I see you wore the white for me." Rand cleared his throat, since swallowing wasn't possible, with his mouth so dry. "I also see you've used something of a local touch."

"Do you like it?" Her voice was unsure, even anxious, perhaps. The curtain she was clenching appeared to have a case of the tremors.

"I don't know if *like* is the word." He advanced, and her kohl-lined eyes darted to the bed, then quickly back to him. Well, he thought with relief, at least he wasn't the only one feeling his feet slip on the high wire.

"I found the cosmetics laid out in the bathroom. I sent Jayna away, so I just used my imagination. They're not exactly what I'm used to." She wet her lips, which were glossed to a deep shade of wine. "I mean, the makeup I usually wear is different back home."

"I wish you'd try to think of this as our home until we get back to the States." He found her feminine uncertainty immensely appealing, especially since he'd never seen a woman look as desirable as she did now . . . standing there, wringing the curtain, afraid she'd put her makeup on wrong.

"Is it too much?" Her kohl-lined eyes, as mysterious as the Orient, glanced at him for reassurance. "I'm going to wash my face."

He caught her by the arm as she tried to leave and insistently pulled her to him. Twining a hand through her hair, he urged her head back. The tiny beauty mark she'd penciled into the low hollow of her left cheek dipped as her lips parted to accommodate a soft gasp.

"Leave it," he said, his voice a little rough. "You do realize, don't you, that you're the kind of woman a man wants to stare at to the point of being rude."

"I—I like it when you look at me. I always wonder what you're thinking behind those one-way windows."

"One-way windows?"

"Your eyes. Sometimes I peek in when you don't think I'm looking. That's when I see the most."

And how much had she seen today? How far had she looked when he'd been half out of his mind with desire to take her willing body, only to find that his moral fiber was stronger than his rutting instincts?

"Do you peek in while I'm busy staring?"

"I try to." She took a quick breath. "But usually they're too steamy to get a clear picture."

"Steamy windows . . . Hmmm . . . It does feel foggy in there sometimes. Especially when I imagine kissing you, wondering what makes you tick, and if you're as much of a hissing kitten in bed as you are out it. But the way you look tonight gives a whole new dimension to anything I've ever imagined before."

Her fair skin heightened in color, and she smiled nervously. She seemed to be blooming in enticing and unexpected ways. She'd lowered her guard earlier, but he'd forced that. Dare he hope that she was opening herself up to him freely? If she could trust him that much, then maybe, just maybe, he could trust them both enough to let her into his shadows. Shadows that wouldn't be so dark if she would share her light with him.

"Thank you, Rand. No one's ever said anything quite like that to me. But I guess you're more familiar with flattering a woman than I am with being flattered."

"The way you say that, I get the impression you think this is one of my standard seduction lines." He felt the faint tremor as her muscles tensed.

"Is it?"

"That's something I like very much about you, Rachel. Upfront and direct. I find that quality in a woman to be a rare and valuable asset. You don't go for deceit, or play the tease to manipulate a man to your advantage." She glanced away, and he caught her chin, forcing her to look directly at him. He searched her eyes. "You wouldn't ever do that, now would you?"

"Of course not." Her eyes dilated and he felt her go from tense to stiff. Rand raised a brow, and his lips thinned. Feeling his hopes threatened, he searched for the familiar hardness of self-protection. It seemed to have moved, because he couldn't find it. Suddenly he was desperate to get rid of Joshua's interference and cling to what he knew.

"No, of course not," he said flatly. "You're above that. Just as I don't resort to flattery to entice a woman into my bed. Seduction under false pretenses isn't my style."

"But buying a woman under false pretenses is. You are using this situation to your personal advantage, aren't you?"

How easily she'd tripped him up. He should have known better than to take her appearance and the sensual bent of her words for what he wanted them to be. Damn Joshua for putting him through this. Damn him for insisting he accept the blow because he deserved it, when Rand Slick was champing at the bit to silence her pert mouth with a punishing kiss.

He waited a full minute before one of them gained the upper hand.

"I asked for that, didn't I?"

"That. And more."

"You're right. Why don't I make up for my earlier advantage-taking and show you around our house before dinner?"

"You mean I'm actually free to tour the premises?"

"Not only tour, but have the run of the place. Just as long as you don't get this disrespectful in front of the servants." *Whew.* That was close. Too close. Before he could stop himself, Mr. Slick demanded some retribution. He was squirming uncomfortably and wanted some company.

"Don't forget where we are, Rachel," he said sternly. "I'd be expected to punish you for such a sharp tongue. If I didn't give a proper show of taming you, we'd raise suspicion. Do us both a favor and don't put me in that position."

"Tame me! Punish me! With what? One of those whips the auctioneer was screaming for? Or maybe you've got some chains or leather bindings stashed away, along with a black face mask."

"Actually, no." A grin tugged at his lips, but he squelched it. She was riled enough as it was, though he did find the flash of her eyes, the agitated heave of her breasts, very much to his liking. "I'm adventurous, but more status quo than kinky. The servants would think everything was aboveboard if I simply hauled you into the bedroom and made you scream."

"I'd bite my tongue off before giving you that satisfaction."

Rand traced her mouth, sliding his thumb over it, savoring its glossy texture. The internal war raged on, as did the voice demanding that he take her lips, kiss them until they were too swollen to talk back and she simply accepted that he needed her spirit, her acceptance—and if she could find it in her, even perhaps something called love. *There*. He'd let himself think it. *Love*. A four-letter word he was compelled to explore for himself, Rand, because no matter how much of Joshua was left, he would still be what life had made him. He wanted her to accept all of him, the good and the bad. Wanted? Needed. Desperately, just as he needed the security of knowing she couldn't run away from him here.

More important, neither could he. Rachel seemed to think she was a prisoner of sorts. The truth was, he was more a prisoner than she, cut off from all the avenues of escape that were so plentiful back in the States. He found these walls a comforting sort of prison, and Rachel, its sweet warden.

If only she knew how close to the mark she'd come today, tearing out his insides with her accusations. *See how he runs!* He'd wanted to defend himself, to tell her that old habits, even destructive ones, were hard to break.

He hadn't then. He couldn't now.

"Temper, temper, Rachel." He made a clicking noise, a reproving tut-tut. "You wouldn't really want to bite off your tongue, would you?" He stroked the supple interior of her lower lip, careful to avoid her teeth. "Judging from the sample I had earlier, I'm certain that would be a terrible waste."

"You are *the* most impossible, infuriating man I've ever met in my life. Maybe chivalry *is* dead, since chauvinism is apparently alive and well."

"I'll take that for a compliment, since I'm not in the mood for *The Taming of the Shrew* as a prelude to dinner. But I always did enjoy cherries jubilee for dessert. There's something about a room with muted lighting and a dish going up in flames against a white cloth that appeals to even the most jaded connoisseur."

Rachel was doing a slow burn. "I won't even dignify such a lewd insinuation with one of the many names I'd like to call you at the moment."

"I'm disappointed. Names can tell a lot . . . angel."

"I agree." She fixed him with a level stare. "Who's Joshua?"

14

His THUMB TENSED, but then he commanded himself to go about his sensual play as if she hadn't struck a nerve.

"Joshua's a boy who grew up the hard way. He's a mutual acquaintance of mine and Sarah's. I've seen him more recently than Sarah, but I'm sure she remembers him well. Once you locate her, that's the password to clue her in that I'm here."

"Why not use your own name?"

"Because..." He should tell her. And yet the thought made him feel more exposed than he already did, and this was torture as it was. Later, perhaps. When he had his footing. Or in a moment of intimacy, when Rachel was as defenseless as he. "Because this way my identity remains a secret. Anyone who might overhear could inform Sarah's owner and blow the cover we have to maintain until we leave."

The room felt claustrophobic, cloying, as memories rushed back to him, memories he'd relegated to a lockbox long ago, because that was the only way he knew to survive. And how well he'd done it, slamming the lid shut before the past could injure him further.

He abruptly turned for the bathing chamber, leaving his lockbox behind, only to feel it being dragged after him on some invisible chain.

"I thought I saw some ointment in here earlier. Let's get those wrists tended to, then go for that tour. Big place. Could take an hour to show you around, and I'd hate to ply you with an overdone dinner."

"Rand?" She stood at the door, and he kept his back to her as he rummaged through a drawer full of household supplies, his mind shunning the unwanted baggage and casting about for an avenue of escape. He found it in an unexpected form.

Girl stuff. Opening a tube of salve, he waved her to the sink while his attention focused on the cosmetics she'd used. Her things. How would his things look next to hers? Lipstick next to a shaver. Panty hose draped near his bathrobe. Strange to imagine, but he found the idea unaccountably appealing.

"Let's have a look at those wrists." He scowled as he gently smoothed the healing balm over the abrasions. "Bastards. I'd like to strangle them for this."

"I need to ask you something, Rand. I wish you'd look at me, because it's important, and I want to see the truth in your eyes. None of those shutters you're so good at drawing."

Her voice was soft again, as it had been before she'd gone for a confrontation. As much as he wanted to trust it, he feared to. Undoubtedly she was resorting to her initial strategy since he hadn't taken the bait. Maybe Joshua's tempering influence was good for something.

"What do you want to know?"

"I keep wondering something." She winced, and he kissed the thin red lines at her wrist. He was indirectly responsible for this. It gave him a sick feeling.

"And what something do you keep wondering?"

"What would you have done if the prince had agreed to pay a million and a half?"

If they were going to get closer, he knew he had to start letting her in. There was danger in that for both of them, and he didn't want her to get hurt should his demons decide to race out. But this seemed a safe place to start. Rand risked letting her have more than a peek.

"No shutters, Rachel. Look inside and tell me my answer."

She searched his eyes, and then she smiled.

"You would have bid two, wouldn't you?"

"I don't stoop to haggling." Rand tipped her chin up and darted his tongue between her parted lips. "I would have bid five. Where my personal portfolio's concerned, you're one investment that's invaluable. Case or no case."

She fairly glowed as she shook her head in amazement.

"You must be about the richest man I've ever met in my life, Rand Slick."

"If it's money you're counting, I do okay. It tends to buy respect and fear and favors. I've got plenty of all that, but I've learned there are some things that money can't buy."

"My dad used to say it couldn't buy love."

"Your dad was a smart fella. Money can induce people to fake emotions for the person carrying the money clip, but it doesn't guarantee genuine feelings."

"That's shallow. Only someone with a lack of character would pretend to care for another person just because they've got something to gain from it."

"And you have more character than anyone I know. Maybe that's why I never believed money was the reason you agreed to risk yourself for me."

The look they shared was one of rushing memories—her earlier insistence he was a client, a paycheck, and the way he'd twice called her bluff. Rachel had every right to resent his methods, but it just wasn't in him to be sorry for having touched her intimately. Those moments had changed the course of their relationship, those hot, precious moments when he could forget everything but what touching her did to him.

The memories arced between them, and he wondered if she would turn away, rather than confront his unspoken need to let what was between them flow and not fight it anymore. He had to fight himself enough, without her fighting him, too.

She touched his shaved cheek, and he felt a surge of tenderness. From her. And in him. It left him off balance, wavering between the bittersweet lure of the contents of his lockbox and a quick dive into his concrete bunker.

"I know what I said that night at my home, Rand, and to-day. You found out for yourself that I was lying, but I'd like to take it all back just the same. Lies don't sit well with me, and the truth is, even if you were poor I'd still . . ."

He waited on edge while the four-letter word beginning with *L* flirted with his senses.

"Yes, Rachel?"

She seemed unable to go on, as though she'd painted herself into a corner and was frantic to find a way out. How well he could relate to that.

"Because . . ." She wet her lips, and her eyes darted about, looking at the sink, the tub, the ointment, anywhere but at him. "Because even if you were poor I'd still think you were a beast, and wonder why I was crazy enough to take your case," she said tartly. "No doubt you would have smuggled us in and we'd be sharing dinner out of a can while I posed as a masseuse in that spa I'm supposed to get greased up in to find Sarah."

"I can think of worse things than having to spend the day getting massaged and relaxing in a sauna." He managed a faint smile, masking his disappointment at her retreat.

"I'll still be on the job. All the massages in the world can't take the tenseness out of asking the right questions while your insides are upside down."

"You'll do fine. And don't forget, Jayna will be there, too. One word and she'll come get me. If you even sense a threat of danger, I'll be there. I give you my word."

"No, Rand. You could make a bad situation even worse. You can do your bit after I make contact. Until then, you stay scarce. It's my job. And my neck."

He touched the neck in question. The pad of his thumb rested over the thrum of her pulse, which both of his personas would protect at all costs, whether she liked it or not. Without Rachel, neither he nor Sarah stood a chance.

The urgent need to rescue Sarah, and the gut-deep drive to solidify this bonding of man and woman escalated to a dizzying pitch. Both hinged on protecting the neck he longed to put his lips against, to taste and suck until she bore his mark. His, and only his.

"I thought we had this settled. We're a team, Rachel. Don't try to take back what happened today. You should know me well enough to realize I don't give up ground I've gained."

"You weren't very ethical about gaining it."

"Ah, now it comes back at me. Well, let me tell you, lady, you gained some ground of your own that was hell for me to give up. Between the two of us, I hope we can win more than one war."

"There's one war we're going to win for certain." Her chin got that stubborn little look to it that he found so appealingly saucy. "I've come to realize how imperative it is to get Sarah out. After walking in the other woman's shoes, I want more than anything to give her a new pair."

Shine your shoes, mister? It hit him out of left field, jarring loose the lockbox. He tried to close it again so fast he stung from the snap.

"It could take awhile, Rachel," he said in a vague voice while he shoved and kicked at the contents trying to slither their way out. "Even if it's the most popular hangout for the elite concubines, you can only spend so much time making small talk in the sauna."

"I'm sweating already. If this takes longer than a few trips, I'll start looking like a prune."

"Not once your skin's anointed." He passed a hand over his eyes, praying that when he looked again he'd see nothing but her, that the unwanted garbage had packed up and gone home. Home...

I'll come back when I've got lots of money. Then I'll buy you and me a brand-new house... Whenever you feel sad, just think about that.

"Anointed, huh? Then I'll be a prune with zits. Should be a real experience, dehydrating then getting my pores clogged with perfumed butter."

She laughed, and he felt the memory subside. Thank God for Rachel. Even now she could make him want to smile. But he didn't. He considered her, and this elixir effect she had on him, at length.

Rachel's laughter trailed off, and she began to fidget.

He continued to stare; she fidgeted some more. The staring and the fidgeting had a way of taking his mind off the little monsters. *Well, well, Mr. Slick, the wooly bullies seem to be gone for now, but watch where you step, 'cause there's some smushed guts laying around. 'Nough to slip on.*

He could feel himself begin to relax as Rachel's discomfort with his perusal gave his jagged state a sense of companionship. And he did like her company under any circumstances.

Deciding to go for the rose at the expense of a few thorn pricks, he chuckled. "Perfumed butter? Don't you mean oiled and prepared for your lover?"

"Whatever, but I suppose getting it slathered on is better than being the one working it in."

"I wouldn't mind working it in."

"Rand!"

"The oil, of course. We could take turns practicing and slide all over each other like a couple of greased pigs oinking their heads off at the county fair."

Rachel's throaty hoot of laughter washed over him. Just what he needed to forget the threat of slippage. He was okay now, his gut emotions all stuffed safely away.

"I like it when you talk my kind of language. It's a lot more comfortable than that hoity-toity way you can act sometimes."

"Oh, I can get down and dirty when I want to. Comes from having too much practice at eating out of cans."

Her teasing expression softened, and he read a hint of the pity he had learned to abhor in leaner days.

Taken off guard by it, he cringed inwardly. With nothing more than a sympathetic look, she'd managed to shove him back into the same dark place that her laughter had momentarily banished.

"Are you feeling sorry for me?" he demanded.

"A little. Maybe because you don't feel sorry for yourself."

"Don't do it," he warned. "Laugh with me. Fight with me. Work and possibly even make love with me. But don't ever let me catch you pitying me. I won't have it."

"But there's something inside you, something that's marked you for life. I don't know what it was exactly, and I'm positive it wasn't fair. But if pride goeth before a fall, then you're very close to the edge."

"You're right—I am close to the edge. One that you'd better back away from. Let it lie, Rachel, because the pride in question sure as hell doesn't need your sympathy."

He turned, determined to cut her short before he could undo the progress he'd made. If he didn't get out fast, he feared he'd slip and come down on her like an avalanche.

Rachel caught his arm and yanked him back with surprising strength. He glared at her, silently warning her not to persist.

"Quit running, Rand. I've got something to say that I think you need to hear." She leveled a stern gaze at him that he admired, even as he cursed her foolhardy courage. "The kind of pride that refuses a sympathetic ear is false pride. Why don't you talk about it for a change? What happened to you, what made you this way. If you got it out of your system—"

"I don't want to listen to—"

"You'd feel a lot better for it. Stop hiding from things you can't change. Your roots are permanent, whether you like what they are or not. Share them with me. I know it must be bad, and if I feel sympathy for what you went through, just try to accept it. Accepting compassion won't make you any less of a man. Maybe it could even help you accept yourself."

He felt as though she'd slapped him with her concern, caring in a way he didn't want her to care, trying to make him confront the past by jarring his lockbox wide open. And she wouldn't let him shut it. It was as though she were reaching inside and searching through the muck to find some hidden treasure. It was like being stripped of all the power and prestige he'd earned, to be thrust back into a soup-kitchen line.

He wanted to lash out at her for serving up his insides on a hellish platter, compliments of her compassion.

In reflex, as automatic as deflecting a blow, he thrust his hand into her hair and leaned her back against the sink. He hit the handle. Water spilled from the faucet. He cupped it and quickly poured several handfuls onto her chest, wetting the silk until it was transparent and clinging to her breasts.

"What are you doing? Rand! Rand, please, you're scaring me. Please, stop it!"

"We're going to play a game, Rachel. It's a simple game. I get you wet, and than I get you hot. You've got beautiful breasts, did you know that? And your nipples look— Oh, poor things, they look so cold the way they're puckering. I think I need to mouth them, warm them a bit for you. It's the least I can do, since I'm the one to blame. Just out of compassion, you understand. Because I feel so sorry for you."

"Rand—"

"I'd rather you call me a beast. You called me that before, and I'll take it over your pity any day. Again, Rachel. Let's hear it. *Beast.*"

"Beast!" she sobbed. "Beast!"

In that moment, he loved the beast within him, clung to him, because he was invulnerable, and strong in his weakness.

"Much better. How can you pity a beast like me? Do you still want your beast? I hope so, because he does want you.

Now let's cut the crap, because we both know this is no game."

He palmed a breast, bent on his self-serving mission, the eradication of her hurtful compassion, and the assuagement of his never-ending lust. He'd almost succeeded in burying Pandora's legacy when he realized she was crying.

He stopped cold. He stared at her, unblinking. And then, as if he'd stepped outside his body, he saw the ugly scene as an onlooker might, with a sense of disbelief.

Was this what he'd become? This monstrosity that passed itself off as human? This creature that had squelched the man who was capable of heart and depth, the man who deserved this rare woman?

"Heaven help me," he groaned. "What have I done?" Rand's hands were shaking as he traced the path of her tears, the kohl streaking black down her cheeks. The makeup she'd put on so painstakingly and then anxiously wanted his approval of was being washed away by the proof of her hurt, compliments of the man who owned her—a man who was no prize himself.

No prize, but you've still got your precious pride. Satisfied, Slick? The stupid pride that he wore as protective armor had been penetrated by the strength of her softness, her acceptance. The very things he craved, and yet he'd punished her for offering them unconditionally. Money he understood, but something this priceless he had smashed, then ground to dust.

"Sweet Jesus—" His voice cracked. He turned off the water and lifted her, oh, so tenderly, until she was burrowed, limp and sobbing against his chest. He stroked his hand, the one that had so cruelly turned against her, into her hair and then gently rubbed her bare back. He made a shushing sound, a long *shhh, shhh* of comfort that hadn't passed his lips since the day he jumped the boxcar. He kissed the tears from her face until she was done crying.

"Angel . . ." he whispered. "Angel . . ."

Rachel latched on to his wrists so hard her fingernails bit into his skin.

"Why did you do it, Rand? If you won't tell me anything else, tell me that. Help me understand."

His neck felt stiff as he jerked out a shake of his head. He didn't want to go back into that dark place, that place that had driven him to this belly-scraping low.

"I can't tell you, Rachel. I don't know why."

"You do. Somewhere, somehow, you have to."

For her, he forced himself to peer inside the stash of jumbled treasures and trash. Plowing his way through, he fingered the priceless, smashed down the ugly filth, and emerged with something of value: the truth.

"All right," he said unsteadily. "You're dealing with someone who's gone a hard path, and he's afraid of what you're doing to him. Worse, what you can do. It's like waiting for the other shoe to fall, and feeling it hit can't be half as bad as fearing the blow."

"But what am I doing? What did I do to deserve this? I don't know what I've done, what—"

"You dug too deep." He pressed his lips to her forehead while he grappled with an emotion that tore through his insides like a runaway train. "You let me know you would have eaten out of the same can as me."

15

"MORE WINE, RACHEL?"

"No, thank you, Rand." Uncertainly, she watched out of the corner of her eye as he concentrated on his own glass. The purple garb she had changed into matched the grape of the vintage.

"I could call for white zinfandel. I know that's your favorite."

"This is fine, really. It's much better than any wine I've ever had before."

"You must have a discerning palate. Some people can't appreciate a fine wine."

They continued their meal in a stilted silence. Rachel forced herself to sample the exotic fare on her plate. Not that she was hungry, with her stomach tied up in knots, but she'd been taught that wasting food was sinful when others went without. Now she had cause to wonder just how many meals Rand had gone without.

What had life done to him? How had it twisted him so? Doubtlessly with brutal jabs and blows he'd learned to return with an ugly finesse to survive.

She shivered, wondering if she had the stamina to survive him. The problem was, she was already in so deep her heart was hocked to the limit, and he was holding the pawn ticket. It was too late to get it back. She saw only one way to emerge intact. She had to find enough inner strength to get through the emotional land mines he had buried in more places than the government had warheads—and shatter his one-way windows.

"You didn't say much about the house. I'd hoped that you would find it to your liking."

"It's very. . . opulent," she said tactfully.

"But you don't like it."

"No. No, it's not that. I'm just accustomed to more lived-in surroundings."

"You could decorate it however you want." He caught her hand on the elegant tabletop of white linen. "Jayna could take you to some of the local dealers. Friday's six days away, and there's always the chance we could be here awhile. I'd like you to be comfortable, however long the stay."

She stared at the dark fingers grasping hers in what felt like earnest hope. Or perhaps a silent apology. It would be easy to turn that against him, to spite him for what he'd done; and yet she sensed he had suffered more than she, and the price he was paying was the vulnerability in him now.

Remembering her own survival strategy, she decided to take a step forward, hoping she wouldn't hit one of those land mines of his.

"I'd rather you go with me instead, Rand. Maybe we could take a day to go to a market and find some things we both like. You know, some knickknacks, souvenirs." Her smile was hesitant. "We could even buy a few more pillows for me to throw at you."

"Sounds like a plan." He squeezed her hand, and she took it as a thank-you. "I'll work it into my schedule."

"When?"

"Soon. I have a lot of business to take care of in the next few days. But maybe you gathered that from the mess in my office."

Rachel thought of the high-tech apparatus, the whirring computer with staggering numbers on the screen, the neat stacks of paper and printout sheets piled high. There was a clinical starkness to it that she hadn't liked, the only indication of warmth being the faded snapshot of two youngsters hugging within the protection of a gilded frame that sat prominently on his massive desk.

It seemed typical of him, this picture, out of sync with the tools of his trade, which allowed him to pay megabucks to buy a woman. A woman he'd said he would have given any amount for, case or no case.

Maybe it was a good time to try out Jayna's sage advice and see if she couldn't influence his decision.

"I'd like to go tomorrow."

"Why tomorrow?"

She took a deep breath and leaped. "Because I want you to give up working in your office so you can spend time with me. It goes back to what you said about my feminine ego being pricked. I hate to admit it, but you were right. This way I can tell myself your priorities suit me, even if nothing else you say or do makes any sense yet."

Rand chuckled. "You're a pistol, lady. The first day we met you should have warned me you always end up on the other side of the trigger." He scooted his chair out and patted his lap. When she didn't move, he said quietly, "Please, Rachel. I just want to—well, to hold you while we talk."

Risky. Damn risky when he could easily yank the ground from beneath her feet and bring her to her knees. The emotional strain she'd endured in a single day had bled her dry, and though she'd survived—barely—she wasn't sure she could manage a repeat performance.

"Do it? Please, angel. For me."

In his own way, she realized, he was reaching out to her. She could refuse and remain safe, but with that came the very distance she longed to bridge. Drawing a steadying breath, she complied, but managed not to drape her arms about his neck.

"Okay, I'm sitting. Now, how about making that date for tomorrow?"

"Done. Now, how about me telling you something a lot more important?" He cleared his throat, and she felt his hold tighten. "I'm sorry, Rachel, deeply sorry, for what I did to you tonight. Apologies are hell for me. If it tells you anything, I've been rehearsing this one all through dinner."

His guard was lowered; she tested the chink in his defenses.

"I could make this difficult for you."

"Indeed, I've left myself wide open for a quick jab, if not a devastating blow. You could even go for the jugular, and I wouldn't blame you. You've got every reason to wash your hands of me after this. But I'm asking you, please don't."

She searched his eyes and saw his honesty, his anxiety. She was moved to the compassion he'd refused earlier. She wouldn't speak it, though something told her he wouldn't spurn her offering this time. Letting her actions speak for her, Rachel draped her arms about his neck and tentatively stroked the tense, corded muscles. She thought she heard a relieved sigh just before he laid his head against her breast.

"I can hear your heart beating," he said gruffly.

It beats for you, Rand, she thought. *It beats too fast and too sad and with too much hope, because you are who you are—the man who can either love me or leave me with nothing but shattered glass.*

"It took a licking, but it's still ticking," she said around the squeezing sensation inside her chest. His low, throaty chuckle vibrated against her, and she felt her heart accelerate at his intimate touch.

"So's mine," he whispered. "It's not too steady or reliable yet, but . . ."

She urged his face up, compelled to see through what she thought just might be the beginnings of a broken window.

"But what, Rand?"

"Hang tough, Rachel. When a rusty engine gets a jump start, the going's usually rough before all the gears remember how to work." He shifted, and she realized there was one piston that was sure as heck in working order. "You look tired. What say we call it a night? You can find out for yourself if I steal the sheets."

Oh, Lord, she wasn't ready for this. Not yet. Not until she felt sure she wouldn't make a fool of herself again, not until she was better able to handle whatever lessons Rand might dish out. The core. She had to get to his core, because there she'd find protection and heart and him.

"What say we have another glass of wine first?" she suggested. "I'd like to talk. Tell me what your favorite pastimes were when you were little."

"Popping tar bubbles with a stick. Racing on my bike. Braiding Sarah's hair." He latched on to the bottle, then got up, still holding her in his arms. "Grab the glasses, angel. No? Okay, we can forget them. Drinking straight from the bottle isn't so different from open cans."

His directness surprised a smile out of her. "I believe you're letting your rough edges show, Mr. Slick."

"Goes with the package. Your feminine ego should be flattered that I'm not making my usual effort to cover them up." His stride was decisive as he took the stairs. "I just hope you don't already regret it, or end up disappointed when the mystery man's exposed for what he is."

When the mystery man's exposed. Not *if*. Could it be that something had been jarred loose by the nightmarish scene of water on silk? Taking the gamble, she dealt him the unvarnished truth.

"I don't think I could possibly be disappointed. But I am afraid there's a price attached. One that's so high it scares me."

"And that is?"

"That you'll take a part of me with you that I'll never get back."

"Works both ways, angel. I'm a little afraid for myself. You've already taken a part of me that I know I'll never get back, and Lord knows I've got too many missing pieces as i is. Maybe that helps? Knowing you have that power over me?"

"It does." She rested her head against his shoulder, feeling the strength of muscle, and the inner strength his admission built within her.

"Then are you still afraid?" He stood at their bedroom door.

"No," she said, willing herself to believe she didn't fear what might await her there.

"Prove it. Open the door," came the soft command. "Open it, and give me the chance to put your fears to rest."

Her hand was visibly shaking, and the brass slipped in her grip twice before the door yawned open. She gasped, amazed.

"Who did this?"

"I left instructions to have the bedroom made ready. I understand it's the custom, but I took the liberty of requesting a few personal touches. You like, or no?"

"It's...breathtaking. There must be a hundred candles lit, and is that music I hear?"

"Sound familiar? Seems like you said it evoked images of *Arabian Nights* and a brass lamp that belonged to Aladdin." He leaned into the door, a click sounded loudly like a hollow gong announcing their absolute seclusion.

Rachel tried to wet her lips, but even her tongue was dry. "I thought you were going to put my fears to rest."

"I didn't say which ones." He settled the wine bottle on a bedside table, then slid her slowly down his length. His hands strayed over her back, wisping and teasing her flushed skin to a prickling chill. She shivered and tried to move away, trusting herself less than him.

"Tell me your worst fear, the one making you pull away from me when I simply want to hold you. Is it me? Did I hurt you so deeply tonight that you don't want me to touch you?"

"You did hurt me," she admitted. She searched his eyes and found remorse there, a need for acceptance in spite of what he'd done. She gave it, slipping her arms about his waist.

"I want you to touch me," she said. "But even more, I want to touch you. Inside, where you wouldn't let me in before. That's my worst fear, Rand. That you'll close me out and I'll die from the cold."

He hesitated, his lips pursed. Then he sighed heavily and embraced her, resting his cheek against the top of her head. She felt the tenseness of his muscles, the faint shake as he tried to force them to relax.

"The ice is part of me, Rachel. It probably always will be. But you've been thawing it out. I feel like I've been slipping and sliding through dark tunnels I can't see my way through anymore, while I keep straining to reach a faraway light. You're holding it, and I just pray to God I don't snuff it out before I can hit the finish line. Be patient with me. Be strong when I stumble, like I did tonight. If you can do that, you'll be saving someone besides Sarah." He tilted her face upward. "That someone is me."

16

SHE REACHED OUT, daring to touch the flame that could both sear and warm.

"Rand," she whispered, touching his lips, desperately needing to touch them with her own. But the moment was ripe for a deeper discovery, one more urgent than the need to kiss. It was the need to *know* him. "Tonight I hit a tender spot with you, and we both suffered for it. Maybe I'm a glutton for punishment, but I don't think so. Tell me what you wouldn't before."

"It's not pretty," he warned. "You might not like the answers you get. I know I don't."

"I'm not asking for anything pretty, or a dressed-up truth. And as far as liking your answers goes, they can't be half as bad as I feel not knowing."

His pause was a terrible timelessness as she waited . . . and waited.

"All right." His nod was curt. "Stay here. I have something for you."

He kissed her quickly, then disappeared into a connecting room she'd learned was his dressing chamber. On edge as she waited for whatever it was he might bring back, she knew the victory of courage, of having endured the hurtful and emerging with the prize of his willing exposure.

The hypnotic leap of the candle flames, their white tips dancing to the tune of the soft breeze billowing through the open window, was a seductive companion in his absence. It wisped through her heightened senses, while she listened to the ripple of music enhancing the scent of spice and . . .

Bay. She turned.

No robe. His chest was bare. Loose black silk pants rode low on his waist, revealing the indentation of his navel. It was garb befitting a dark, powerful genie, but he looked to her more sleek and dangerous than that.

A savage in silk.

Her legs took on the substance of no substance. She tried to swallow and almost choked on the immediate surge of un-adulterated desire that followed.

"I have two things for you. Give me your hand." Rand folded her fingers over a vial, keeping one arm behind him as he did. Her palm touched glass. The shifting weight of liq-uid. Liquid in the glass; liquid between her thighs.

"What is this?"

"Your freedom of choice."

Rachel held the vial to the candlelight and saw that it was the color of burgundy.

"This looks like blood."

"When the cook wasn't looking I drained it from an un-cooked lamb she'd stored in the refrigerator. It's a little thin, but it should serve the purpose."

She guessed the purpose and its emotional significance. Rand's show of respect for her rights induced her to trust him implicitly.

"You're offering to let me keep my virginity. When you have every legal right to take it here, and you want to, you're not." Rachel rolled the vial between her palms like the talisman it was. "The blood of a lamb."

"A sacrifice on my part, believe me." He glanced down at the front of his silk trousers. Rachel followed his gaze and in-haled sharply. She did indeed believe him.

"A stained sheet is expected by the slavers tomorrow," he explained. "It's the custom for the slave to show proof of her virginity, if she is so sold to her master. A great store is put on that, especially since an owner can demand the return of his money if he has reason to think he's been sold used property."

Forcing her attention back to his face, she could feel her own grow warm. With pleasure. With an answering arousal. And with a little embarrassment that he'd caught her staring at him with undisguised interest.

"You're a man of many colors, Rand Slick. Every color but black and white."

His face darkened a shade, and he said, "Put the vial aside. I'm going to give you a piece of my past. Just remember what I told you. When the ice melts, I tend to slip."

"I'll catch you," was her soft vow as she laid the blood beside the wine.

"Just so I don't crush you when you do." He took a deep breath and slowly brought his arm from behind his back. He extended a delicate doll to her, and she took it. As she did, she felt the quick retreat of his hand as he rid himself of it.

She studied it, unable to imagine why anything so sweet and comforting to hold would affect him as if he thought it vile. He turned and passed his finger through the lapping flame of a bedside candle. Several times he repeated the motion, as if he'd rather court a burn than face another, deeper pain.

"I bought that for you today," he said in a tight voice. "I almost didn't."

"I'm glad you did. I'll treasure it as much as the doll I have at home. My dad gave it to me. Maybe that tells you how much this means to me." She closed the small distance and tried to see his eyes. Flat. Turbulent. Resentful. Tender. Emotions merged together as his fingertip descended again and again.

She gripped his hand and forced it away from the dancing heat. He shook off her hold and reached for the wine bottle.

"I bought one for Sarah, too. Santa gave her one a long time ago, but I doubt she's still got it." He laughed; it was a bitter sound that jarred her with its harshness. Rand took a long swig, then swiped his forearm over his mouth before offering Rachel the bottle.

She took it and drank as a comrade might, while she clung to the doll as if for protection from the beast she knew he could be and feared might emerge with a vengeance. Courage, she told herself. And then she acted on it.

"Tell me about Sarah's doll."

"Not much to tell. Just that that's all I left her with when she needed a brother." He turned to her, his eyes glittering with fury. At himself. At her, for making him relive this. Rachel forced herself not to shrink back.

"Did you run away?"

"Oh, yeah. I ran. I was so damn good at it I can't seem to stop."

"Why did you run?"

The sound he made was close to a snarl. She drank some more, needing some borrowed courage. He jerked the bottle from her hand and helped himself.

"It's like this, Rachel. See, we had a home. Not a rich one. Fact is, we were probably on the poor side by most folks' standards, but me and Sarah never knew to care, 'cause we had plenty when it came to what counted. Then our old man croaked. Penniless. No insurance, so you might as well forget a will. You got any idea what happens to kids without parents? Kids that got no money, so their white trash relatives don't wanna take 'em in, since they're nothin' but extra mouths to feed."

She felt as though he'd struck out at her with each hateful word. Words that he spoke in a dialect as foreign to his usual speech as the language of this country. But it was the picture that he'd painted with broad, slashing strokes of black that stunned her into silence. She saw the tight swallow he made, saw the watery shimmer in his eyes that seemed closer to acid rain than tears.

"Tell me." She wanted to shed the tears that he refused himself, but she didn't, knowing he would refuse them from her, as well. "Tell me what happens to kids who are left like that."

"They get split up, that's what. One gets sent to a stranger's home, the other gets railroaded to an orphanage. Unless he tucks his sister in nighty-night with her doll, climbs through a window, jumps a train and never keeps his pro—" He choked on the last word.

"Oh, Rand. I'm so sorry." She made to lay her palm against his cheek, and he slapped it away.

"Keep your pity to yourself," he snapped. "I've had enough of it for one night."

"Not pity, Rand. Caring." *Love.*

"Yeah?" He snatched the doll from her grasp and flung it on the bed. "Then why don't you kiss me and make it better?"

He raised the bottle to his mouth, then slammed it down on the table. She was staring at him, loving him, shaking with fear of what he might do next.

He jerked her against him. He crushed her open mouth with his lips. Rubbing them hard, as if to punish her for his exposure. She whimpered. And then she embraced him.

Stroking his back, she tried to soothe away something she knew she couldn't make right, while he thrust against her belly as though he could find release that way and flush out all that was ugly inside him.

His thrusts gave way to a gentle bump and grind, and then he was moaning, opening his mouth and giving her the wine that he hadn't swallowed, so that it swirled warm and rich over her tongue, trickling sweetly down her throat.

"Rachel," he groaned, "you're killing me, tearing down what it's taken me a lifetime to build."

"Build again. Build with me." As her eyes beseeched him, she thrust forward to topple his last defenses.

"I want to. God, I do, but I'm empty. Used up. Right now, I've got nothing left to give. You deserve more."

"I'll make up for it. I can give enough for us both."

"That's not my idea of a relationship." He fumbled for the vial and raised it between them. "This is." He uncapped it with his thumb and set her away from him.

Rachel watched as he drizzled the blood onto the pristine sheet and then strode to the window. He hurled the vial down to the street beneath, then braced his hands against the windowsill as the tinkling shatter of glass sounded below. His head hung forward as he took deep breaths of air.

She came to him, wrapped her arms about his bare waist and pressed her cheek to his back.

"You amaze me, Rand. You may have some missing pieces, but you make up for them in the most unexpected ways."

"Do I? I'm selfish, Rachel. What I just did was selfish, because I'm hoping it makes you want to give even more than you already have. Manipulative of me, don't you think?"

"Maybe. But this time I rather like it."

She pressed a kiss to one of his vertebra, and then another. He sighed raggedly and clutched at her wrist. Expecting him to disengage her arms, she was taken aback when he flattened her palm against bunched muscle and male chest hair. Hair that gave way to a thinning as he led her hand down, down, until he slipped it just beneath the drawstring of his pants and then let go.

"I'd like you to manipulate me for a change. Whether you do or not is up to you. But I am asking you to touch me. I need that much from you, if you can give it."

What she felt was trepidation, excitement, and a need that mirrored his. She slowly inched her way down, her heart pounding against her ribs to drum against his back. His abdomen was flat, taut, and one or both of them were quivering as she reached to grasp him.

Air sluiced through her lips. "My God," she whispered. "*Rand.*" His flesh was sleek, and so warm it was hot. But what she hadn't expected was his pulse filling her palm, this part of him assuming a life of its own.

"Stroke me?"

"I—" She began to pant in time to the movements she was making by instinct. "Am I doing this right?"

"The mechanics don't matter, angel. The truth is, I've never been touched by a woman this way before. What you're doing is better than right. It's so right it's a little scary."

He moved his hips, guiding her uneven strokes into a smooth, perfect rhythm.

"It could be more right," she whispered as she kissed his back, tracing his spine, so curved and deliciously salty, with her tongue.

"I can't make you any promises."

"Then don't."

"But you want them."

"I want you."

"Then take the only thing I've got to give you tonight." The evenness of his speech shifted with his groan as he cupped her hand over the plump end of his flesh. And then his fingers were interlocked with hers and he was pulling her hand away.

"No," she protested. "I want more."

"That's what I'm giving you, angel." He kissed the hand that had stroked him, then wrapped it about his neck. His embrace was gentle, desperate, and so very encompassing. They held each other tightly, for how long she didn't know. And then he lifted her chin and pressed a deep kiss to her mouth.

"Thank you, Rachel. For everything. I hope I can make it up to you someday."

He released her and started for the door.

"You're leaving?" How could he leave after this? *I'm so good at running, I can't seem to stop*. His confession came back to her with a clarity she didn't want to acknowledge. She wanted to tear at it, to rip it to shreds and burn it for the waste it was.

"As the master, Rachel, I can sleep wherever I choose. And until I can give something back, I choose not to sleep with you."

"Did it occur to you that just maybe I'd be satisfied with a warm body for the night?"

"Don't devalue yourself like that. Hold out for something more substantial." He softened the gentle rebuke with a gaze that held both kindness and heat. "Sweet dreams, angel. With luck, maybe I'll have some for a change, too."

When he'd denied her before, she'd felt angry, rejected. But this denial was worse. She had touched him. Reached inside him and grasped his being in far more ways than the physical. And that was what made her heart contract now, and her unfilled body do the same.

She could beg him. She could possibly seduce him with her minimal skills.

She could let him go and wait for him to come back—a different man, perhaps. But still a man who held her captive more surely than money or the laws of Zebedique could ever guarantee.

As he made his way across Persian rugs and marble floors, she watched the departure of two very different people sharing the same body. Two men, not one . . .

It was a flash, one of those stark insights that come out of nowhere but emerge clear as a conspiratorial whisper.

His hand was on the brass doorknob when she stopped him with a single word.

"Joshua," she called.

He paused while her recognition echoed in his head. *Joshua, Joshua, Joshua . . .*

How many years had passed since anyone had called him that? Sarah had been the last. And here he stood, hearing the past roar in his ears as loud as a freight train flying by.

Joshua waved to him from a boxcar, a memory resurfacing and demanding his due. But he wasn't Rand. They were both tied up in him, struggling to reach a compromise.

"Joshua's at an impasse, Rachel. As soon as I can manage it, I'll introduce you. Something tells me the two of you would have a lot in common."

He left then. Went straight to his office and a bottle of bourbon. It kept him company, but not very good company. It wasn't Sarah. And it sure as hell wasn't Rachel. Rachel, who had recognized his dual identity, who continued to summon the remnants of Joshua's spirit.

The thick, ribbed glass that held the whiskey was infinitely more satisfying and more true to his real nature than a crystal glass. Tonguing the bottle's mouth, he pretended it was Rachel's virginal lips, the warm liquid inside the nectar of her arousal, the boozy nirvana sensations those that her strokes had evoked.

They hadn't made love, and yet it had been the most sexual experience of his life. Maybe because she'd given and asked for nothing in return. There was a word for that, wasn't there? *Selflessness.* Or was the word *love*?

Rand considered the word, or rather the actions that spoke it. He thought she loved him, selfish bastard that he was. But now he had cause to wonder if maybe even selfish bastards could fall in love, too.

Messages flashed on the computer screen. Probably important, but for once he didn't give a tinker's damn.

He wasn't drunk yet, but his mind was racing so fast his head was spinning. Love. Could it be that he was in . . . Was it possible that his refusal to accept her offer meant that . . .

Rand got up and rummaged through his desk. As he put pen to paper, he decided that getting sauced and staying put sure beat the hell out of shutting windows and running.

17

A LIGHT TAP SOUNDED at the bedroom door. Rachel peeked over the top cover, wondering if it was Rand. Her heart accelerated. She scrubbed at her cheeks and wiped at her puffy eyes, hoping her crying jag didn't show. The doll that she'd held on to in the night lay on the pillow, where Rand's head should have been. She quickly and carefully shoved it underneath the bed.

"Come in," she said shakily.

"Good morning, mistress. The master requested that I bring you breakfast. He said . . ." Jayna averted her gaze as she rolled a table next to the bed.

"Yes?" Rachel looked at her hopefully as she clenched the sheets, wrapping the top one about her and wishing for her granny gown back home.

"He said you should eat well to keep up your strength, since he had exhausted your favors."

Rachel understood the double message. He'd kept up the front while secretly extending his regrets to her.

"Um . . . Jayna . . . How was the master when you saw him this morning?"

"Not well." Jayna flashed her a discreet smile. "He looked to be a man with favors more exhausted than yours."

So, Rand had had a bad night, too. She wasn't surprised, but there was comfort in knowing he'd shared her misery.

"Did he say when he would visit me again?"

"You are eager?" She gestured to Rachel to get out of the bed and began to strip the bottom sheet. As she studied the bloodstain, she shook her head. "This is surprising. He is kinder than most masters, I think, but I would not guess it from this."

Rachel ducked her head, embarrassed by the implication and by being privy to the deceit. He is kind, she wanted to say, in his hidden places he is kind. Places, she thought with a private smile, that he had let her into.

As Jayna took her leave, the sheet tucked neatly in her arms, Rachel came to a decision. Enough of this sleeping in separate beds while she cried into her pillow. Rand meant well, she knew, but her woman's instincts insisted that last night's protectiveness had only kept them apart.

"Jayna!" she called. "About what you said yesterday, you know, about even slaves being able to influence a man? Well, I thought about that, and it reminded me of something. Have you ever heard you can catch more flies with honey than vinegar?"

Her brows drew together. "It is not familiar. But there is an old truth each concubine knows in the harem. If the master is good, and she desires he lie with her and not another, she lures him with the scent of jasmine oiling her body, and promises him the greatest pleasure with the slant of her eyes, the tight binding of her robe."

"Seems to me that those gals in the harem know a lot about flies and honey. Think you could come in here and oil me up before dinner, maybe help me out with some makeup and get that robe bound real tight?"

"With pleasure, mistress. It is what the master requested, as well." She paused, and then she winked, catching Rachel off guard. "No cards today, mistress. He has ordered you to be made ready to shop after you bathe."

Rachel smiled as Jayna bowed out of the room, feeling very differently about his dictates from the way she had only twenty-four hours ago.

He'd sent her breakfast. He'd even taken the time to order her bath drawn. He was taking her shopping!

Rachel laughed at herself. Even here she could still get excited about going shopping. Maybe after they were back in the States, she and Sarah could become friends and go shopping together. They could exchange Christmas and birthday presents, watch as Rand opened up a box with a tacky tie inside . . .

She stopped herself from taking the image further. Her thoughts had implied permanency. And then she knew. She had lied last night, lied to them both. Because she did want promises. She wanted forever. As in a wedding ring and children who would never be subjected to what he'd gone through.

Be patient with me, he'd said. *Be strong when I stumble.* He'd also said he hoped he didn't crush her when he fell, or snuff out her light before he hit the finish line.

Her excitement dampened, she felt the threat of a loss she couldn't bear. *Courage.* Her jaw clenched, as did her fist, and she scrambled under the bed for the doll he'd given her.

Rachel hugged it to her, along with an unwanted truth: No woman could force a man to love her or commit to her, especially not a man who admitted to compulsive running.

If you love something, let it go. If it comes back to you, it's yours. If it doesn't, it never was.

The old cliché had never held so much meaning as it did now. But she'd learned a lot from Rand, and her latest lesson was about finding the courage to take personal risks.

A month ago, even a day ago, she would have held out for the promises she wanted. She wanted them badly enough to give him her all and pray he could come to love her as much.

Setting the doll in a chair opposite the table Jayna had left, Rachel tried to take her mind off her borrowed worries by playing her favorite childhood game.

"Would you care for tea?" she asked the doll. "No? Then perhaps you'll join me for . . ." She raised the stainless steel globe off a steaming plate of some interesting-looking items. "Well, I'm not sure what we're eating, but it smells good. And just look, Jayna left an orchid floating in a brandy snifter. How did she know we have a weakness for flowers and—"

Her conversation with the doll was cut short when she spied an envelope peeking out from beneath the glass. Quickly tearing the seal open, she scanned the bold script on the parchment.

"Listen to this," she told the doll confidentially.

"Dear Rachel,

"Old garbage has a way of piling up when ignored, and I haven't aired out the house for a very long time. You told me that I'd feel better for it, and you were right. Long way to go, but thanks to you I'm getting there."

Rachel paused, a warm smile brimming from her lips.
"You know," she confided to the doll, which she'd named Sarah sometime in the long, lonely night, "it's not so scary to let someone go when the scales are tipped in your favor."
Clearing her throat, she continued reading.

"It's very late, and I'm not exactly sober. I can't sleep, because you're keeping me awake. Maybe if I just keep writing I can keep from acting on what I want to do to you now. I can see you in bed. I'm imagining you in it without any clothes . . ."

Rachel stopped reading, her eyes wide, her breathing shallow. "I'm not sure if you should be listening to this," she said to Sarah while she fanned herself with the hot sheet of paper. "Cover your ears."
Scanning the lines, she went on.

"I'm very affected by this little imagining. It arouses me. In fact, I'm damn close to throwing down this pen, barging into our bedroom and taking back what I gave.

But as long as I can put one word in front of another I can keep myself from acting too soon.

"I'm pretending that I'm with you now, that I've pulled away the sheets and you're sleeping on your back. I like you this way, uncovered, unconsciously responding to my hands as they take what they want without asking. I can feel your bare skin hot against my palms; your breasts are wet where my tongue is teasing them.

"I know it's wrong to take advantage of you this way, but that doesn't stop me from doing it. But you don't want me to stop, do you? I can hear the sounds you're making as you slowly come awake, realizing I'm kissing my way down, until my mouth fits between your legs. How good you taste, Rachel. And I do love the feel of your hands gripping my head to you.

"Are you hot? Do you want me inside, angel? God knows I want to be there. But I'm not, and I think I know why. It's the reason I left you when more than anything I wanted to stay. For once in my life, I don't want to take, but to give.

"What I'm sharing with you on this page has very little to do with sex and a lot to do with something I'm not too familiar with. It's called lovemaking. A mutual possession.

"You haven't asked me for promises, and I'm grateful for that, because promises are something I have a problem with. But I will make you one now: I'll never make a promise to you that I won't keep.

"Our days are numbered before the plot thickens— let's make them count. Sleeping without you, well, it does leave something very much to be desired. I hope that soon we'll wake up together sharing rave reviews."

"Good Lord," Rachel moaned. Rand had said she was thawing him out, but he was doing a doozy of a job of turning the thermostat up to scalding. Was she hot? As far as she could tell, hell couldn't compete with the fever she was in.

Rachel glanced at the doll. Then she reread the letter. Two gifts from the same man. The man who'd signed off with "Love." She studied his signature, realizing he'd written Rand over something he'd whited out.

Rachel began to scratch. She almost tore a hole through the parchment, but she managed to uncover a thin, blurred word. Holding it up to the light, she smiled slowly. She pressed her lips to the name, then held it to her breast.

"Love, Joshua," she whispered.

She ate breakfast in a dream state, sharing her hopes and dreams with her Sarah doll but keeping her libidinous thoughts to herself. A walk on the dark side, indeed, she thought. Rand had crooked his finger, or pen, and summoned an anxious companion. Her. At least she thought it was still her. She was changing. But so was he.

When Jayna tapped on the door and announced that her bath was drawn, Rachel floated toward the scent of jasmine emollient. She realized, belatedly, that she should hide Rand's—or rather Joshua's—note.

With a womanly sigh of delight, Rachel reached for a book and tucked the letter inside.

"Just thought I'd read what the master sent yesterday," she said to Jayna, who nodded her approval.

Climbing into the tub, Rachel set about gaining some knowledge from the *Kama Sutra*.

JAYNA ADJUSTED the veil covering Rachel's face, leaving just enough room to peek out with her kohl-lined eyes.

"How do women around here stand to wear so many clothes?" Rachel tugged at the full-length crimson silk robe, checking out the gold brocade fastenings that ran from her neck to her sandal-clad feet. "This getup is ridiculous. I'll bet Zebedique holds the world record for heat rashes in women."

"You will grow used to it." Jayna shook her head with a weary sigh. "I have."

"And I thought panty hose were a drag," Rachel muttered.

"It could be worse." Jayna fussed with the head covering, then nodded her satisfaction. "You please the master, and he is treating you well. Many concubines are not so lucky."

"No concubine is lucky, Jayna. Everyone deserves the right to freedom."

"I agree." Jayna covered her mouth as though she'd spoken treason. "But we must keep these things to ourselves."

Rachel reached for her elderly hand and patted it, carefully choosing her words. "Maybe someday, Jayna, you and I can play that game of poker and I can tell you what you're missing out on. What would be even better would be if we could play it where we're both free to call our own hands."

Jayna shook her head. "I, too, was a concubine, many ages ago. My master was not kind, and I tried to escape. Do you wish to see what he did to me?" She lifted her robe and exposed two burn marks on the inside of her thighs. "These are signs of shame. But that is not all. A man may be made a eunuch, but a woman may be cut, too." Her mouth trembled, then grew hard. "In ways that make her no longer a woman."

"Oh God, *no!*" Rachel choked, nearly gagging on the sickness in her throat. Her vision blurred, and she clasped Jayna to her. "I hurt for you." She could hardly get the words out, her horror and compassion were so complete.

Jayna patted her back—oddly, the one who was offering consolation.

"You must not cry for me. My next life will be better. And yours can be good now." She held Rachel away then, gripping her by the shoulders. "I tell you this so you will be warned. But if you should ever be foolish, as I was, I will turn my back when I should be guarding." She gave her a small shake. "Tell no one of this talk."

The desire to tell her all was great, but Rachel knew better. Too much was at risk, and Jayna had suffered enough without being dragged into this, too.

The bedroom door opened without a knock of forewarning. Jayna quickly stepped away as Rand entered, looking as powerful and demanding as his role dictated he appear.

"Leave us, Jayna. I wish a few words with my bed slave."

Jayna bowed out, catching Rachel's eye, then touching a finger to her lips in warning.

As soon as the door shut, Rand's stern mouth gentled into a smile. If she hadn't been so upset, she would have been struck by his almost-boyish charm.

"Hi, angel." He quirked a brow. "How did you sleep last night? No better than me, I hope."

Rachel shook her head. "Rand, we have to talk."

He frowned. "What's wrong?"

For a moment, she was too overcome to speak. He opened his arms, and she sank into them, grateful for his solidity and strength and moral substance.

"We *have* to get Sarah away from here."

"Of course we do." He lifted her veil and brushed a soft kiss to her lips. "We're walking to the market so that I can point out her house and you can get a feel for the general territory. It's a good excuse to time the distance."

She gripped his robe in both her hands. "It's not just that. We *can't* fail. If we do, what could happen to her would be worse than if we'd never come at all. This country is vile. Slavery isn't even half of it."

"Explain."

She did, feeling his own grip tighten with each appalling word. His expression revealed shock, grinding anger, and something else, something she hadn't expected. A protective intensity.

"Forget the shopping and get packed. I'm calling for my plane."

"What?"

"You heard me."

"But Sarah—"

"Sarah means the world to me, Rachel. But so do you. Having one woman I love at stake is bad enough, and I'm not going for double or nothing. Now get packed, while I get ahold of the men I've had watching her house. We'll just have to come up with a plan to abduct her. You're leaving."

Rachel knew a momentary dizziness, one part of her mind sifting through what he'd said about not going double or nothing with the women he loved, turning it this way, then that, afraid she'd misinterpreted it. Meanwhile she grappled with the realization that he was sending her away. What if he failed? What if Sarah's owner caught them? This was far riskier than their original plan. Sarah could be mutilated while Rand rotted away in one of this stinking country's many prisons.

"You can't do this, Rand."

"Watch me. It's my decision to make, and it stands."

"But you already told me how she was guarded, how your men couldn't make a successful snatch. It's why you hired me. I can get to her where you can't. Don't do this, Rand. Don't do it to Sarah." She yanked the robe at his throat and brought his eyes even with hers. "Don't do it to *me*."

She saw concern slowly replaced by an implacable hardness, a calculating expression.

"Why? I'll still pay you in full."

She almost slapped him. Instead she gritted her teeth and tore aside her veil, making sure he could see that she wasn't put out. She was livid.

"Oh, no, you don't. You dragged me in too deep to expect me to swallow that line of tripe. As far as I'm concerned, you can stuff your stupid money where the sun doesn't shine. Forget the plane, because I'm staying. Either we all leave together or we don't leave at all."

"Sounds like you've got it all worked out, Ms. Tinsdale."

"That's right, Mr. Master. I'm not going anywhere today but shopping with you."

They had a staring contest that was a draw until his flat gaze softened and he sighed heavily. "I'm only trying to protect you, Rachel. I'd never forgive myself if anything happened to hurt you."

"The only thing that could hurt me now is if you sent me away. Let me stay and do my job. We're partners, remember? I can't go back without you, because I—"

She caught herself. Were her eyes giving her away, she wondered frantically, while his own narrowed, probed, ascertained?

"Because . . . why, angel? I'm waiting."

What few defenses she had left were crumbling, crumbling, leaving her like so much raw wood he could torch, then leave in ashes for the wind to scatter.

Rachel shut her eyes and prayed for courage.

"Because I love you. That's why."

It was out, and she couldn't take it back. She had the sudden compulsion to run, and she felt a strange empathy for Rand's nonstop flight from emotion and commitment.

She forced herself to look at him, and wasn't sure what she saw staring back. He was unblinking, too still. As if he were absorbing, considering, making some decision.

She couldn't stand the taut silence, the churning inside her head and in her stomach while she wondered if she might just have given him the impetus to run faster than he ever had in his life.

Rachel beat him to it. She spun away, ready to dart for the door.

Rand grabbed her wrist and jerked her back, so fast her breasts collided with the ungiving width of his chest, pushing a soft gasp from her lungs.

"Where do you think you're going?" he demanded, whipping the covering from her head and thrusting what seemed an uncommon number of fingers against her scalp, twisting her hair round and about them so that she had no choice but to stay put.

"I'm going shopping," she said between a gasp and a pant.

"I don't think so." His mouth was against her neck, and then it was busy drawing an earlobe slowly between his teeth as he growled, "Neither of us is running this time around, Rachel. You left yourself wide open with that enlightening bit of news. We're going to explore just how far it goes, and find out if I can manage a return on the same emotional investment. Let's get started with a promise from me to you."

Trying not to hope for too much, Rachel focused on simply getting her vocal chords to work. "What kind of a promise?"

Her heart was in her throat, the throat he was nuzzling and sucking, while the brush of his fingers connected with her skin as he impatiently worked the brocade fastenings, slipping them free, then tugging and snapping them loose when they didn't obey. Somehow her own hands began to make themselves useful, pushing at his robe, searching for his bare chest.

"I'm going to make love to you, and take my sweet time doing it. By the time we're through, we'll be too exhausted to crawl to the door. You'll be my slave and I'll be yours, both of us slaves to our mutual pleasure. Angel, that's a promise you can take to the bank. Or, better yet, to bed."

18

SHE LOVED HIM. As unlovable as he'd been at times, she had still said the words. His mind was reeling with them, even as he feared to believe them. What if she changed her mind? What if she took it all back once she knew everything there was to know about him? To lose this after having had it would be worse than never having it at all.

His hands worked in fevered tandem with his thoughts, her soft little moans making it hard to think clearly. *She loved him.* His filthy lucre carried no weight with her. *She loved him.* He'd exposed the beast he could be, and she'd soothed him, helped him reach out to Joshua.

Rand came to a decision, a manipulative decision, but one that her love meant enough for him to make. He'd bind her to him with the senses so thoroughly that she'd keep coming back for more. He'd use that to solidify the love she professed, let her touch that part of him that retained a tattered nobility, the ability to love her back as much as she deserved. By the time she saw him in all his unglory she'd be in too deep to retract the love he ached to have.

Nobility. He called on it now.

"You love me," he whispered. He was on his knees now, flinging her sandals away and taking a soft bite from the inside of her leg. "Even the unlovable, you love."

She seemed too busy grabbing at his hair and urging his face against her, then arching back with a tormented wail that might have been his name, to grasp the importance of what he was demanding to be reassured of.

Rand gritted his teeth and forced himself to rise. Soon, he told himself. Soon he'd lose himself inside her and, he hoped, find that part of his soul that continued to play hide-and-seek. But not until he had a promise from her that, more than ever, he craved to return.

He backed her against the cool silken wall and stilled her thrashing head with his forehead pressed against hers, all the while making soothing noises and stroking her hair.

"You want me."

"Yes, yes . . ." she murmured.

The hot silk of her panties came into contact with his fingertips; unable to stop himself, he slid around the thin barrier and rotated her cleft as he repeated himself in terms that left no room for doubt.

"If you do love me, Rachel, heaven help you, because I can't help what I am. You said once that you wanted it all, but damn, I want it, too. Joshua can make love to you, hold you, and be what you deserve. Rand can screw you until you can't walk, hurt you without blinking an eye, and manipulate you, because it's his stock-in-trade. You asked who I was, and there's part of the answer. But you have to want them both. There's no having one without the other. Tell me you understand."

Her eyes were so glossy he thought she might be close to fainting. But there was a spark of cognition that showed she had grasped the essence of what he had said.

"Can you love me like that?" he demanded. "Choose your words carefully, angel, because I won't let you take them back in a saner moment."

"I meant what I said. I love you. I've never said those words to a man before." Her palms rubbed, pressed and slid from his cheeks to embrace his neck. "Much less to two men sharing the same body."

Her kiss was severe. It was the sweetest heat he'd ever taken, and the sweetest he'd ever been given back. He was staggered by the totality of the acceptance she offered. She, a woman who had left herself so vulnerable to him that he could easily destroy her. And yet he felt he was the one being destroyed, torn apart and put back together with her touch.

Her hands didn't have the practiced feel of expertise, but held an urgent and emotional sincerity that was so much sweeter, so much better, and infinitely more arousing, than anything he'd ever experienced before.

He wanted to tell her that he loved her, and he tried to push the rusty words past his lips.

"Rachel, I—" Stuck. The words hurt, echoing the rigid hurt in his groin. She made it worse by tilting herself against the remaining barrier of the thin pants he wore.

"Walk with me, Rand. Lead me through the dark side."

With a groan, he dropped to his knees and urged hers a generous distance apart. Against her panties, his mouth breathed the heat of promises he longed to make. His tongue bathed them until they were wet—or perhaps it was her own arousal he could taste through the silk. The barrier of the soaked cloth became intolerable, and he slid the panties off, then hooked them over his wrist. A medal of sorts, they seemed, a trophy of her yielding, and of his claiming.

Each darting lick was a message, a message of loving sensitivity transmitted from his heart to her very core.

She screamed. He had no mercy left to give her. Her body was a vessel for murmured words, words that said all the things he ached to make true but needed time to make a reality. But he was making it so now, wasn't he? With each second that passed, wanting only to give, he created a new reality in himself.

She cried out to him, cried two different names, and he made her weep for more. He gave it to her, and felt her rippling thrill as though it were his own.

She climaxed against his mouth, and as she did she heard his own tortured sounds mingle with hers as emotions too long dammed up were released in a rush.

"I . . . love . . ." he murmured into the wet haven of her juncture. Then, with an ease he hadn't expected, he said the rest, whispering against the shudders from her womb, "I love you."

Without further prelude, and with his vow and her sobbing cries of the names still singing in his ears, he rose and tore off his pants. Her legs were shaking uncontrollably, and he caught her as they gave way.

He absorbed the remnants of ecstasy contorting her tear-streaked face and lapped the salty liquid with his tongue. It occurred to him then that he had triumphed, that for once he had given without taking. And he felt wonderful, better than he would ever have believed possible, even with his own body gripped by this grinding ache.

She covered his face with kisses, whimpering as though she were distraught. He'd never seen a woman so . . . He searched for words to describe what he was seeing. What he was seeing touched him deeply, because it was something he'd never witnessed before in a woman. Fragmented, that was it. She seemed fragmented. While he had never felt so whole.

"Are you all right?"

"No. Yes." She sniffled, and he wiped her nose with the panties dangling from his wrist. "I don't know."

"You're beautiful standing there like that. All flushed and weepy. I can still hear you screaming my name. It was sweet. Moving." His kiss was tender. "Orgasmic."

"You were listening." She cast her gaze downward. "God only knows what I said. It's frightening, losing all control. I had no idea. I feel . . . I feel like I'm in a thousand pieces."

"I wish you'd look at me." He lifted her chin, and he looked into the eyes of Woman. Woman discovering the enormity of passion's price—the total forsaking of reason and self. And she was awed by the discovery. But the discovery wasn't hers alone. A possessiveness gripped him, so intense that his vision momentarily blurred, and he knew he'd die before ever letting her go.

"It's powerful, Rachel. People have killed in the name of passion. We haven't even hit the tip of the iceberg. . . ." He smiled slightly, for once enjoying the thaw. "Already I know there's a part of me that wouldn't hesitate to kill any man I found daring to touch you like this."

His palm fit over her mound, and he cupped her, using their mingled moisture to prepare her for discoveries yet to be made.

Rachel gripped his wrist. She was panting; her eyes were wide and uncertain. Her reaction thwarted him; it created a determination to go on without stopping, to trample down whatever the hell was holding her back, to cement his feet to the floor if that was what it took, to bind her to him for good.

"What's wrong?" he quietly demanded. "I gave you a taste of what's to come. It's time for the feast, and I'm starving."

"I'm scared, Rand."

"If it's the pain, I'll ease it. I want this to be good for you. Trust me."

"Not the physical pain. I'm shattered, and it terrifies me to think of how deep it can go after we make love."

"Ah, I see. Fear of the unknown. Don't worry." He kissed her reassuringly. "I'll know when you fall, and I'll be there to catch you when you do."

No, Rand, she wanted to say, you don't see at all. His windows were open, and he was waving her inside, but the courage she'd found earlier was deserting her when she needed it the most. Nothing could have prepared her for this. She felt bound to him more completely than she could ever have dreamed. She quaked with the knowledge he could hold her here, inside him, and then cast her out again as soon as Sarah was found.

How she wanted promises. Promises that he would never do that. Because she wouldn't be able to survive. At least she didn't think so—and she had no desire to find out.

"What happens after we go to bed, Rand?"

"Maybe take a bath together, rub each other with oil."

"But what happens to *us?* Once we're out of Zebedique?"

His eyes were dark with wanting her, and sharp with sudden understanding of her question.

"We are talking forever, aren't we? As in—" he cleared his throat, as though the word wouldn't come "—marriage?"

She nodded, the short jerking movement cutting off the air in her throat. At least he'd gotten the word out, which was more than she'd hoped for.

"You want a commitment from me that I'd sever my right arm to make. But the truth is, you're going to have to be a little more patient. I'm close, Rachel. Closer than I ever imagined was possible for me." His face clouded. "And, too, you deserve time to learn some things about me before you make such a long-term commitment yourself. Now enough about that. We've got plenty to deal with here as it is."

He wrapped her fingers around him, and she felt his hips jerk as her hand sheathed sleek, turgid flesh.

"We can do this one of two ways," he whispered. "We can make love, which is an act you can never take back. Or you can tell me to leave, and remain intact. If that's what you want, you'd better tell me quick, before I lose what little control I've got left."

Rachel was stunned that he would still offer the choice. It told her a lot about him as a man, about his principles. It told her that he might return her love, though he hadn't spoken it.

The silence lengthened, and she felt his hands fan over her buttocks, felt his intimate strokes as he lifted her up, wrapping her legs about his hips. The wall was cold against her back, and she so wanted to feel it against her while he pressed deep inside her. The image of him entering her begged to be embraced, begged her to forget any promise but his body's offering.

"Think of my letter," he urged. "Think of me doing all that and more to you." He pressed himself lightly against her entry. His touch was flirtation and tantalizing temptation.

"Does thinking about it make you hot, make you want me now?"

"You're manipulating me." She knew it, accepted it, and found she wanted more of the same.

"You're right, but it's not manipulation the way I could take this. I could tell you that if you pressed me into you, I'd give you that commitment you think you want. Or I could seduce you, and after it was over remind you that you wanted it as much as me and promises weren't part of the bargain. But I'm not going to do that. Instead, I'm offering you the truth—I want forever, and it's just beyond my grasp. Take me inside, and it might help me get there a little quicker. My fear is that once I'm there you may decide you don't want me."

Her breasts rode against his chest, urging her to mate their nipples, to bear down and plunge him inside. *Courage.*

"Love me," she pleaded. "Say it. Just say it once."

"I . . . I . . ." His breathing was shallow. "I love you." The words spilled from his lips in a rush. And then he said them again, slowly, with feeling. "I love you, Rachel. Now choose."

"There never was a choice, Rand. Even if you hadn't said it, I'd want this. But hearing the words makes the risk a lot easier to take." Her fingers were unsteady as she closed the tiny gap and sought to fit him against her. It was not unlike a sprung cork seeking to reenter a wine bottle's mouth. "Rand." His name was a gasp. "Help me?"

She expected him to bang her against the wall. She expected an immediate and forceful invasion. What she couldn't have counted on was his withdrawal, the feel of his arms scooping her up and holding her against his chest as he carried her to the bed with haste and decisiveness.

He knelt over her there, his palms bracing her knees apart, his phallus positioned to enter what begged to be entered, and his face above hers. Dark passion was illuminated by a spark of light. He appeared to be not only in the throes of heated passion, but also . . . happy? Pleased with himself?

"I want to practice," he said. "I love you. There. I said it. And it didn't hurt one bit. In fact, it felt so damn good I'm saying it again. I love you, Rachel Tinsdale."

"And I do love you, Rand. Both of you."

"Don't ever try to take that back. I won't give it up."

His hands began slowly working her over, finding erogenous zones she'd had no idea even existed.

Do you like this?

God, yes.

Touch me this way, angel.... Ah, perfect... Your eyes, what are they saying? Tell me what you want . . . just say it. . . . .

I'm hurting. Please make the hurting stop.

I don't want to hurt you. Let me do this.... There, isn't that good? And you do feel so good to me, angel. Relax... relax...that's my girl. Damn, you're tight. Wet. Now feel me just this little bit inside you.

You're making it worse. You're teasing me.

I'm not teasing. I'm caring. And I'm loving you enough to go slow. But . . . stop that. Did you hear me? Dammit, Rachel, be still. Quit—Oh, Lord! Hold tight to me!

Her cries he took within his mouth. So soothing, his murmurs of possessive consolation. So sheltering, the arms that gathered her in ultimate possession.

Pain became a memory, and then all she knew was bliss. Rachel returned his careful thrusts, her improvised movements meeting with his whispered approval, delighting her and giving her an ample taste of what it meant to be a woman with power, heady with the knowledge that she pleased her man.

Then patience fled, and tender lovemaking became a primal rutting. She should be shocked, came the distant thought, yet she found it stunning. Their coupling was beautiful, because it was who they were, the guts and the grit of what they felt for each other. She lost all thought of caring about promises she was more desperate than ever to hear, about what sounds she made, about whether she was losing all pretense at dignity as they rolled and wrestled and mated without any manners at all.

She was hanging half-off the bed when he begged her to come, to meet him in that dark place where he would catch her if she would please, please, just fall. She shattered like glass, her body battered and lush, as she felt his liquid release. It was tingling and hot and not where it should be, but upon her belly. They slid over each other, covered with sweat and the scents of bay and shared ecstasy.

For a long time, their murmurings made no sense, and yet all the sense in the world. When she shivered, he pulled the tangled covering about them, stopping to scowl as his hand searched the bottom sheet for blood—human, not lamb.

Rand groaned. "I was rough. I'm sorry, angel."

"I'm not." She exhaled a languourous sigh, that of a woman who was well loved and well bedded. "No matter what happens, I'll always remember this as one of the most amazing moments of my life." She touched his cheek, feeling a wondrous bonding, a deep and abiding affection that nothing he could ever do would steal. But he was frowning, concern etched on his brow. "What's wrong?"

"A couple of things. You weren't protected." He rubbed his hand over her belly. "I've never skated so close to the edge before, tempting fate like that. I promise to be more careful in the future."

A promise. One that signified his wish to protect her. One that raised a question that she hadn't considered.

"What happened to you, Rand—has it made you turn against ever having children?"

"I've never wanted children. I'm not sure I'd exactly be a good role model."

"But what if—"

"What if I didn't pull out in time, and you're pregnant?"

She nodded. She had always wanted children. But that wasn't the issue, was it?

"I get the feeling you want to know if I'm the kind of man who'd get you pregnant, push for an abortion, and then, if you wouldn't go for one, salve my conscience with an offer of money instead of assuming the responsibility."

"I didn't mean to imply... Don't look at me that way."

"Like I'm angry, hurt? The fact that you had to ask just goes to show you still have a lot to learn about me." He stroked back the hair clinging to her face, and she saw a depth in him that was honor, a refusal to shirk duty. It was a surprising turn of the Rubik's Cube. His unscrupulous reputation might be valid, but he held to some very traditional values.

"I'm sorry, Rand. I didn't mean to offend you or question your principles. I wish I could take it back."

"We're learning, that's all, angel. But your question does bring up something else that's bothering me." His kiss was lingering, persuasive. "I want you to leave. It's not likely that you're pregnant, but if you are, I don't want to risk our baby. If you're not, I don't want to risk you. Go home, take this memory with you, and wait for me to come back."

Our baby. He might not want children, but that one word told her how far a commitment from Rand would reach. It augured well for the future, and it told her that the question of children could be worked out in time. It strengthened her resolve to stay, to lessen his and Sarah's risks, even if her own was increased.

"No, Rand. The answer is an unequivocal, flat-out *no*."

"Trust me to come back."

"This isn't about trust. You have mine, won with a vial of blood." She traced his lips, lips she wanted to touch when they were surly and tight, soft and open, old and drawn. "What it comes down to is this. Even if you can't commit yet, I have. For me, that means we're in this together and there's no way I'm leaving when you, and your sister, need me the most."

"I don't like it."

"I'm not asking you to." She offered him a smile that he didn't return. "Take me shopping tomorrow and show me Sarah's house. We *will* succeed, Rand. Trust me."

"You're a hardheaded woman, you know that?" He sighed heavily, giving in, but not gracefully. "All right. We'll do it your way. After I have mine with you." The sure glide of his palm from breast to cleft moved on to the bedside drawer. He slipped on a sheath, and without further ado he was inside her.

"I love you," he said, the rhythm of his words matching the gentle rocking of his hips. "Strange, how it gets easier to say every time."

It was a promise of sorts, she decided. One that was hers to treasure, to climax yet again upon, and forever keep.

19

As SHE WALKED ten paces behind Rand, Rachel was glad the veil covered her mouth. It wouldn't do to be seen in the open market wearing the euphoric smile of a woman supremely sated after two days of alternately tender and ravenous love-making. She was, after all, expected to play the role of a just-bought bed slave getting a public lesson in submission.

A sigh of relief filtered through the thin cloth. She was glad for this taste of limited freedom, and even more glad that Rand had bowed to her judgment.

He'd been anxious to walk past Sarah's house en route to the market, and his anxiety worried her. It made her nervous. One screwup was all it took, and no matter how in control Rand thought he was, one chance glimpse of his long-lost sister could set off some dangerously instinctive reactions. It had taken some doing, but Rachel had won. Today's destination was saved for last. At dusk, when the shadows would mask their faces and the hired surveillance team tailing them at a discreet distance wouldn't be as easily noticed.

That had been her reasoning, though in truth it was more a gut feeling that something could go wrong, a feeling that she couldn't have justified. The feeling was still there, but Rachel shook it off, determined to enjoy this bit of sight-seeing while she could. Friday would come soon enough. Today she'd savor.

The descending sun slanted into the huge canvas tent as they filed down one row and then another, Rand the leader, she the chattel, and Jayna bringing up the rear as her guard.

Jayna had kindly, but sternly, laid out the rules. A slave was not permitted to speak to her master unless spoken to first. A slave was not to make eye contact with any man but her master. A slave was to keep the expected distance at all times, unless signaled to trot to his side should he want a quick fondle, then fall back the required ten paces once he was ready to move on.

To break any of these rules was to risk a public whipping.

Trinkets and fabrics and hand-carved wood all vied for Rachel's attention. She paused to admire an ivory necklace. Jayna gave her a gentle push.

"Hurry, hurry," she urged. "The master walks on."

"But I want to know how much this—" A high-pitched wail stopped short her protest. Rachel searched for the source.

She gasped. Close to where Rand stood, a good twenty paces ahead, was a spectacle that caused her stomach to lurch and her blood to boil. A fruit vendor was grappling with a dirty, urchinlike child, who dropped a banana as the man shook him.

Acting on impulse, she began to run toward the child. Jayna grabbed her arm and spun her around.

"Do not be foolish, mistress. Else you suffer a beating."

"But that man, he can't abuse the poor child! Somebody has to do something. Let me go!"

Jayna's grip tightened as Rachel struggled to intervene.

"You can do nothing. It is sad, but common, to catch hungry thieves. The child will be punished. I do not wish for you to be punished, also."

"Punish a starving child for stealing a banana? That's inhuman. What's his punishment, a spanking?"

"His hand will be cut off. It is the price all thieves must pay."

Such was her shock that Rachel stared dumbly at Jayna, and then at the weeping boy, who was begging for mercy. *What could she do?* She had to do something, anything, to stop this atrocity.

Rachel broke free of Jayna's hold and rushed forward. When she was just shy of the fruit cart, Rand confronted the merchant. She was close enough to hear his halting speech in the Zebedique tongue, which the other man replied to with a rabid snarl and another shake of the wailing child.

Just when she was ready to join the fracas, Rand held out a thick stack of local currency and gestured to the fallen banana. The merchant hesitated. Rand withdrew the bribe.

Before Rachel could yell at him to give the man however much money he wanted, the child was dumped on the hay-strewn floor and a bunch of bananas thrust into his grimy little hands by the vendor—who quickly held his own out, palm up.

Rand shelled out the payoff. The child kissed his feet and, hugging the fruit to his skinny, bare chest, darted from sight. His savior appeared to take no notice. Rand's gaze had turned on Rachel, and she saw mirrored in his eyes the distress, anger and compassion she herself felt. She stood only a few feet away, far closer than she was allowed.

"Woman!" he bellowed, and raised his hand as if he meant to strike her. "Will you never learn your place? Get back where you belong. Ten lashes await you at home."

He was so convincing that she instinctively fell back two paces and collided with Jayna. Several passersby shouted their hearty approval, no one needing an interpreter to know that she'd just been royally admonished by a most masterful master.

She caught his playful wink as he turned and studied the vast array of exotic fruit. The rat. The stinking, naughty, marvelous, sweet rat. Rand was the only man she'd ever wanted to cover with kisses and slap senseless at the same time. He had a hard heart, she knew that, but it was just as big and gentle and good as it was hard.

She did love him. She loved him so much that her throat constricted and her mouth trembled beneath the veil while she watched him select an assortment of cherries and figs, dark grapes and ripe persimmons. When he offered the vendor a handful of coins, the man refused payment and tumbled the fruit into a thin cotton sack.

Rachel assumed it was Rand's generosity in exchange for the child's hand that had earned him the freebies. But she was wrong, she soon realized. The man pointed at her and laughed, apparently impressed with Rand's hold over his concubine.

Rand slapped the man's back, as if they shared similar philosophies on the treatment of women. She knew better. Though he smiled a tight smile, Rand's jaw was clenched, and so was his fist around the sack. He looked mighty close to shoving the vendor's face into the wagon of fruit.

Fearful that he might give in to the urge, Rachel stepped forward. Jayna clamped a firm hand on her shoulder.

"Do you wish for twenty lashes, mistress, not ten?"

"For heaven's sake, Jayna, Rand wouldn't—" Rachel bit her tongue. She'd slipped, just like an amateur—or a woman in love standing up for her man. Amateurs and women PIs falling for their clients were not mutually exclusive. It was too late—from the beginning it had been too late to fight the inevitable—but she rushed on to salvage what she could. "What I mean is, the master seeks his own pleasure. He'd rather make me pay up in bed than beat me to a pulp."

"Yes. I think this, too." Jayna's soft laughter was that of a wise old woman who'd endured enough pain to recognize love, no matter what its form or its disguises. "Do not make him shame you again when it is not his wish. Be still, child, for he comes."

Before she could utter a single questioning word, Rachel was staring up at Rand's madder-than-hell face. He gripped her wrist and shoved the sack into her hand. If not for the soothing rubbing of his thumb over her pulse point, or the apology she read in his eyes, even she might have bought his act.

"Carry this," he commanded harshly. "You will feed it to me later." And then, to Jayna, he said, "How long before the sun goes down?"

"One hour, perhaps."

"Shit."

His impatience relayed itself with a yank of the clasp at Rachel's temple. Thrusting the still-attached veil to one side, he immediately took her mouth, which was open in an "Oh!" of surprise.

His kiss was immediate, greedy and rough. It was a long kiss, so long she wondered if he meant to make out until dusk set in. Not that anyone around here took notice of such matters, judging from the activity that bustled around them.

Staying as true to her role as possible, Rachel refrained from gripping him close, though she returned his kiss with a fervor equal to his. He was her lover, her friend, and her only link to Western civilization. Their kiss was confirmation of all three, and his lips left her with no doubt that he needed this bond as much as she did.

In this place, this evil place, they kissed with a madness they both clung to for their sanity. These people weren't right, not right at all, but in their midst was rightness. Call it love, call it lust, call it truth.

Whatever she called it, it was *them*. She and Rand, two strangers in a too-strange land. His hands were kneading her buttocks, and her own were clutching the bag between them to keep herself from returning his show of possession.

His mouth was still open when it skimmed her cheek and settled beside her ear.

"I hate this country," he said, so quietly that even Jayna couldn't hear. "I'm close to hating myself for being the one who got you into this. But, Rachel, there's no one else I'd rather be with."

"Me, too," she whispered. "Me, too."

"Good enough. And so was that kiss. It'll get me through sundown. How about you?"

"I'll make it, but I'm counting the minutes till we're home."
While she still had the chance, she reminded him of her earlier warning. "Don't forget, if we see Sarah or her owner when
we pass their house, you *have* to keep going. Don't stop.
Don't even look their way."

"Gotcha. In the meantime, I think it's a good idea if you
pretend I'm that jerk by the fruit stand who's watching us. Get
uppity and give me a reason to play your master. Who
knows? Maybe he'll toss me a pineapple or two."

It was almost as hard not to snicker as it was to let Rand
go. Rachel wiped the back of her free hand against her wet
mouth and refastened the thin cloth. Indulging a grin, she
cherished their moment of shared humor.

Rand's sardonic laughter echoed through the tent.

"Just a taste of what's to come, wench! Wipe your mouth
again and I'll slap it."

He turned on his sandaled heel and didn't glance back. She
waited until Jayna gave her a nudge.

Only Rachel heard her low chuckle. Only Rachel and the
patron saints of harmony and justice and love.

TRAILING EVEN A PRETEND master home should have ran-
kled, but it didn't. She knew they were equals, and just as
important, so did Rand. In fact, as they approached Sarah's
street, Rachel was all too aware that she was his professional
superior when it came to this kind of risky business.

The nagging apprehension she'd felt earlier came closer to
an alarming unease with each step toward their destination.
She told herself she was being ridiculous, that nothing could
go wrong simply because they passed the place where Sarah
was kept.

Even so, Rachel said a silent prayer that they'd make it
home without incident. She shifted the assortment of pack-
ages in her arms while she kept her gaze locked on the back
of Rand's head. An elegant black car whizzed past and turned
into a driveway two houses down. The houses were man-

sions, and she and Jayna were a good half block away. Rand
sped up.

She might have been the perfect concubine, instead of a
sweaty-palmed PI, the way she immediately matched his accelerated pace over the redbrick sidewalk.

Her heart kept time with her feet, beating faster, faster. The
swish-swish sound was so loud in her ears that she didn't hear
Jayna panting as she rushed to pick up a fallen package.

"You carry too much, mistress. Let me help."

"Thanks, Jayna," Rachel muttered distractedly. She thrust
the bulk of her load into Jayna's arms, hardly aware that the
elder woman was struggling to grasp it all, while she herself
now carried nothing but a bag of fruit.

For a split second, Rachel chanced a backward glance. The
hired men, dressed in Zebedique garb, were making tracks
behind them. They appeared to be deep in conversation, but
she was certain from their quickened pace that they were
aware of the sudden switch in what had been an innocuous
walk home.

"Damn," she groaned, cursing herself for taking her gaze
off Rand for even that little bit. And then she silently damned
him for sprinting ahead at an aggressive saunter. He was
closing in too fast, but, thank heaven, not fast enough to beat
the wrought-iron gates that swung shut behind the car.

He stopped in front of the gates. He stood there frozen, so
still he might have been an ice sculpture. The driver got out
and opened the back door of the car.

*What in the world did Rand think he was doing, calling
attention to himself like that?* It was exactly what she had
feared. He didn't know what he was doing, wasn't capable
of thinking past the need to reach for, to rescue, his sister.

By the time she'd regained her ten-pace distance, a man and
two women had emerged from the back seat. Rand was leaning forward, his own hands reaching for the bars and his
mouth opening.

"You bastard!" Rachel dug into the sack and hurled a soft persimmon as hard as she could. *Smack!* The juicy orb splattered against his upper arm. Rand's mouth snapped shut, and he whirled around. "You son of a bitch, who do you think you are, expecting me to bow to you?"

Fruit began to fly. A handful of cherries hit his chest, zapping the target like buckshot. Next she launched an attack of grapes, from his face to his crotch, screaming insults at his genital endowment as she advanced. By now the car's occupants had turned to observe what appeared to be a mutinous slave turning her owner into a living work of abstract art.

Several figs landed between Rand's stunned eyes before she pounced and knocked him on his butt. Rachel punched at his chest and kicked at his shins. She wrestled in earnest, until he had no choice but to flip her on her back, sprawl over her and lock her in a stranglehold, unless he wanted the stuffings beat out of him.

Once his face was within inches of hers, she wheezed out in a whisper, "Get a grip, Rand. Get it fast, or you'll blow the scam. Hurry up and apologize to our audience for your wayward slave, and let's get the hell home while the getting's still good."

He shook his head, as if to clear it. Rachel pushed him off and sprang to her feet. There had to be a God in heaven, because Rand had regained his senses enough to follow suit.

He shook her hard, then thrust her away with ample momentum to send her stumbling backward into Jayna and the two hired men, who'd caught up.

While Rand made a stilted apology to the small gathering on the other side of the gates, Rachel insinuated herself between Jayna and the hired guns, hoping against hope they passed for locals enjoying a cheap thrill.

"Scram," she hissed at the two men. "Get the hell—"

They took off, laughing as if they'd just gotten their jollies for the night.

These guys that Rand had brought in were good, really good. But not as good as Jayna—gentle, wise Jayna—who sized Rachel up with a withering glare before scourging her with a string of scalding epithets, throwing down bags and shoving her to her knees.

Her hands pressed against her charge's shoulder blades, then moved to urge Rachel's face to the ground, until her forehead rested by Rand's foot in humble, beggarly fashion.

Once the onlookers retreated to the house, Rachel felt Jayna's soft pat of reassurance and then Rand's tight grip as he pulled her to her feet.

The trek home was made in silence. Rand, ten slow, deliberate paces ahead, as if he had to struggle against nature to take each step. Jayna, just behind her, murmuring a litany that might have been a lullaby or a prayer.

And she, Rachel, thanking the stars for their narrow escape and cursing, yet understanding, Rand's near fouling of their master plan.

And while she thanked heaven, she thanked Jayna in silence. Jayna deserved better than what she'd been born to, and Rachel was ready to go to the mat to see that she got it.

But why stop there? Why not go for broke?

Rachel wanted it all. Freedom for Sarah and Jayna. The screws put to this country and the slavers who benefited from its twisted mass psyche. They'd earned her enmity, and she wanted their heads. And Rand. She wanted Rand. With all his secrets, his flaws and his darkness and his marred beauty, she wanted him. No other man would do. They all faded in his shadow. Here, there, anywhere, she loved him. Would always love him.

The question was, once this nightmarish dream was over, would he still feel the magic, too?

20

RAND DIVIDED THE LENGTH of Rachel's hair into three portions, rubbing the inviting texture between his fingers as he began to braid.

"Only two days left till Friday," Rachel said, snuggling her backside between his open legs on the bed. He nudged his hips forward and was rewarded with a girlish giggle.

"No thanks to me, Friday's still on. I still can't believe I almost blew it yesterday—and Sarah wasn't even one of the concubines that got out of that car. I owe you, Rachel, I owe you really big."

"You owe me nothing but a back massage tonight."

"You're too easy on me, angel. I'd feel a lot better if you'd slug me, instead of being so nice and understanding about my major-league screwup."

"It's easy to go easy on you. After all, you've been so hard on yourself, you've saved me the trouble." She caught his hand, which had strayed to her breast, and brought it to her mouth. Even his knuckles responded to her gentle bite, sending an immediate message to his groin. "C'mon, Rand, give yourself a break. You're human. You acted on instinct. There's no crime in that. And besides, no harm was done."

"Thanks to you. You tried to warn me, but it's like I heard and didn't really listen. If you'd been me—"

"I would have reacted exactly the same way. She's your sister, not mine. And that's why, no matter what, once you drop me and Jayna off at the bathhouse, you don't budge from the car until you see the whites of our eyes."

She kissed his palm, giving him the reassurance he needed, the trust she still had in him when he'd lost it in himself. He loved her. Lord, but he did. He loved her so much that fear for her safety was gnawing away at the pit of his stomach. If he ever lost Rachel, he'd never find himself again. And Sarah, sweet little Sarah—who had long ceased to be little, even if that was how he remembered her—she needed Rachel just as desperately as he.

They were bound, the three of them, parts of a whole, Rachel, the crucial link. Without her, Joshua would forever be missing. He gathered her as close as he could, nuzzling his cheek to her neck, his hands cinching her waist.

"I'm scared, Rachel. I'd never admit it to another soul, but my skin's crawling just thinking about you walking into that bathhouse without me."

"Don't borrow worry, when chances are it won't even come. We've got our backup, a plane on standby, and maybe even an ally in Jayna, if push comes to shove. A week from now we could even be back home . . . Joshua."

He felt her slight stiffening and knew it came from her reference to home and promises he hadn't made. Promises of marriage. The word was an ominous one, but he'd begun repeating it to himself in silence, as if by doing so he could make himself immune to the punch it packed. It held a strong and heady lure for him, being one of the few things he'd never compromised his standards on.

In his mind, marriage was a sacred union, binding, irrevocable. Divorce, as far as he was concerned, was breaking a promise—and that was something he'd done one time too many.

He asked himself how he could be so deeply in love and even think about divorce. Maybe it was because most everyone he knew had been divorced at least once, though they'd probably never even considered it as a possibility. Rachel was like that. She saw only what they had now. It was a naive, seductive part of her nature—part of what he loved about her.

Marriage. What a concept. Rachel needed time more than he did, though she had yet to realize it. Marriage to him would not be easy. Marriage to him would be for life.

She was so everything he could ever want that it made him go gentle on her hair and absorb the utter delight it gave him to hear her sigh again, "Joshua."

"You've taken to calling me Joshua. Why?"

"Because it makes me feel good. Joshua Smith. A boy who ran away, shined shoes, and became Rand Slick."

"Rand Slick," he repeated with a laugh. "Right out of a comic book or a gangster movie."

"I wonder if that's where the real Rand Slick's parents came up with his name."

"Damned if I know. Dumb luck finding the same name on a local gravestone with a close enough date of birth."

"You never told me how you got his birth certificate."

Rand continued his braiding and shook his head at the memory. "Amazing what kids can learn from watching the tube. I wrote to the county department of records and asked for a copy, since the original had been lost. Five bucks for the fee, and Rand Slick I officially was. Wish I'd chosen better, but after I got it on a social security card, it was as good as engraved in granite. The government doesn't seem to know I've been officially dead for twenty years. Selective memory, I suppose, considering what I've paid in since."

He could have finished the French braid twice by now, but still he took his time. Rand absorbed the domesticity of their easy companionship; it reminded him of the days he'd braided Sarah's hair. He was getting much better at peering into his lockbox. Lifting the braid, he kissed Rachel's nape and thanked her silently for giving him such freedom.

"Had you paid your first visit to Sarah by the time you managed to change your name?"

"No. That was two years later." Memories. This was one he didn't like, and he told Rachel so.

"Remember it anyway. Tell me why you didn't approach her then, or the second time, either."

Rand hesitated. He hadn't slipped recently. Maybe it was a good time to test how much progress he'd made.

"It's simple, Rachel. I was ashamed. I can still see her when she was ten, coming out of the school, laughing, talking to some other wholesome-looking kids. And what was I? Just this vagabond who survived on the streets. I wanted her to remember me the way we parted. Her big brother who hung the moon, not the hardass I'd become."

"But what about your second visit?"

"I was twenty-one and didn't even have a high school diploma, much less the home I'd promised to give her. I was working odd jobs, making ends meet and putting aside a dollar here and there. She looked happy, and I had nothing that could compete. So I decided leaving her was the most loving thing I could do. As it turned out, turning my back when I didn't want to was the incentive I needed to get where I'm at now."

"But how did you get there? That's a mystery you still haven't spilled."

"You'll be disappointed. And I hate to destroy the last of my mystique." He tied a ribbon in the middle of her back, then swished the scarlet tail over his lips.

Rachel turned, and they locked in an embrace that was almost too good, to all-encompassing, to be true. So good he was afraid it was too good to last.

"Indulge me," she said. "I won't be disappointed. Everything else you've told me's been better than a Saturday matinee. But it has more daring and courage, more twists and turns than a movie could ever pull off. It's human. It's you. I'll love it. Guaranteed."

If she loved him, really loved him, it had to be warts and all. Rand took a deep breath and braced himself to expose a few that, though he'd tried to cauterize them, were there to stay.

"Okay, it's like this. I got mad. At life and myself. I'd worked hard, been honest. It got me minimum wage and little else. The only thing I could do better than a Wall Street executive was play pool. I had two hundred dollars saved and took it to a pool hall to hustle nickles and dimes."

"You must have racked up quite a bundle."

"Enough to take to the racetrack while I devoured every finance book, money magazine and *Wall Street Journal* the public library had to offer. I got lucky and knew when to cut my losses before my wins took a dip. In six months I had twenty thousand smackers. I was ready for higher stakes."

"The stock market?"

"Commodities. They pay off bigger and faster than stocks. Twenty grand turned into a hundred. A hundred to a million. In three years I had my nest egg. By then I'd hooked up with some professionals who didn't play by the rules and found out I had a knack for arbitrage. I had what it took."

"You mean a self-taught profession, and lady luck."

"They got me started, but that's about it. I had the instincts of a shark, the ethics of a snake, and the hunger of— well, the street kid. I'd been so poor that I couldn't get enough. A million, ten million in the bank, and every morning I expected to wake up in a roach-infested shack and find out it was all a dream. For years I've put in sixteen-hour days and slept more nights in my office than at home in bed. That's been my life since I last saw Sarah." His smile was no smile. It was a grimace.

"Everything you heard about me from my competition is true. I played dirty pool, bet on fixed races, and came out on top at the price of my morals. And by the time I could offer Sarah a good life, she was nowhere to be found. So here I am. With so much money it's indecent, tracking down a sister who has every reason to hate me, and holding a woman in my arms who's crazy if she gambles on the likes of me."

"The likes of you?" Rachel kissed him softly. "The likes of you are very special, Rand. You shouldn't beat up on yourself for doing what you were driven to do."

He stared at her hard. "Were?" he repeated. "You used the past tense. But we're in the present and wondering about our future. You've asked me what happens to us once we get out of here. That depends a great deal on what you can accept and what you can't. I've cleaned up my act some, but—" He gritted his teeth and took the plunge. "Rachel, I still play dirty pool. Barring a miracle, chances are I always will."

He waited for her to recoil, or at the very least judge and hold him in contempt.

"C'mon, angel," he bit out, unable to endure her silence. "Aren't you impressed with the secret of my success?"

"Are you?"

"Impressed? Hardly. Sorry for it? Absolutely not."

"Then I suppose we see eye to eye, to a point. I don't like how you've gotten where you are. But I understand your motives. Maybe that's why, even knowing what I do, I can respect what you've accomplished. You did it the only way you knew how. Life dealt you a dirty hand and you just learned a little too well how to deal it back."

Considering her entrenched ethics—the kind of ethics he now wished he'd never traded away—her reaction was a lot to swallow, despite his need to drink it up. He had to test her. Besides, he might learn something new if he watched her real close.

"You could make a load of money yourself if you wanted to give an exposé. I'm sure the money magazines, and maybe even the reigning rags of trash, would love to get the scoop."

"Shut up, Rand." She shoved him down on the mattress, her braid whipping against his chest. "I've always known you played dirty. But you've changed even more than me, and I imagine that's something you're going to take with you when we get back. Whether you stick around for me or not."

He felt a little mean, and a whole lot threatened. But Joshua tempered his words, even as Rand slipped and struck back.

"And you're just champing at the bit to find out which direction I head for once we escape, aren't you?"

"You bet I am, Mr. Master. But for the time being, you're not going anywhere except to bed with me."

"You still want to sleep with me after this? Lord, Rachel, either you've got a worse case of lust than I gave you credit for, or you give new meaning to love being blind."

He waited, on edge, her reaction so important it somehow seemed to be the very key to the future.

"You idiot," she said softly. "How dare you even suggest such a thing? I resent the hell out of your ugly implications, and I've *never* had blinders on when it comes to you." She kissed him full on the mouth. "You've sold yourself short, Rand, but don't try sharing the wealth. I could never love you less for showing your life to me."

She proceeded to chastise him with velvet lashes, strokes of acceptance that touched him down to his roots.

Deep into the night, Rand stared at the canopy overhead, while Rachel's even breathing soothed his savage breast. It seemed he was still learning lessons from her. She was young but wise. And she was strong and sharp, cutting into him as cleanly as a surgeon's blade with her uncompromising acceptance and her uncanny insight.

He wondered what she would think of the insider trading information that had arrived earlier that day. He hadn't stooped to that lately, but this deal had been too sweet to pass up. She'd hate it if she knew. But he didn't think she'd leave him for it. Unbelievable. That a man like him could marry a woman of her substance . . .

It made him want to deserve what she offered. It made him think of who he'd been and who he wanted to be while the words *marriage* and *divorce* jousted in his head.

The night wore on, and eventually he got up. Rand went into his office and hit a button on his phone that immediately connected him with the other side of the globe.

"The deal's off," he said flatly. "From now on, I don't know you and you don't know me. Keep any future information to yourself, unless you want a visit from the SEC."

With that, he hung up and fed a pile of papers that spelled pay dirt into a shredder. A smile of supreme satisfaction curved his lips as he watched the equivalent of millions of dollars swirl into the trash can, like confetti raining down on a hero returning from war.

RAND JERKED to a sitting position. Sweat-drenched sheets clung to his skin. For heart-palpitating seconds, the stubs of flickering candles guttered into the dregs of his nightmare.

Only the dream had a new twist this time. Or was it prophecy?

Rachel. His disoriented gaze locked on the form huddled by his side. Peaceful, sweet. She reached for him.

"Rand?" she murmured groggily.

He was breathing fast. Was she really here, or was this the dream and she was climbing a flight of stairs while he fell straight to hell?

His hands were shaking as he cupped her face. Her skin was smooth, and warm, and reassuringly *there*.

"Rachel," he groaned. "Rachel."

"Is something wrong?"

"Bad dream."

"Tell me."

He didn't want to relive it, not now, when he needed more than anything to assure himself that she wasn't an apparition, that she was truly real. He was so afraid of losing her, just as he'd lost Sarah.

Her gentle strokes down his chest were comforting. In his naked need, her touch was fire in barren, dry grass.

"Rachel," he said, his voice ragged against her mouth. "Hold me. Hold me tight."

His kiss was desperate. She draped an arm about his neck, and her free hand clasped his. Their fingers interlocked.

"I need you, Rachel. Tell me you need me, too."

"I do need you. Both of you. All of you."

"Then take me. Help me to forget."

She sheathed him with an intimate assurance and followed his entreaty, mounting him with feline grace.

"Tell me about your bad dream," she urged.

"It's a nightmare I've had forever, and you're a dream chasing it away. Get rid of it, angel. Ride me."

"Is it about Sarah?" She followed the direction of his grip, rising and descending in time to their words.

He didn't want to relive the awful thing, but maybe, just maybe, he could kill the old monster if he shared it with Rachel. At the least, it was sure to lose some power with her by his side.

"It was always Sarah. Until tonight. You took her place behind a glass wall. I saw you but I couldn't get to you."

His upward thrust was urgent; her downward reply met it, stripping away the scene replaying in his head. He felt her cloaking him in the darkness, her empathy so strong it was palpable, giving him the strength to go on.

"I tried to break the glass until my fists were bleeding, but it was no good. The black fog came, and when it lifted you were gone. Harder. *Harder.*"

"Where did I go?" She met him with rapid strokes, her breasts rising, then crushing against his chest.

"Up the stairs. Out of sight. I ran through the endless tunnel while a train chased me down." His breathing accelerated as though he were a marathon runner in the race of his life. "Elevator," he gritted between his teeth, then gnashed out, "I make it to the elevator just before the train eats up my feet. No way but down with . . . with . . ."

"With what? Who? Oh God—"

"No God. A demon. He's winking at me. Taking me... My feet leave the floor. My—my head's striking the ceiling." His movements echoed the sensation. "I've lost you."

"No," she whispered sharply. Her nails bit into his tensed shoulders, and oh, how he loved the sharp bite of it. So real. So good. "No," she assured him. "I'm here."

"Make it true. End the nightmare." His plea was desperate, his hips were locked, up, up, and fixed. "Drive it away. That's it, angel. Love your beast. Ride him to dust, break his dream like glass."

She obliterated the horrid vision in front of his wide open eyes. Her own were pinched shut, her neck was strained back, and her mouth was stretched in an oval cry of . . .

"Joshua."

Her convulsions gripped him, taking the hated dream into her. He ejaculated, and knew not only the sweetness of soulful release, but also the regret that it was a condom and not her that he had spilled himself into.

Nightmares. Marriage. Children . . .

In that telling moment, he knew he could want them with her. There was so much he wanted, and so little time before this woman he loved too much would put her life on the line to make up for the grave mistake he had made. To help him keep his promise at last.

She collapsed on top of him, using what strength she had left—very little, he sensed—to stroke his face.

"I hate your nightmare," she whispered. "I hate it for hurting you."

He pressed his lips into her palm, then studied the ring finger of her left hand in the muted light.

"I hate it for making me feel what it would be like to lose you."

"But I'm here. Feel for yourself that I am here." She rocked slowly forward.

"I feel it, all right." He felt a lifting of his heart from nothing more than her pleased smile. She rubbed her cheek against

his chest in a soothing back-and-forth movement that reminded him of a kitten brushing figure eights about his legs.
Such a contrast to the woman who had practically ridden him
into his grave. "You ride me well, angel. You love me even
better."

Her chuckle was soft, a welcome sound that challenged the
mean, dark demon. Rand joined her, chuckling until it gained
momentum and he laughed aloud at the nightmare. It was
just the same as spitting in its face. It felt good. No, it felt
damn good.

He kissed her soft. He kissed her hard.

"This time, ride me," she demanded. "Ride me until we're
both too tired to move or even dream...."

21

"READY, ANGEL?" Rand tucked a stray curl beneath Rachel's headdress. She caught his hand and kissed it. He realized they were both shaking.

"Ready as I'll ever be, master."

He tried to chuckle at their standing joke, but the sound caught in his strained throat, and he groaned in distress.

"My guts are like water." Pulling her close, he felt the pooling of their strength.

"You'll be okay, Rand."

"It's not me I'm worried about."

"I know." She patted his back. "I know."

"I don't want to let you go into that bathhouse alone. It's hell already, and we haven't even left yet."

"Jayna will be with me. Just remember that, while you stay posted in the car. With luck, I'll be hustling Sarah out with me and we'll all be on the plane before her guard can find her owner and sound the alarm."

"With luck. Backup. And no delays on the runway. I just hope if we pull this off Jayna doesn't get punished for our success."

He caught a spark of determination in Rachel's eyes. He knew that look and guessed what it meant.

"You want to take Jayna with us, don't you? Rachel, she doesn't have a passport, and we're going to be running for our lives as it is. She's old. She could slow us down."

"To hell with a passport. We're bypassing check-in and customs anyway, and our own government won't have the heart to send her back."

"No government, not even ours, has a heart. If we get caught, they're going to be more worried about the political situation and keeping Zebedique's oil than getting us out."

"But you have that contact, the official you said you could count on to throw his weight around if need be."

"The men following us have orders to get to a phone fast if we run into problems." He snorted with a wry kind of humor. "My guess is, our ticket out would be the tasty bit of dirt on Zebedique and American slavers that my lawyer would turn over to *The New York Times*. Wish I could've just done that to begin with. But there was no way, with Sarah caught in the middle. Her owner might have gotten rid of the evidence. Permanently."

Rachel nodded. "You did right. It does make me feel safer, though, knowing that if the political machine lets us down the public will raise enough Cain to get some action."

"I imagine so. A high-profile citizen incarcerated for trying to rescue his sister sold into slavery? Front-page news, sure to incite some good old-fashioned moral outrage."

"And speaking of moral outrage . . ."

"Jayna." Seeing what this meant to her, and aware of his own reluctance to leave Jayna to the wolves, he relented. "Okay. If she wants to go, we'll take her, and I'll use my clout to make sure she doesn't get sent back."

"Thank you, Rand."

"Thank Joshua. Better yet, you can thank them both properly, once we're out of here." A weary sigh sifted through his lips. "You know, you've got this damnable way of stirring up my conscience. I just hope to hell you haven't done irreparable damage. I could end up out of business if the competition senses I've lost my edge. They'd love to pick my bones."

The sound of her soft laughter as he exposed this very real possibility would have ticked him off at one time. Instead, he took it, savored it, and slowly smiled. At the moment, the idea of his financial demise did seem a petty consideration, hardly worth considering.

"You could retire today if you wanted to and leave them to tear each other apart. Besides, if you did lose your money, you'd still have me. And Sarah. We could all sit around and pass the cans at dinner. Maybe see who won the spoon in a hand of poker."

The quip was light, but the question of where their rapidly accelerating future was heading was still there.

"I guess it could be romantic. Sharing cans. Sharing the spoon." *Sharing lives* came the persistent thought. On the heels of that was the other one that continued to nag at him. He'd changed in a very short while. Her mention of open cans even gave him a warm glow. But how much of it would stay with him once they were back in their old reality and away from this artificial scenario?

He saw himself plunged into the manic pace of New York. He saw Rachel returning to her Vegas home with the kind of reputation that would keep the phone ringing forever and a day. And Sarah, free again, free to decide whether she wanted to have anything to do with her black-sheep brother.

He didn't like any of it. He wanted to ask Rachel to marry him and let the dice fall where they might. Only... what if he couldn't retain what he'd gained here; if he slipped too far, could Rachel handle it? And he had a promise to keep, the professional boost she had earned. He wouldn't renege on that promise, though it might prove his undoing. She could get caught up in the fast-track life and decide that a future with him was more thorns than roses.

Rose-tinted glasses. He jerked them off and knew what he had to do. The answer was as incisive as a paper cut: When they returned, he'd keep his business promise and withhold the vow he ached to make. They'd see each other on weekends, until he found out if Rachel's lessons would stick or if she would see him in a different light. This place affected their judgment, and marriage—a forever marriage—left no room for mistakes.

"We need to go, Rand. How about a kiss for luck?"

"Luck's something we're going to need, Rachel. Let's make the kiss good."

As his mouth savored the open invitation of hers, he felt the taint of his decision. An ugly feeling that he was hurting them both in the name of rationalization tore at him. He felt he was reducing their relationship by evaluating it as though he were cutting a high-stakes once-in-a-lifetime deal, rather than relying on the emotions and trust he'd learned from Rachel.

Did this mean he was regressing already? The fear relayed itself in the urgency of his kiss. Crushing her lips as if he could extinguish the unwanted thoughts, then pressing his tongue deep inside, he groaned his need for her understanding as she held him within the haven of her mouth's womb.

Time weighed heavily upon them, its tick-tock-ticking a suffocating pressure. Did she feel his tumult, he wondered? Then he knew that she did, because her own embrace was desperate, and held a fear that went beyond their immediate danger. In this silent understanding they reached for a fleeting comfort.

He hiked up her robe and pushed down her panties. Her own hands were equally frantic to expose just as much of him as was necessary before they fell to the floor together.

It was not a graceful coupling. She parted her thighs, and he sank into her without foreplay. His thrusts were quick, deep and urgent. As she took him, they stared at each other in silence. No words were needed. They both knew what this was. Their need to cling to what they had, to put off the inevitable, while girding themselves for it with this raw act.

Not more than two minutes had elapsed, but somehow what had passed between them in those two minutes seemed to bind them in a way that marked them for life. He felt her contractions, though she didn't blink or utter a sound. He was near to coming himself, fully aware he'd ignored the wisdom of a condom. Rachel knew, too, he was quite certain. And neither of them was pretending it was an oversight made in the heat of the moment.

This wasn't heat. It was desperation.

Rand made as if to pull out. She gripped his wrist and moved for the first time, raising her hips from the floor.

He hesitated, then gave a final jerk—but not in the direction of prudence. The act was done. A decision made, based on anything but rational judgment. Why had he done it, he wondered? Was he manipulating himself now, taking out some future insurance that could spell marriage no matter how far he backslid?

The touch of her palm at his cheek was comforting, though her gaze told him she was wrestling with similar questions of her own.

He offered her his hand, and she took it. They held that between them, this thing that they'd done. Then, breaking the contact, neither of them knowing where it might lead, they adjusted their clothes and exited their bedroom of memories.

They left hand in hand, without a backward glance, and without a word having passed between them.

RACHEL SAT CLOSE to Rand in the back seat of the Mercedes limousine that he'd bought—and planned to leave behind, along with his home, once they shook the dust of Zebedique from their feet. He didn't seem concerned about losing his assets in case the country confiscated them after they escaped. She couldn't imagine shrugging off a loss of those proportions as if it were nothing more than a dime rolling into the gutter.

She couldn't imagine a loss of the proportions she stood to lose herself. Was it the uncertainty of where they went from here that had caused her to do what she'd done? Had it been a last-ditch effort to keep something of Rand if stateside reality tore them apart? She'd been foolish; she knew she'd be foolish again in a heartbeat, given the choice.

But what if they were caught? How horribly selfish of her to bear a child here. But it wouldn't happen. She knew it in her bones. They would succeed. And if they didn't, the hired men trailing two cars behind them had their instructions. They'd get out—whether it was clean or messy.

Rand reached for her hand and stroked it over and over. "We're almost there, angel."

Jayna, facing them on the opposite seat, watched them shrewdly, though Rachel couldn't interpret what she might be thinking, because her face was covered, as was her own.

The driver, one of their hired men, parked a discreet distance from the bathhouse entrance. Rand's slight smile of encouragement was forced and tight.

I love you. He mouthed the words. She nodded and gave him a thumbs-up sign as the driver opened her door and she got out, Jayna in tow. Rachel could feel his gaze upon her as she walked away, intent on her destination.

She wished he was going with her, as partner and friend. She wished she'd had another good-luck kiss. Anything to put off this awesome undertaking that had her trembling from the inside out.

But as she stepped through the pair of shiny brass doors, Rachel sensed the strength he willed her, sensed his tough love protecting her even now. It acted as a catalyst for her courage, creating a gritty resolve to see this through. The time had come to do her job. She'd do it right.

Rachel blinked in the soft light of the interior after the brilliant sunshine. The entry itself was immense, and thankfully cool, giving way to columned arches, golden urns housing lush palms, and decadent rooms smelling of jasmine. Groans of pleasure from cushioned massage tables reached her ears, as did murmurs of conversation in various tongues, and the universal sound of laughter.

"You will like it here," Jayna said. She pushed aside her headdress, and Rachel followed suit. "It is a haven. An escape."

Rachel's glance was incisive. Jayna raised a brow and smiled conspiratorially.

"Let's hope so, Jayna."

"For many years I was a masseuse in this bathhouse. It is where I learned to speak your language." She paused, and Rachel experienced the full effect Jayna seemed to intend. "American concubines who were lonely taught me."

"I don't suppose there's a chance you know of some hanging around lately, besides me?"

Jayna's eyes darted quickly in either direction, seeming to ensure they wouldn't be heard.

"Two Fridays past I came to visit old friends. One friend was guarding her slave. American. She reminded me of the master. Not dark, but there is something they might share."

Holding her breath, Rachel whispered, "Blood?"

"Yes." Jayna's smile was kind but sly. "But not of a lamb."

"You knew."

"An old woman learns much from pain and years. It is good to see honor before passion."

Of course, Rachel thought, mentally slapping her forehead. The sheets were changed daily, and the second night would have been evidence enough, even if Jayna's intuition—or eavesdropping—hadn't tipped her off already.

"You're a good person, Jayna. I hope I can help you out one day." She thought she could trust Jayna; she knew she needed her. Time was of the essence. "If I can find the master's sister, you could play that game of poker with me soon. As a free woman."

Jayna waved the offer aside, though her gaze was wistful. "It is too late for me. But not for younger souls. I must be careful, but I will help if I can." The sound of approaching feet had Jayna moving them toward a dressing area. "Now, quickly, undress. I will ask my friends if they know of the American woman while you are tended."

"But what if they—"

"Shhh." Jayna silenced her by efficiently stripping Rachel of her heavy garb and thrusting her arms into a thin silk robe. "They are my friends. They, too, hate bondage."

Before Rachel could question the safety of the ploy, Jayna hustled her to the outer room, where a massage table awaited.

Cries of greeting were shouted to Jayna, who returned them in the native tongue. She shoved a cold glass of sparkling water into Rachel's hands after removing the flimsy robe and helping her onto a cushiony table. A quick wink, and Jayna disappeared to an adjoining room that seemed to be where the workers took their coffee breaks.

The masseuse made grumbling noises as her ministrations failed to work the tenseness from Rachel's bunched muscles. Finally giving up, the attendant took her to the next phase, while Rachel's eyes darted about for a glimpse of anyone who might be Sarah. She fretted over Jayna's whereabouts.

Upon entering a huge chamber, Rachel was greeted by a sight that momentarily stunned the worry out of her.

"Good Lord," she muttered. "What is this, Hugh Hefner's old home away from home?"

Naked female bodies of all sizes and ages appeared to be in a state of nirvana as they soaked in a massive communal tub. It bubbled like a vat of champagne, curling about Rachel's toes as she climbed down the marble steps and seated herself on a vacant ledge.

The water was the perfect temperature, and there was a cool swish of air from overhead fans. It should have been soothing, but she hardly noticed it, every sense she possessed honed to pick up any possible clue.

With half-shut eyes, she leaned back and did her best to blend in as she scanned the assembly. She studied faces, decided who looked friendly and who didn't. She listened for even a single word of English. All the while she stayed alert for the scent of potential danger, the feel of an unseen threat. So sharp was her attunement, she turned at the sound of Jayna's footfall, picking it up over the sound of gurgling water.

"Mistress," Jayna whispered urgently. "You have the luck. Come."

Rachel forced herself to rise nonchalantly while her pulse galloped and blood pounded between her ears. As Jayna wrapped a Turkish towel about her, they exchanged more furtive whispers.

"What did you find out?"

"She has just entered the steam room, this woman I believe you seek."

"Is her guard with her?"

At this, Jayna smiled. "She stands outside, waiting. My friend, Montage, has been tortured as I have been." Her lips thinned. "The master she serves is not so kind as ours. He is a cruel man, but she needs money, and so she plays guard. She does not like doing this to eat. Should she have food, shelter from someone kind, then . . ."

"You think she might be for sale?"

"For freedom. A place where her master cannot punish her for treason."

Yes! Rachel stayed herself from raising a victorious fist in the air and whirling Jayna in her arms.

Anticipation forced adrenaline through her veins until it was all she could do not to rush them both to their destination. Once they were there, Jayna nodded to an elderly woman, who began speaking to her in hushed tones, though no one else was around to hear. Rachel couldn't understand the language, but gathered from their quick hug that they had come to some understanding. Rachel saw the gleam of excitement and hope in the other guard's eyes, just before she made a curt bow.

"It is done, mistress. I have told Montage your word is good. For freedom, she will do this." Indicating the arched door of the sauna, she said, "Enter. Be quick. We will guard, and call if someone comes."

"Be ready to hightail it out of here as soon as I come out. But tell your friend we have to be discreet. You and I, we'll lead the way, and they'll follow until we get to the exit. Then we walk to the car, real easy, like we're taking an afternoon stroll. Got that?"

"You...you bet." Jayna's attempt at Western slang coaxed a tight smile from Rachel as she took a determined step and then another, striding into the chamber, from which puffs of steam were billowing.

The door closed behind her, and a quick survey informed her that two dark women were enmeshed in a private conversation, while another one, blond and very pretty, lounged on a marble bench near the back. Her eyes were closed, but Rachel discerned dark circles of fatigue beneath them. A purplish bruise rode high on her cheek.

Fists clenched, Rachel wasted no time in closing the distance between them. As she drew closer, the impact upon her was immediate and forceful. She didn't need a recent photo to know that this had to be Sarah. This woman bore such a strong resemblance to Rand that there was no room for doubt they shared a family heritage.

"You look like an American," she said quietly.

The woman raised herself up and looked her full in the face. She smiled tiredly, as though the spirit had been beaten out of her, then indicated that Rachel should sit.

"Welcome to the club." She made a derisive sound. "Been to any good auctions lately?"

"Yeah. A man by the name of Joshua bought me." Rachel took note of the immediate flicker of hope in her eyes, which was immediately snuffed out, as if the woman had given up on her brother a lifetime ago. Rachel kept her voice low, but her tone was urgent. "Tell me, does the name Joshua mean anything to you?"

This time the flicker sparked to life. Rachel touched her finger to her lips.

"Just nod, yes or no." She got her answer. "How are you, Sarah?"

"I—I'm . . ." Her voice trailed off, her mouth working but no words coming.

"Just listen, and listen close. I'm sitting in for your brother. It seems there's a promise he came here to keep. He's waiting in a parked car nearby. A car that's headed for an airstrip where a plane's idling, ready to take off."

"Joshua," Sarah whispered in a faraway voice. She choked back a muffled cry. "I can't believe it."

"Believe it." The two dark women continued to talk, and Rachel hurried on, fearful of an intrusion. "We have to move quickly. What I want you to do is count to one hundred after I leave, then get up and follow me out. Everything's set. All you have to do is walk."

"But my guard . . ."

"You only have one, right?"

"Several," Sarah said. She appeared to be battling shock. Rachel felt a sudden sense of alarm. "But today, just one came. Montage. She's kind to me. She tends me when I'm beaten."

"She wants out of here, too." Rachel sent a thank-you to heaven, at the same time feeling a thirst for brutal revenge against Sarah's owner. "Just do your best to stay calm, Sarah. All you have to do is leave after me, go with Montage to get dressed, and the two of you follow me out the front door. After that, we're on our way. Think you can do it?"

"Joshua." Sarah was crying. "*Joshua.*"

"Stop it," Rachel hissed, cringing at the necessary sharpness of her warning. "Please, Sarah. Blank out everything except my instructions. Pulling this off depends on you getting yourself together. Come on, I'll start counting with you. One . . . two . . . three . . ."

"Four...five...six..." Sarah continued the numbers as she swiped at her cheeks.

"Good girl." Rachel squeezed her hand and got up. She nodded amiably to the two other occupants of the room, who sent her a cursory greeting and continued their gossip. At the door, she stole a look at Sarah, who gave her a tremulous smile.

Fifteen minutes later, Rachel and Jayna stood at the entrance to the bathhouse, waiting, on edge, for the anticipated swing of the door. It came with a swish, and they started walking while a quick glance assured Rachel that their company was close behind.

She recognized the nondescript car with their cover about to pull out as she heard the limousine's engine start and purr. The back door opened when she was less than five paces away. Her heart quickened when she spotted Rand's drawn and expectant face. She realized he was assuring himself of her safety. At her nod, he craned for a look at his sister.

It was then that she heard the sudden shout. A cry of outrage, while the sound of running feet sounded too close behind her.

22

RAND'S GAZE WAS FIXED on Sarah—God, could he believe it was really her?—when he heard the man's harsh voice.

"Stop!" His robe was flapping and rolls of flab bounced up and down in time to his agitated jogging. "Stop, you stupid bitch! Where do you think you're going?"

This repulsive insect of a man had to be Sarah's owner. Rand's blood ran hot, and an impulse to mutilate the bastard who was daring to slander his sister had him out of the seat before he could think on their safest course of action.

He grabbed Rachel and shoved her into the limo while Sarah ran close behind. Any thoughts he might have had for a warm reunion fled as he thrust her in the same direction and barked, "Get in!" Her headdress covering came loose, exposing a large, ugly bruise. He fought the urge to kiss it and make it all right.

Rand caught a flash of an elderly woman close behind Sarah, but his eyes remained locked on the unbelievable sight of Jayna hurling herself at the greasy-looking slave owner while she screamed, "Go! Go now! Flee..."

Teeth clenched and bile in his throat, Rand rushed to Jayna as she reeled back from the fist that had caught her in the face. He disentangled the old woman from the enraged brute who had hit her and pushed her to safety.

"Get in the car. Get out of here, and don't wait for me."

With that he jerked Sarah's owner by the robe at his throat and shook him like a mouse caught in a cat's mouth. They were in the middle of the street, and a car whizzed past without stopping. It seemed that in this country a public brawl was nothing out of the ordinary.

In spite of his girth, the man managed to twist free and land a blow to Rand's jaw. Amid spitting curses and the man's screams for "Police! Police!" Rand's street smarts took over.

He fought dirty. He fought mean. An uppercut to the right, a fist to the gut, and a knee in the groin that should have castrated the bastard. It should have been enough. But it wasn't. He wanted to kill him.

"You filthy son of a bitch." Another brutal jab. "That's for beating up on my sister. How d'ya like it, huh?" He grabbed him by the hair and nodded his battered face up and down. "Feels real good, don't it? Big man like you, so tough you go hitting old ladies. How'd ya like a taste of your own medicine?"

He might have literally beat him to death, heaping murder on top of any other charges he might have to face, but for the sudden grip on his shoulder, pulling him off. He whirled around, ready to push the intruder aside. But it was Rachel. She caught him by both arms.

"Rand! Rand!" She shook him hard. "Oh, God, Rand, please stop. He's not worth it. We've got to get out of here while we still can."

He had trouble focusing, he was so blinded by his vengeful purpose, but she was pulling at him, pleading with him, and then raising her own fist as if she might knock him out and drag him away herself. Rand was suddenly aware that a crowd had begun to gather, some placing quick bets and shouting "More! More!" while others called for the police and an ambulance.

He caught Rachel by the waist, and they began to run, almost staggering over their robes and each other's feet in their haste. Somehow they made it into the car. Before the door was shut, the driver was already peeling out.

Rand was breathing raggedly, the fight still in his blood, and blood on his face, his robe. Then he felt a shaking palm cover his hand.

"Joshua?"

As he stared at his sister, who sat by his side, the years rushed in reverse. All the rehearsed words of apology and reunion deserted him and he blinked against an unfamiliar stinging in his eyes.

Big boys don't cry. . . Big boys don't cry. . . .

"I finally kept my promise, angel." His voice cracked.

Then Sarah's arms were around him, and his around her, and they were clinging as tight as the day they'd said goodbye.

"I always knew you'd come back for me," she said brokenly.

"I guess better late than never?"

"In the nick of time, Joshua. Daddy would be proud."

Rand used the edge of his sleeve to dry her tears and wipe her nose.

"I got ya something, angel."

He reached across the seat and discovered that Rachel was holding his gift in her hands. They connected, hands touching, gazes meeting in a silent understanding. *Bless you* was the message his eyes sent. *Bless you for giving me Sarah back.* Rachel's chin quivered, and out rolled two big tears. Rand's throat tightened; he knew she was shedding the tears he couldn't because big boys didn't cry.

Placing his offering in his sister's lap, he said, "I thought you might want to hold your doll on our way home."

"Home," she repeated, stroking the doll's curls. Her eyes met his, and he knew they would make it back there together. And then the words that had haunted him in his nightmares, spoken behind a glass wall he'd finally broken through, were spoken aloud. "I love you, big brother."

RACHEL AND RAND WALKED side by side down the corridor to her office.

"That was some trip back, huh, master?"

"Nothing like getting shot at while you're climbing into an airplane. Good thing those local police weren't too handy with their pistols. They could use a few lessons from you." His chuckle was strained.

Rachel knew they were both trying very hard to keep a lightness in their conversation as their impending departure rushed near. He had a plane to catch, work piled to the ceiling in New York and Sarah waiting for him at his home.

In the month since they'd returned, they'd hardly had a minute alone, what with paperwork for their defectors, statements, bringing in the big guns. Not to mention him getting Sarah settled with Montage, and Jayna moving in with Rachel in Vegas.

Rachel's stomach lurched when they stopped at her door. She made herself busy, refusing to look at him while she rummaged around for her keys.

"Anyone ever tell you that you've got terrible taste in purses?"

"Jayna. And you."

"How is Jayna? Is she adjusting okay?"

"She's fine. Getting Americanized. She threw her old outfit into the trash after I took her shopping."

"Is that why you look so tired? Shopping till you drop?"

Rachel tensed. "No. It's just all this business with the authorities. Exposing slavers is hard work. But now that they've caught one in the act and he's spilling his guts, I think things should calm down."

"Not with all the business that's coming your way. Every time I call, the phone's busy. I guess you're up to your armpits in cases now that you've managed that leg up you worked so hard to get. You deserve every bit of your success, Rachel. I'm happy for you."

"Thanks," she said, too abruptly. "I'm real happy for me, too." Happy? She'd never been such a wreck in her life.

He pushed a hand through his back-brushed hair, and she commanded herself not to run both of hers through it. She feared that if she did she'd break. The tension in her was brittle, with so much unresolved, and no promises for the future. His window-glass eyes were wide open, and what she saw there hurt.

He loved her. But he wasn't going to offer marriage. Not yet.

"I want you to know how much I appreciate what you've done. If you hadn't come after me, I could be cooling my heels behind foreign bars."

"It's nothing. Just doing my job." Her fingers were so icy they were numb. The keys clattered to the floor.

"I'll get it," he offered politely. Too damn politely.

Their fingers touched when they reached for the keys. Neither of them moved. Rachel slowly lifted her face. His breath was on her, and she inhaled the scent of spice and bay.

"Are you pregnant?"

She knew she could keep him simply by telling him the truth.

"Rachel, I asked you a question. Did I get you pregnant that last day in Zebedique? Are you carrying our baby?"

If you love something, let it go. If it comes back to you, it's yours. . . .

She let him go.

"No, Rand. I'm not pregnant. Case closed." Rachel rose and shoved the key into the damn door she couldn't get to unlock.

His hand covered hers, and he leaned toward her, too close.

"Rachel. We can't leave it this way."

She pressed her forehead against the etched-glass door, refusing to let him see the overbrightness of her eyes.

"So how do you want to leave it? What do you propose?"

The last word fell between them like a window that couldn't make up its mind whether to open or close while it shuddered from a storm brewing on either side.

"I need some time, angel. Be patient with me?"

Angel. He'd called Sarah that, she now knew. The endearment meant as much as hearing him say that he loved her. But not as much as a lifetime commitment.

"My patience is wearing thin, Rand. You either want me or you don't."

"Of course I want you. I love you."

"Do you? Do you love me enough not to run away?"

"I'm not running. I'm coming to terms with myself. And the future."

"But your terms don't include me."

"My terms have everything to do with you. Look, I've been thinking it's going to get old fast, jetting back and forth to see each other. How do you feel about..." He tapped his lips, and she shuddered. With so much need to kiss them; with a terrible premonition of what he was struggling to say.

"I'd like you to move your business to New York, use an extra office of mine. There's plenty of room in my penthouse for Jayna. And you. I think it would be a good idea if we lived together for a while before—"

"Don't insult me with some half-assed commitment," Rachel snapped, tears springing to her eyes. Rand reached for her, and she shoved him away. They stared at each other, her eyes glittering with hurt and fury, his dark with apology and a plea for understanding.

She wanted a fight, a fight that would make his Zebedique street brawl look like a schoolyard tussle. Apparently sensing how close to ugly this confrontation was getting, Rand backed off, spreading his hands in a gesture of defeat.

"I'm sorry, Rachel."

"I didn't ask for a character reference."

He winced. Rand hesitated, then took an envelope from his coat pocket and pressed it into her palm.

"Here's your fee, as promised. Remember, any promises I make to you, I'll never break."

"I don't want the stupid fee." She thrust it back at him. Rand's controlled expression was suddenly jarred.

"It's a million dollars."

"And you think I care about that? Keep your damn money. It's not what I want from you." She pushed the door open.

"I'm coming in. We need to talk."

"We're through talking, Rand. And don't you dare step through this door again until you've got your own mind made up one way or the other. Don't call me. Don't write." She stepped over the threshold and faced him point-blank. "In fact, I don't want to see your face again until you've got a ring in your pocket and you're ready to head for the altar."

"But, Rachel . . . Angel . . ."

"No ifs, ands or buts. Those are my terms. And in this case, my terms stand."

She shut the door in his face. And then she waited . . . and waited. It didn't open. And while she slumped against the wall, her face buried in her hands as she heard his retreating footsteps, she repeated over and over, "Big girls don't cry. . . . Big girls don't cry. . . ."

"FULL HOUSE, MISTRESS! I win. Hand over the loot."

"Criminy, Jayna, you're wiping me out." Rachel shoved a pile of pennies over her desk.

"Just call me, how you say, Cool Hand Luke? Or is it Minnesota Fats?"

"You're watching too many movies on the VCR, Jayna."

"I know. So yesterday I went to the casino. All that fruit running around made me hungry. So I ate a hamburger and drank a shaked milk. The commercials say you can't drink the water."

"Lord," Rachel groaned. "Now it's the slots and junk food. Heaven only knows what comes next."

"Once the baby is here, I promise to—" Jayna's brow furrowed. "Oh, yes. Clean up my act."

The mention of the baby, now two months in the making, brought a sudden catch to Rachel's throat. A month since she'd seen Rand. A month spent straddled between the never-ending need to see him, touch him, while she stroked her still-flat belly and remembered . . . too much.

Jayna's gnarled hand covered hers. "Call him. Tell him of the baby you carry. He will come."

"No. Absolutely not."

"But you are so sad."

"Heartbroken, Jayna."

"And stubborn." The kindness of her eyes contrasted with the chastisement in her voice. "You foolish woman. Why must you be so proud? The master, he loves you."

"No one's my master but me. And as far as I can see, he's guilty of being too proud himself. Pigheaded, that's what he is." Rachel snorted, even as her heart nosedived. "He's had a month to come to his senses, and he hasn't shown his face yet. Guess I'll have to rack up my losses, no matter how much it hurts, because it's all or nothing, and I'm not backing down."

"His sister, she calls you much. You say she is worried about him."

"Sarah's a good person. But her brother has to make his own decisions, not her."

"Montage says he sits alone in the dark. He sleeps with your white robe. She finds it when she changes his sheets."

In her mind's eye, Rachel saw sheets stained with lamb's blood. Her robe on the floor, lying next to his. So much they shared. So much he was cheating them of.

"The way I look at it, if he wants to sleep with more than a robe, he knows how to get his butt to a jewelry store. Some trade-off, huh, Jayna? Him in the sack with a wad of cloth, while I cuddle with a doll."

Rachel had to cling to her hard line, because that was all she had. Except for memories—and an unborn baby. And a love that was so strong it took everything she had not to hop on the first plane to New York and settle for no promises and Rand's arms holding her tight.

How she hurt for him. How she hurt for herself. And for the baby that they shared, keeping her company while he remained alone except for his sister.

"Why don't you go cash in those pennies for some quarters and go for the jackpot, Jayna? If it's all the same to you, I'd like to nap on the job."

"As you wish, mistress."

"My wish is that you'd quit calling me that."

"Okeydokey...Rachel."

"You're a gas, Jayna. Oh, and thanks for the shoulder. It helps to have you around, especially since Rand's not."

"Small tomatoes, right?"

"Potatoes, Jayna. But, no, you mean a lot to me. Making sure I eat right and get my rest. You'll be a great nanny when the time comes."

"It is time you should rest now." She drew the curtains together, then pulled down the shade at the door. Just before she took her leave, she turned. "Call him, Rachel."

Once Jayna left, Rachel squeezed her eyes tight, fighting the moisture that was trying to leak out. Reaching beneath her desk, she latched on to the doll she always kept close. Her sleeping with a doll, Rand with a robe. There was no sense in it. Jayna was right—she was being stubborn, and prideful.

She eyed the phone, her hand shaking as it hovered over the receiver. She laid her head on the desk, listening to her heart pound, putting off the inevitable a few moments more.

The door opened and shut. She thought she heard a click of the lock. Jayna, no doubt, playing guard, locking up for her safety. Footsteps. Maybe if she pretended to be asleep

Jayna would decide to go on to the casino rather than watch her snooze. Then she'd make the call.

"I'm looking for a missing person."

Rachel's head snapped up from the desk. Eyes the color of slate pinned her where she sat; a faint whiff of bay and spice tempted and teased. Some Middle Eastern instrument played a distant refrain while Rocky's theme surged in the background.

"His name is Joshua Smith, and I understand you're just the person who can help me find him. He loves a woman. One he can't live without. Rachel Tinsdale is what she goes by, but her alias is Angel." He withdrew a black velvet box and flipped open the lid. A diamond so large it was gaudy winked into her stunned eyes.

"Allow me to introduce myself. Rand Slick. A rose by any other name probably smells ten times better, but if you'll have me, I've got a car idling. Its destination is the courthouse. My mission is marriage."

Before she could absorb the head-spinning, heart-thudding magnitude of what he'd just asked, he was behind the desk and hauling her into his arms.

"I love you, Rachel. I'm no bargain, and life with me won't be a bed of roses. But if you can handle that, I'll spend the rest of my life doing my damnedest to deserve you."

"Rand." She plowed ten fingers into his hair and laid a kiss on him that torched them both to ashes, ashes, all fall down....

"I've been so miserable without you." She was crying, not caring if her mascara was running or even her nose, because he was there, making promises she knew he'd never break. He pulled out an embroidered handkerchief and wiped away her tears.

"I've missed you like crazy, angel. It's just no good without you. I can't work, can't sleep. I can't do anything but think about how right it is with us and wonder why the hell

I ever thought keeping us apart was in our best interests. The truth was staring me in the face, and I couldn't see it."

"And what is the truth, Rand?"

"I'll never be perfect. You'll never quit loving me because I'm not. We're meant to be together. It's that simple."

"Took you long enough to figure that out." She sniffled as she stroked his chest, absorbing and exulting in the solid feel of him, the quickening beat of his heart against her palm. "I've been crying myself to sleep every night. I haul your doll around in my ugly purse along with a bottle of your cologne. I sniff it, close my eyes and pretend you're there."

"I'm here, angel. I'm here. Now, I want to do this right...." He knelt, one knee on the floor, the other crooked, in a formal, gallant pose. Taking her left hand, he held the ring at the tip of her finger. "Will you marry me, Rachel? Think about it before you answer, because marriage to me is for life."

"I wouldn't have it any other way. The answer is yes, Rand. And it's yes again, Joshua." Her hand was shaking; why, even her finger had the tremors as he slipped on the ring.

"For better or worse," he said in a gruff voice. "Though I'm afraid I'll get the first and you'll get the second. But maybe the richer or poorer part will help even things out. Especially since you threw that million bucks in my face."

He pressed a kiss to the ring and got up. Rachel's eyes darted from him to the rock on her hand, unable to decide whether she was closer to tears or laughter. She gave in to both.

"You idiot. You know better than to even mention money. Like my dad said, it can't buy you love. You've got mine, and it's free for the taking."

"And I need you enough to take it. I want forever, Rachel. I want the fights when I slip, I want your arms to be there when I fall. And I want babies. The whole nine yards."

Rachel's gaze froze on the ring. Had Jayna interfered? Was Rand here because he knew about the baby?

"Did Jayna call you?" she demanded.

"Call me? About what?"

"Being a father-to-be, that's what."

Any pretense Rand had to suave sophistication gave way as his jaw dropped in a *Duh, say again?* expression.

"I don't believe it. You said you weren't.... I'll be damned. You lied, didn't you?"

"You bet I did, Mr. Master." She smiled smugly. "I let you go, and you came back."

"Why, you little sneak," he growled. He tried to pull a stern face, but all he came up with was an ear-to-ear grin. With a quick swipe, he shoved the phone and papers and playing cards from her desk. They thudded to the floor as he leaned her back and ran a hand up her thigh. "I think I need to dole out a lesson to my concubine for keeping secrets from me."

Rachel yanked him down by his tie, bringing his mouth a whisper from hers. Angling for a heated kiss, she murmured seductively, "You're a savage."

"And angel, you're silk."

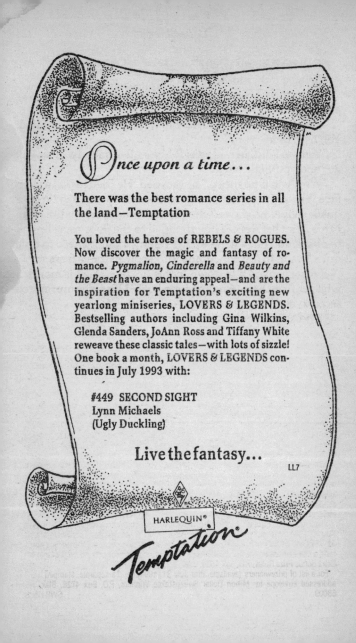

$\mathcal{O}$nce upon a time...

There was the best romance series in all the land—Temptation

You loved the heroes of REBELS & ROGUES. Now discover the magic and fantasy of romance. *Pygmalion, Cinderella* and *Beauty and the Beast* have an enduring appeal—and are the inspiration for Temptation's exciting new yearlong miniseries, LOVERS & LEGENDS. Bestselling authors including Gina Wilkins, Glenda Sanders, JoAnn Ross and Tiffany White reweave these classic tales—with lots of sizzle! One book a month, LOVERS & LEGENDS continues in July 1993 with:

#449 SECOND SIGHT
Lynn Michaels
(Ugly Duckling)

Live the fantasy...

LL7

HARLEQUIN®

Temptation

OFFICIAL RULES • MILLION DOLLAR MATCH 3 SWEEPSTAKES
NO PURCHASE OR OBLIGATION NECESSARY TO ENTER

To enter, follow the directions published. **ALTERNATE MEANS OF ENTRY:** Hand print your name and address on a 3"×5" card and mail to either: Harlequin "Match 3," 3010 Walden Ave., P.O. Box 1867, Buffalo, NY 14269-1867 or Harlequin "Match 3," P.O. Box 609, Fort Erie, Ontario L2A 5X3, and we will assign your Sweepstakes numbers. (Limit: one entry per envelope.) For eligibility, entries must be received no later than March 31, 1994. No responsibility is assumed for lost, late or misdirected entries.

Upon receipt of entry, Sweepstakes numbers will be assigned. To determine winners, Sweepstakes numbers will be compared against a list of randomly preselected prizewinning numbers. In the event all prizes are not claimed via the return of prizewinning numbers, random drawings will be held from among all other entries received to award unclaimed prizes.

Prizewinners will be determined no later than May 30, 1994. Selection of winning numbers and random drawings are under the supervision of D.L. Blair, Inc., an independent judging organization, whose decisions are final. One prize to a family or organization. No substitution will be made for any prize, except as offered. Taxes and duties on all prizes are the sole responsibility of winners. Winners will be notified by mail. Chances of winning are determined by the number of entries distributed and received.

Sweepstakes open to persons 18 years of age or older, except employees and immediate family members of Torstar Corporation, D.L. Blair, Inc., their affiliates, subsidiaries and all other agencies, entities and persons connected with the use, marketing or conduct of this Sweepstakes. All applicable laws and regulations apply. Sweepstakes offer void wherever prohibited by law. Any litigation within the province of Quebec respecting the conduct and awarding of a prize in this Sweepstakes must be submitted to the Régies des Loteries et Courses du Quebec. In order to win a prize, residents of Canada will be required to correctly answer a time-limited arithmetical skill-testing question. Values of all prizes are in U.S. currency.

Winners of major prizes will be obligated to sign and return an affidavit of eligibility and release of liability within 30 days of notification. In the event of non-compliance within this time period, prize may be awarded to an alternate winner. Any prize or prize notification returned as undeliverable will result in the awarding of that prize to an alternate winner. By acceptance of their prize, winners consent to use of their names, photographs or other likenesses for purposes of advertising, trade and promotion on behalf of Torstar Corporation without further compensation, unless prohibited by law.

This Sweepstakes is presented by Torstar Corporation, its subsidiaries and affiliates in conjunction with book, merchandise and/or product offerings. Prizes are as follows: Grand Prize—$1,000,000 (payable at $33,333.33 a year for 30 years). First through Sixth Prizes may be presented in different creative executions, each with the following approximate values: First Prize—$35,000; Second Prize—$10,000; 2 Third Prizes—$5,000 each; 5 Fourth Prizes—$1,000 each; 10 Fifth Prizes—$250 each; 1,000 Sixth Prizes—$100 each. Prizewinners will have the opportunity of selecting any prize offered for that level. A travel-prize option, if offered and selected by winner, must be completed within 12 months of selection and is subject to hotel and flight accommodations availability. Torstar Corporation may present this Sweepstakes utilizing names other than Million Dollar Sweepstakes. For a current list of all prize options offered within prize levels and all names the Sweepstakes may utilize, send a self-addressed, stamped envelope (WA residents need not affix return postage) to: Million Dollar Sweepstakes Prize Options/Names, P.O. Box 4710, Blair, NE 68009.

The Extra Bonus Prize will be awarded in a random drawing to be conducted no later than May 30, 1994 from among all entries received. To qualify, entries must be received by March 31, 1994 and comply with published directions. No purchase necessary. For complete rules, send a self-addressed, stamped envelope (WA residents need not affix return postage) to: Extra Bonus Prize Rules, P.O. Box 4600, Blair, NE 68009.

For a list of prizewinners (available after July 31, 1994) send a separate, stamped, self-addressed envelope to: Million Dollar Sweepstakes Winners, P.O. Box 4728, Blair, NE 68009.

SWP-H693

LIGHTS, CAMERA, ACTION!

Hollywood Dynasty

HARLEQUIN®
Temptation

The Kingstons are Hollywood—two generations of box-office legends in front of and behind the cameras. In this fast-paced world egos compete for the spotlight and intimate secrets make tabloid headlines. Gage—the cinematographer, Pierce—the actor and Claire—the producer struggle for success in an unpredictable business where a single film can make or break you.

By the time the credits roll, will they discover that the ultimate challenge is far more personal? Share the behind-the-scenes dreams and dramas in this blockbuster miniseries by Candace Schuler!

THE OTHER WOMAN, #451 (July 1993)
JUST ANOTHER PRETTY FACE, #459 (September 1993)
THE RIGHT DIRECTION, #467 (November 1993)

Coming soon to your favorite retail outlet.